JACK HARKAWAY AND HIS SON'S ADVENTURES IN GREECE

EDWIN J. BRETT,

BOYS OF ENGLAND OFFICE, 173, FLEET STREET, E.C.

AND ALL BOOKSELLERS.

HOW TO FIND THE FOX.

FIND THE TIGER.—A PUZZLE.

EDWIN J BRETT'S

JACK HARKAWAY
AND HIS SON'S ADVENTURES IN GREECE.

"THE MONGOLIAN STARTED UP, DRENCHED WITH CHAMPAGNE, AND WITH THE CORK HALF-WAY DOWN HIS THROAT."

JACK HARKAWAY
AND HIS SON'S
ADVENTURES IN GREECE.

CHAPTER I.

SPIRILLO—A MYSTERY—HIDDEN DANGER.

MAGIC ISLAND. It was happily named by young Jack.

"If that is Magic Island," cried little Emily to young Jack, "this I will christen Fairy Creek."

"Hurrah! bravo, Emily!" cried Jack.

This was not less happy than young Jack's name, and it was as generally adopted.

A consultation was held upon deck between Jack Harkaway, Dick Harvey, Mr. Jefferson, Magog Brand, Spirillo, Nabley, Pike, and lastly, Isaac Mole.

"Before we land, Spirillo," said Jack Harkaway, "tell me, do you think that we have to apprehend anything like a surprise?"

"Hardly," was Spirillo's reply, "while we are in any force."

"Do you think there is any danger?" asked Jack.

To any one of us venturing about alone—yes, great danger. While we are in parties—no. But I must not disguise from you, gentlemen all, that we have an ugly enemy to face in the owner of this island."

"Who have we to fear?" said young Jack, coming up at that moment.

"Monastos, the pirate chief, boy," said Spirillo. "He has the patience of the cat watching for the mouse, and to this quality he adds the ferocity of the tiger."

Mr. Mole coughed.

"This is a most objectionable party," he said, "and I propose that we give him a wide berth."

"You had better, Mr. Mole," said Dick, "or he'll make short work of your scaffolding?"

"What?" cried Mr. Mole. "My scaffolding."

"I beg pardon. I mean your woodwork, your understanding."

Mr. Mole gasped.

"Mr. Harvey, if you were not my old friend, I should certainly demand satisfaction."

"By all means," returned Dick, cheerfully.

Harkaway put an end to any further discussion, by plunging at once into the arrangements for the safe conduct of the expedition against the pirates.

"Mr. Nabley must be left in command with Mr. Pike," said Harkaway.

"Very good, sir."

"The watch must be kept with the greatest vigilance night and day."

"Of course."

"Each watch must be composed of at least three persons."

"Yes."

"During the night watches, a patrol must pass along the deck, at intervals of not more than ten minutes."

"Good!" said Spirillo, nodding approvingly.

"We show our confidence in you," said Harvey, taking Pike and his comrade, Nabley, each by the hand, "by leaving in your care our wives, and all who are dear to us in the world. If we betray a little anxiety in making our parting conditions and rules, it must not surprise you."

"It does not."

"No," added Pike, with warmth, "we are indeed grateful for your confidence—eh, Nabley?"

"Indeed we are."

"Rather."

"You may count upon our zeal," said Nabley. "We have been used to watching, and waiting too, for the matter of that, eh, Dan?"

"Ah! indeed."

"Now then, my friends," said Harkaway, earnestly, "for our parting word. We are going upon an excursion of some danger; we mustn't attempt to disguise that fact to ourselves.

"It only behoves us to show that better part of valour, discretion, upon all occasions, and if I don't mistake, we shall do big things. There must be one fixed word of understanding between us. Should there be great danger on either side, a blue light shall be burnt, and that shall be the signal of recall," continued Harkaway.

"Good!"

These words sank deeply into everybody's mind.

"In other words, the blue light shall be an appeal to the others for aid."

"That's an understanding," said Jefferson; "but, please the pigs, there will be no need for blue lights."

"Amen to that," said his little friend, Magog.

"Well, now, Spirillo," said Harvey, "when you are ready."

"Forward!"

"One word more," said the ex-pirate. "Let us refer to the maps we have got, and do everything in proper orderly style."

"Of course."

"Let us have the charts up."

"Good!"

A man was sent to the saloon for the maps and charts in question, and they were spread out on the top of a big chest on the deck.

"Before we go into this job deeply," said Harkaway, "I propose that we adjourn to tiffin."

"I second the honourable member's motion," said Mr. Mole, with great gravity.

"And I too," said Harvey, "for I am beastly hungry."

"And I'm filthily peckish," added Jefferson.

"This language," exclaimed Isaac Mole, much shocked, "this language is not parliamentary. I rise to order."

"Hear! hear!" cried Dick Harvey; "So do I. I rise to order chops and a pint of wine, for one."

"This is levity," said Mr. Mole, indignantly.

"It is wasting good time," said Jefferson, laughingly. "What do you say, Cæsar Augustus?" he said, turning to Sunday, who stood close by.

"Dat's my platform, colonel," retorted the darkey, laughing all over his ebony face. "Dis chile could jest eat enough to open a shop with."

"I have no appetite," said Spirillo, who had grown suddenly downcast. "No

heart for eating, and I think I shall run on shore to stretch my legs while you eat. Master Jack!"

"Hullo!" cried young Jack, from up aloft.

"Don't venture far from sight."

"All right."

"I shall join you, Spirillo," said Harry Girdwood, "eh?"

By all means."

And the two clambered up on to the rock and found young Jack, who was playing all kinds of merry antics with Nero, in sight of the company generally on board.

From this eminence, they could obtain a pretty fair view of the country in all directions.

It was a lovely place, and merited fully its fanciful appellation of Magic Island.

The fruitful vine met the view on every side, and the eye was dazzled with the brilliancy of the flowers.

Jays, parroquets, parrots, and other birds of the gayest plumage filled the air with their cries.

"Do you see that place there, Master Jack?"

"That narrow between those two high banks?"

"Yes."

"I do"

"That road lies our way. We have to go down there, and then off to the left."

"Is it far?"

"Not very."

"That would be an awkward place for an ambuscade, Spirillo," said Harry Girdwood.

Spirillo shook his head, and looked serious.

"That is what we have most to fear with Monastos, the pirate chief," he said.

"We must be very careful, then."

"Yes."

"Why," remarked Harry Girdwood, gravely, "a single rifle could protect that ravine from a whole troop."

Spirillo nodded a grave acquiescence.

"Before the party disembarks," he said, thoughtfully, "I'll climb up the right bank, scramble through the trees and bushes, and see that there are no signs of an ambuscade."

"Be careful," said Harry Girdwood.

"Trust me. But we must not risk the whole expedition for want of proper precautions. Remember, the pirates on this island are desperate men."

"True."

"Stay here," said Spirillo. "Don't venture further inland; and we shall see all the excitement that the greediest adventurer can desire."

"Very good."

"Be careful."

"I will."

"But, Spirillo," said Harry Girdwood, "one word."

"What is it?"

"If you go further and don't come back in twenty minutes from this time, we shall come and seek for you."

Spirillo smiled.

"Yes—but no," he added, suddenly growing serious, as an ugly thought crossed him, "if I don't return, you can guess what it means."

"No."

"Something will have happened to me; so that it will be madness for you to venture into danger. I must see that all is safe for you, my brave boys."

The two boys looked very serious at this speech.

"You don't suppose, Spirillo, that we could rest if we thought anything had happened to you. Pray return at once."

"I will not, but you must!" said the ex-pirate. "I am not going to have it on my conscience, that I ran you into danger —you must promise me to obey."

They paused.

"Well, remain here," said Spirillo, "or you may endanger the safety of the whole party."

This settled the discussion at once.

"Very well, Spirillo," said young Jack, "we consent."

"You promise?"

"We do."

"Good," said Spirillo, apparently quite relieved by this.

Then, his gloomy looks vanishing, he nodded gaily to the two lads, shook them warmly by the hands, and made for the heights.

Jack and Harry watched him in silence.

They saw him climbing up with very great difficulty, and they judged shrewdly that the place would be utterly inaccessible to an ordinary biped, but for the thick vegetation growing up the slope which gave the climber a hold for hand and foot.

And when he had reached the summit of the embankment, he turned, prior to plunging into the thick wood, and waved his hand in silence at his two young comrades.

"Good bye, old friend," said young Jack. "I hope you'll soon be back; I don't like you going alone on this job. We ought to share the danger."

"Look!"

"He's gone."

Spirillo waved a final farewell, and disappeared in the thicket.

Poor Spirillo.

They waited and watched in silence.

Their minds were filled with most unpleasant thoughts, and they did not care to impart them to each other.

They watched the thicket where Spirillo had disappeared, until their eyes ached.

"Jack."

"Yes."

"Did you hear."

"What?"

"A noise from there."

"No."

"I thought I did, but it was my fancy perhaps."

"Must have been."

"Hark! was that it?"

"No. What I heard, or what I fancied I heard, sounded like a groan."

"A what?"

"A groan."

"Fancy," said young Jack, determined not to admit anything so unpleasant.

Just then a voice called him by name, and he started and changed colour so rapidly that you could see how fiercely strung his nerves were under the present excitement.

"Jack."

"Hullo, sir."

"Tell Spirillo that I want him," Harkaway senior said, "ask him to come here."

"I can't; he's gone."

"Gone?"

"Yes."

"Where?"

"Gone up the heights there to reconnoitre."

Harkaway made his way ashore, and joined the two lads at this.

"Gone alone?"

"Yes."

"That's very imprudent," he said, "very."

"I wished to join him, but——"

"You?" ejaculated Harkaway, aghast.

"Yes."

"You dare to, young—young jackanapes. You think to throw us all into a fever of nervousness again, I suppose?"

"I, sir."

"Yes, you."

"Indeed, I never thought anything of the kind, father."

"Nor of anything," sighed the elder Harkaway. "Your great fault is just that."

"What, sir?"

"Thoughtlessness; but now listen seriously to me—you, too, Harry."

"Yes, sir."

"I wish you both thoroughly to understand that you are not to venture out of sight, or to court unnecessary danger."

"Dad is anxious and out of temper," said young Jack to his comrade Harry.

"There, there," said Harkaway the elder, "I only want you to promise me that you will be prudent."

"We do."

"Yes, yes, sir," said Harry Girdwood.

"Good; and now where the deuce can Spirillo be?"

Where, indeed!

They were destined to ask each other that question pretty often.

An hour passed away.

An hour from the time that Spirillo had pushed his way into the thickly-wooded summit of the heights.

Yet no signs of him.

Jack Harkaway got to be very uneasy indeed.

So he went on board and consulted with the assembled party—the two lads joining them for this purpose.

And when young Jack had related all the circumstances of the case, they all pulled long faces.

One decision they all came to.

Something had happened to their guide and comrade.

"There is one way of accounting for it," said Daniel Pike, "a way that no one has appeared to think of yet."

"What is it?"

"Supposing it is part of a scheme to bag us all?"

"What?"

It made them all jump again.

"Impossible!" ejaculated one of them.

"Absurd!" cried another.

"Utterly unlikely," added another.

"Monstrous!"

"Ridiculous."

And so forth.

All were dead against the detective's explanation of the mystery.

"Wait a bit," said Pike, "before you decide so positively against me, listen to what I have to say in support of my supposition."

"Go on."

"Let us hear."

"Supposing it has been a planned thing from the beginning, suppose that all his plans and charts were part and parcel of a big scheme, to throw the ship and all into their clutches?

"You will admit that it is a scheme worth any amount of outlay and labour to accomplish.

"It will represent an immense fortune, for not only is there the value of the ship and all our effects, but there is also the question of ransom, and my life upon it, they will want a princely sum for each of us, or——"

The detective drew his forefinger ominously across his throat.

The gesture was too significant for them to misunderstand.

However, there was present one man who was not to be led into any wild belief about Spirillo because of the strange circumstance of his disappearance.

And this was the good old doctor who had escaped with him and the two boys from the pirate junk.

Now, just then the meeting was joined by an unexpected visitor. Nero.

Young Jack's monkey had also nb on an exploring expedition, and he had just returned without anything to show for it.

"Hullo!" cried Ben Hawser, coming up with a scrape and a tug at his forelock. "Blow me, if he ain't got a hat."

It was true.

Nero had managed to get a hat from somewhere, and this Ben Hawser took from him.

"Well, wherever he has been, he has come across some human beings."

"That's true."

"Stop!" cried the American doctor, growing strangely excited by now. "Give it me."

Ben obeyed.

"Hah! I thought so," exclaimed the doctor.

"What?"

"This hat is the pirate Spirillo's; it is the hat he wore when he left here.

And then, looking about to assure himself that none of the ladies were within hearing, he sank his voice to a whisper and said—

"Do you see that?"

"What?"

"Blood! The hat is stained with blood. It is Spirillo's.

CHAPTER II.

THE END OF SPIRILLO.

STAINED with blood.

An uncomfortable thrill went through the whole assemblage.

"Nero, Nero," cried young Jack, piteously, "What have you seen? Why can't you talk for once?"

"Talk," echoed Ben Hawser; "he can talk fast enough if he likes, only the cunning rascal's afraid he'll have to work hard. Confound his artful carcase."

"Something has happened to Spirillo," said the doctor. "This is clear."

Young Jack and Harry Girdwood exchanged glances.

They thought of Spirillo's parting words.

"What's to be done?" asked Jefferson.

"Mount the heights with our revolvers in hand."

"That is very dangerous," said the doctor.

"Why?"

"They have such splendid cover, that they could pick us off one by one before we could get to the top."

"Or even get the satisfaction of a shot in return," said Magog Brand.

"This is a case calling for Indian warfare, for a trusty scout, who could creep upon this hidden enemy without being seen."

"Dat's me."

They all instinctly turned round, as our old friend the Prince of Limbi stepped forward.

"Monday."

"Yes, gentlemen. We'll see if we can't make my old savage life of some use once more."

"What do you propose?" demanded Harvey.

"I shall find my way a-top of dem hills—but not as Spirillo went; I shall go in de grass."

"The grass!"

"The grass!"

"I shall go in de grass, I say like a snake—like a serpent, and if I find anything in my way, I shall sting like a serpent."

Saying which, he took out a short axe he carried under his waistcoat, and made a vicious dig with it.

Thoroughly civilized as he was, the prospect of going on the war-path aroused all his old savage instincts.

Harkaway looked around at the company.

"What do you say?"

"Monday's the man!" said Jefferson.

"Right."

And so it was unanimously voted that Monday's offer should be accepted.

The Prince of Limbi cast off part of his clothing, and concealing several weapons about his body, he started off.

They watched his progress in great anxiety.

Now, Monday did not scale the heights as Spirillo had done.

He went a circuitous route to the point aimed at.

And then they waited.

A weary waiting it was.

Nervous anxiety and apprehension were depicted upon every countenance.

All stood there, upon the rocky landing stage, watching in silence the crest of shrubs and trees, hoping every second to see Monday reappear.

"Something has happened to poor Monday," said Harkaway, unable to bear the silence any longer.

"Patience, patience," said the doctor; "we do not know yet."

"I, for one, have too much confidence in Monday to believe that, until I learn the worst——"

"Wait."

"If harm should have befallen him, there will be but one course open to us."

"And that is?"

"To mount the heights in force, and clear the wood. We must not be cut off one by one without so much as——"

"Ha!"

"What now?"

"I can see a something crawling along there" said Magog Brand, who was looking through a telescope.

"Up above?"

"Yes."

"Is it Monday?"

"It is—it is! See——"

"He makes a sign to us!"

"Thank Heaven for that!" exclaimed Harkaway, fervently.

"He's not hurt?" exclaimed Mr. Jefferson, full of eagerness.

"No, no."

"Thank goodness for that, say I."

"As far as I can see, at least."

"Where is he now?"

"Coming this way."

"He is crawling on his stomach," returned Mr. Jefferson, "to keep out of sight."

This proved to be the case, for as soon as Monday got clear of the thick growth of shrubs, he started off at a run, and soon rejoined his party.

"Well, Monday," they exclaimed, in great excitement, "what have you seen?"

"Bad—bad!" he answered, shaking his head.

"How bad?"

"Dreadful," answered Monday, shaking his head.

He showed, clearly enough, by his manner that he had seen something which had considerably upset him.

"What is it, Monday? Why don't you speak?"

"Come, out with it."

"Have you seen Spirillo?"

Monday nodded gravely.

"You have seen him?"

"Then he is a prisoner, I suppose," said Dick.

"No—no prisoner. I have seen him, or part of him."

They started again at this.

"What do you mean by that! What part of him?"

Monday's reply was brief, characteristic, and very terrible.

"I have seen Spirillo's head stuck on a pole."

They shuddered.

They wanted no further explanation, for it told its own tale.

Poor Spirillo!

He had been full of warnings for them about the dangers of the enterprise, and he had been the first to slight his own warnings.

And fatally had he paid the penalty of his rashness.

"I leave Spirillo's head on the pole," exclaimed Monday, quietly, "until I can take it away, and put in the place the head of the man that did it."

"Mind you do not lose yours, Monday," said Dick.

Monday laughed at this.

"No fear of dat, Massa Dick. I shall have the fellar what did it before we leave Magic Island.

Would he?

He looked very confident as he spoke; but the hidden enemy was as crafty as cruel.

Whether Monday carried out this threat time will show.

CHAPTER III.

A BRACE OF VILLAINS—THE STORM AND ITS DANGERS—A DIRE CALAMITY—
THE ARM AND ITS LEGEND.

WHEN Hunston made his wild appeal for help, Toro resolved to rescue him if possible.

The Italian villain knew that his English friend knew something of seamanship, which knowledge was the only chance they had of safety.

There were some fragments of cordage in the boat.

Toro hastily joined these together, and prepared for a good throw.

The line whistled through the air.

Hunston just managed to clutch the end with his real hand, and then to his great joy he found himself gradually drawn towards the boat.

But by the time Toro managed to drag him over the gunwale, he was insensible, nor did he regain consciousness till an hour had elapsed.

When his senses once more returned, he began to arrange matters as well as he could for their perilous voyage.

Oars or sail they had not, but in the bottom of the boat were three or four rough planks, two of which they carved with their knives into rude oars, while of another they formed a kind of mast.

The sail was made of a canvas bag, in which their store of biscuit had been placed.

With these rude contrivances, they found they could guide their craft, and make some, though slow, progress.

Two days passed.

Upon the third day, towards sundown, black and threatening clouds fringed the horizon.

The wind came in fitful gusts, moaning dismally as it crossed the weary waste of inky waters.

"We are in for dirty weather," said Hunston. "You had better rest, Toro."

"What for?"

"Because you will have need of all your strength and endurance this night."

"And you?"

"Oh, I have slept this afternoon," replied Hunston, "whereas you haven't closed your eyes since last night, and it is no joke passing the night without sleeping."

"Do you think there is any chance of that?" asked Toro.

"I do."

"Humph!"

"Take in the sail, Toro," said his companion.

"Must I?"

"Yes."

"Perhaps you are right," said Toro.

So he set to work to reef the sail which had been hurriedly rigged the day before.

This done Hunston prevailed upon his companion to try and snatch a few hours' sleep in order to brace himself up for a possible night of weary and anxious vigil.

The huge Italian stretched out his arms and yawned, and then he coiled himself up.

"I shall never be able to sleep," he said.

But barely were the words uttered when he dropped off into a deep slumber —and snored.

And while he snored, he dreamt of fair countries—of lands flowing with milk and honey.

And he seemed in his dream to recollect having been set adrift in a boat on the dreary ocean, with Hunston, and he thought that he was comparing his present lot in life with that dreary time.

Pity that he should ever be interrupted in such pleasant visions.

*   *   *   *   *

"Toro!"

"Ugh!"

"Toro—Toro! wake up, I say."

"What is it?"

"Out with your oars—quick! pull, man, pull!"

The Italian opened his eyes, and

blinked and winked, and stared stupidly about him, before he could recognise the situation.

It was indeed a sad awakening.

"What now?" he growled. "What's the use of asking me to go to sleep, if you want to disturb me at once?"

"You have been asleep two hours, Toro."

"Two minutes!"

"Two hours, I say—more than two hours, I swear. The gale has increased, and now we want your strength and your skill both to save us."

While Hunston was speaking, the Italian looked about him, and began to understand.

It was high time.

The gale had increased, until it assumed a really alarming aspect.

Huge waves broke over the boat in a way that seriously threatened its safety.

They shipped heavy seas more than once, and it needed all Hunston's prompt attention to bale out the water fast enough to keep them afloat.

But the fury of the gale increased, and it was evident that at any moment they might ship a heavy wave that would swamp them.

"Lower your oars," cried Hunston, eagerly.

Toro obeyed.

"Now take the word from me," he said.

"When I give the word pull for your life."

Toro looked up, wide awake, when Hunston gave the signal of danger.

"We mustn't let another of those waves break over us, or we are lost. Do you understand?" said Hunston.

"Yes."

"Now, then!"

"Ready!"

In spite of the darkness of the night, Hunston could see the huge hill of water slowly rolling on in pursuit of them, and threatening to engulf the boat and its living freight.

It was a very mountain, and let this break over their boat, there would be a speedy and awful end to their plotting and scheming, and their criminal career.

Hunston watched it draw nearer and nearer, and then, picking well his moment, he gave Toro the signal.

"Pull!"

The oars struck the water.

"Pull, pull, man!" he exclaimed, earnestly. "Pull, for the love of Heaven or we are dead men!"

Toro obeyed.

Three or four desperate strokes jerked the boat along before the threatening wave, so that, finding no opposition to its march, it simply helped the boat with it, and the danger was past.

The danger for the moment, we would say.

The perils of a fearful night were yet before them.

These bold, bad men—these scoffers at everything good and righteous—could invoke divine help, you may see, in their hour of great trouble.

There is nothing so calculated to fill the heart with awesome feelings, to show man what a helpless atom he is.

* * * * *

"Now again!"

"Right!"

"Pull—pull for your life!"

A desperate tug at the oars shot the boat through the water before the advancing wave.

Yet, dexterously as the movement was effected, they were well-nigh swamped.

The rain came down.

Drenched to the skin with the blinding rain, and sitting knee deep in water—bale it out as fast as they would—they shivered like palsy-stricken wretches.

"There's an ague in this for me," said Toro, his teeth chattering as he spoke.

"Rheumatic fever for me," groaned Hunston.

"Here it comes again."

"Pull then, both together! take the time sharply—now!"

"Right!"

And pull together they did with a vengeance.

The wave rolled its inky crest under the boat's stern, lifting them high aloft.

Saved again!

Saved by their indomitable perseverance and skill of no mean order.

Indeed, both were possessed of gifts which might have achieved for them great things in life, had they turned those abilities to good account.

Well, so they passed through that dismal night, and when morning dawned, it found them both well-nigh exhausted with fatigue—with white, wan faces, and eyes sunken in their sockets, in spite of their frequent recourse to their flasks of spirits to keep up their circulation and their courage.

And Hunston looked about to ascertain if the gale had done them any damage

"No harm done?"

"Not much."

"I thought not," said Toro. "We're precious lucky."

"Yes; if you can call it luck to be able to protect yourself, instead of sitting down and giving way as some men would have done, for we took every possible precaution to secure our provisions and the like."

"We did."

"And—hullo!"

Hunston paused, and looked hastily about him.

He lifted the tarpaulin from off some object at the bottom of the boat.

But then he looked in vain.

"What is it?"

Toro looked full of impatience as he put the question.

"What now?"

"Wait."

"Wait! why don't you answer?"

"I'll tell you," answered Hunston, "though you need not be so impatient and so eager to hear bad news."

"Bad news!"

"Yes."

"What news?"

Hunston gave a final glance about him.

And then he told, in hollow tones, the dire calamity which had befallen them.

"*The keg of water has been washed overboard!*"

Toro said nothing.

But as he sank back in his seat, the look of unutterable dismay upon his countenance showed that he realised the full extent of this great calamity.

"Are you sure?" was all he could falter presently.

Hunston nodded.

"Sure. I was looking for it for some minutes before I spoke. My arm has been very painful; the strain upon it in pulling has been too much for it, I suppose. I thought that I would try what cold water bathing would do for it. I know it is gone."

"That is a dreadful thing, Hunston."

"It is, indeed."

"Your arm getting bad, too," said the Italian, reflectively. "Shall I look at it?"

"Yes, do."

"Probably there is something out of order with the machinery."

"Perhaps."

Hunston started involuntarily as he spoke.

Instinctively he remembered the murdered inventor of the mechanical arm.

The hapless Robert Emmerson.

He thought of the legend on the arm itself.

"FOES, BEWARE ME; BUT WOE TO THE WEARER IF RAISED AGAINST A FRIEND."

He thought of the murdered man's dying words.

Indeed, they were ringing in his ears night and day.

He heard them ever as plainly as when he saw the unhappy Emmerson dying before him.

He felt, too, that he was yet to be punished through that arm with its menacing legend.

CHAPTER IV.

THE HORRORS OF SHIPWRECK—A FEARFUL FRAY.

NEITHER Hunston nor Toro realised the full extent of their calamity at first.

They were by no means ignorant of the value of fresh water in their position.

But being barely out of the greatest possible danger, their minds were in a great degree occupied by other matters, and they did not think of the great trouble which had overtaken them.

The trouble would soon make itself felt.

A pang was felt by Hunston, and for this reason, he had an unpleasant reminder in that afflicted member whereon hung Emmerson's masterpiece of mechanism.

This shot and twinged unpleasantly from time to time, and Hunston would have given much for a little cold fresh water to bathe it with.

"I'm thirsty," said Toro presently. "Where is the water?"

"Overboard."

Toro started.

"Yes, yes, I understand; there is plenty overboard, as you say—plenty of water."

"You don't understand," returned Hunston. "What I told you was that the keg of fresh water had gone overboard in the gale."

"But have we none left on board?"

"No."

"Then we are lost," cried the Italian.

"Lost!"

"Lost, unless a passing vessel picks us up to-day or to-morrow."

"Small chance of that," said Hunston gloomily.

"Well, who's responsible for getting us in this mess—that's what I ask?" cried the giant Toro.

"Am I?"

"Of course."

"It is a lie!" said Hunston.

"Did I strike the blow?" cried Toro.

"What has that to do with the matter? We agreed that the boy should die."

"Harkaway's brat, you mean."

"I do."

"Well."

"Well, then, Emmerson opposed us; he would have pushed matters to extremes, and he fell, as others have fallen before. If the same squabble occurred again, I should do the same again probably. Still, Toro, I will confess that I regret that blow—I regret Robert Emmerson's death more than any act of my life——"

He stopped short as his arm gave him a twinge.

An expression of pain deepened on his face as the pain increased, and in spite of his efforts to restrain it, a deep groan escaped his lips.

Toro looked on, while strange reflections passed through his mind.

What if Robert Emmerson's work should be poisoned?

It was just possible, indeed, he thought, but he kept his thoughts to himself.

The pain which Hunston now experienced was more than a passing annoyance.

The paroxysms commenced with a faint and sickening sensation, and grew gradually more and more unbearable, as the suffering man's face clearly indicated.

"I wonder," thought the Italian, as he watched his companion, "I wonder if these symptoms are the beginning of mortification?"

How strange!

The same thought had entered Hunston's mind.

But he resolutely thrust back the unwelcome fancy.

It could not be.

No.

He had dwelt upon the death of his late comrade Robert Emmerson, until his mind grew filled with all kinds of ugly thoughts.

He would no longer allow himself to be tormented with such idle whims.

But the same thought would ever return.

* * * * *

Many hours passed.

They had all they could desire to satisfy their hunger, but they could not quench their thirst.

And soon they began to suffer most acutely.

Yet they did not like to acknowledge it.

If the truth be told, they did not like even to acknowledge the fact to themselves.

It was an evil conviction which they tried to ward off as long as possible.

As for Hunston, his bad arm grew worse rapidly, and having no means at hand for tending it, the fever increased, and soon his whole body was parched with it.

His throat was dry as parchment, and then, in spite of all he could do, the fearful truth would force itself upon his notice.

They were about to suffer all the horrors of death at sea in an open boat!

They vented their feelings in cursing their late comrades.

They wished them to be assailed by all the ills of mortality at once, and finally to perish in the most miserable manner.

These two wretched men worked themselves up into a perfect frenzy over the thoughts of their enemies, and when they had lashed themselves into a perfect fury, they fell foul of each other.

In the midst of the squabble another small keg fell overboard.

It contained meat, and for a minute it floated adrift.

"We mustn't lose that," ejaculated Toro.

"What's to be done?"

"I'm after it."

And as he spoke, the Italian cast off his coat and hat, and dived into the water.

His action was so sudden that Hunston was taken by surprise.

His first impulse was to pull away from the spot, and leave his friend Toro to perish.

"It is his life or mine," said Hunston to himself. "He might get the best of a squabble, if it came to that."

So he pulled sharply for four or five strokes.

Then his arm pained him so excessively that he was forced to stop, and as he shipped his oars, he perceived Toro rise to the surface, with the keg.

Toro managed to push it on before him as he swam after the boat.

Hunston looked at his comrade earnestly, and as he looked, murderous thoughts took possession of him.

But this was all.

It went no further than thoughts.

As he looked, reflections came of the " for and against " in this matter.

If Toro persisted now, it would leave him master of the boat and its contents, it was true, but it would also leave him alone.

Alone.

The very sound of the word was dreadful to him.

And so the temptation to leave his comrade to perish miserably was abandoned from purely selfish motives.

He could not do without him, at present.

Instead of knocking him on the head

with the oar, he stretched it for him to rest upon.

"Push the keg nearer to me," he said.

"Phew, pooh!" spluttered the Italian. "It has taken all my wind away."

Hunston lifted the keg into the boat.

"I could put an end to him now if I wished," he thought to himself.

Could the swimmer have known how his chances trembled on the balance just then, he would scarcely have felt so comfortable.

He wavered.

Toro held out his hand for help, and Hunston assisted him to scramble into the boat.

"That was a precious hard swim, *caro mio*," said the Italian, shaking the water from his hair, "quite a breather—but it was worth the venture."

"It was."

"But for more reasons than one," remarked Toro.

"What other reasons could there be?" asked Hunston.

"It has refreshed my body completely, and cured my thirst."

"Indeed."

"Aye, that it has."

"I wish it would cure mine," said his companion.

"I'll warrant you it would," said Toro.

"Then I'll——"

He stopped short.

An ugly thought crossed him.

What if Toro should be seized with fancies similar to those that he had had?

No.

This would not do.

He had better not throw temptation in his way.

And as these fancies flitted through his mind, he could not help reflecting how glad he would have been to bathe his fevered body.

Such was the nature of the bond of crime which united these two guilty wretches, that there was nothing approaching confidence between them.

They could never trust each other even after all those long years of close companionship.

*   *   *   *   *

Morning came.

The broiling sun scorched them up,

and what with fatigue and thirst, they were in a truly pitiable plight.

With haggard faces and staring eyes they sat facing each other, supporting, with what patience they could, the torments of thirst.

The silence at length became unbearable.

"Toro," said Hunston, in hollow tones, "I suppose you have read of shipwrecks?"

"I have," returned his companion in much the same strain.

"And you have read of all the horrors that have been experienced by miserable wretches in our condition."

"Yes."

"Why, men have been known to seek each others' lives for food."

"Food."

"Aye."

"What do you mean?"

"Mean? Why, that hunger, despair, madness, have made men cannibals."

"Horrible!"

"Well, well," said Hunston, with a sickly look, "we have not come to that yet, for our stock of food holds bravely out, and we are not likely to lose our reason. The burning, killing thirst that is upon us——"

"What of it?" exclaimed Toro.

"Nothing."

"Of course. How could the death of one or other of us advantage the survivor?"

"Not at all," was the reply. "We could not well drink each other's blood!"

It was an unlucky speech.

Barely had the words been spoken ere he would have given much to recall them.

But it could not be.

They were spoken, and do what he would, they could not be recalled.

But they rang in Toro's ears for many a long hour after, and when he felt the horrible pangs upon him, the terrible reflection came that if his companion lay dead at his feet, it meant a day's more life for him.

And Hunston?

What thought he?

His guilty mind was ever full of such fearful fancies, strive as he would to drive them back.

And now their food remained untouched beside them.

An all-devouring thirst absorbed their thoughts, and they thought only of ministering to it.

* * * *

Night came, and they both sank back in the boat asleep.

But their slumbers were fitful, and broken intermittently.

Towards daybreak, Hunston awoke from his restless sleep, dreaming the most horrible things about the last and most dreadful episode of crime in his guilty life—the murder of Robert Emmerson—and as he opened his eyes, he saw a dark figure bending over him.

He saw that a knife was held over him, and seeing this, he was wide awake immediately.

"Toro!" he cried.

"Ha!" cried the Italian. "You're awake."

"Yes. Stand off."

"Hunston," hissed his companion in his ear, "the time has come that you or I must die; the chance is mine. Die!"

And so saying, he struck downwards a fearful blow.

But Hunston jerked himself aside, and the Italian's knife penetrated deeply into the seat whereon Hunston had been resting.

Then, before Toro could get it free, the Englishman grasped his weapon, and was upon the defensive.

By dint of a desperate effort, he raised himself up to the Italian's level.

"You're wrong!" he cried, in the same mad manner; "it is my turn, and you, Toro, shall die."

And Hunston dug fiercely at Toro.

The blow took effect, but not fatally, in the latter's shoulder.

This blow served to bring Toro to a full sense of his danger.

Quickly recovering himself, the giant sprang back and faced his adversary.

"Hunston," said he, slowly, "you'll never live to repeat that blow."

And he bound his knife in his hand with his handkerchief as he spoke, his fierce eyes being fixed all the while upon his comrade and adversary.

"It is your life or mine," said Hunston.

"Your life or mine," returned Toro.

And the two men, alone in that small boat, on murder bent, fell knife in hand upon each other.

CHAPTER V.

MAGIC ISLAND AGAIN—THE EXPEDITION—A BRACE OF SCOUTS AND BEN HAWSER'S
ADVANCE GUARD—NERO MAKES AN ALARMING DISCOVERY.

To return to Fairy Creek and the Harkaways again.

The news that Monday brought back from his excursion cast a gloom over the whole party.

This may be readily understood.

Spirillo had been a very loose character in bygone days beyond all doubt—they had it in point of fact upon his own admission—but his conduct since he had been with his new-found friends was irreproachable.

Poor Spirillo!

He had just lived to bring them to his reputed El Dorado—this isle of Monte Christo—and then he had met his doom.

He had made himself highly popular with the whole of the party, and now his loss was most keenly felt.

* * * * *

"Jefferson," said Harkaway, to the big American, "we have a duty to perform over this."

"We have," returned Jefferson significantly.

"I mean we must not let this go unpunished."

"Not if we are men," replied Jefferson.

"This Monastos must suffer for it."

"He shall."

"And as there is no time like the present," said Harkaway, "I propose that an expedition should start now."

"At once. Give the orders then."

"No; you give the orders, Jefferson; I'll call the ladies to say good-bye for the present."

"As you please, Harkaway," replied Jefferson; "although I should have preferred your taking the command at once. But stay."

"What now?"

"Not a word to the ladies."

"Of what?"

"Spirillo."

Harkaway shuddered.

"Of course not," he replied. "We should leave them in a desperate state of mind to no purpose."

"I question if we should leave them at all," said Jefferson; "they wouldn't listen to our going if they only knew what had occurred."

"Where is Harvey?"

"Close by; he was here just now—Harvey!"

"Hullo!" replied Dick, from the deck of the vessel.

He had gone back on board to get away from the long faces and heavy hearts about since the sad fate of poor Spirillo had been ascertained.

"Here, Dick!" shouted Jack Harkaway.

"Want me?"

"Yes."

"I'm there."

"We are about starting to discover the retreat of Monastos, the pirate."

"When do we start?"

"In a few minutes."

"Good; I'm ready."

"Call the men together, then."

* * * * *

And so, within an hour from that time, the party started.

It was carried out in this manner.

Monday and his comrade Cæsar Hannibal, both armed to the teeth, crept forward, observing the same tactics as the former had already carried out so successfully.

"Now," said Harkaway, seriously, to his two trusty darkeys, "you must get off—turn to the left or the right, so that each of you will scour one side of the heights above the ravine."

"Yes, sar."

"There must be no imprudence—no rashness."

"No, sar."

"Trust me, Master Harkaway," said Monday.

"Oh yes, sor—you can trust Monday,"

said the other darkey slily; "he'll neber get into danger."

The bystanders grinned a bit at this dig.

This insinuation nettled Monday to the quick.

So he retorted with great asperity—

"As for Sunday, sar, you couldn't have a better man for dis sarvice."

"Glad to hear it."

"That's generous," laughed Dick Harvey.

"Decidedly," said Magog Brand.

"Oh, yes, sar," continued the Prince of Limbi, "Sunday awful cautious man —'fraid of his own ugly shadder."

"Ha, ha, ha!" laughed the bystanders, while poor Sunday was furious.

"Now, then," said Harkaway, "no quarrelling between yourselves. I know you have both courage, and I know that you need it now, for, my good friends, you have the honour of the most dangerous place in the expedition; and after poor Spirillo's fate, it shows no ordinary courage in you to accept the post of scouts."

"Hear, hear!" from Harvey.

"Very true, indeed," said Mr. Jefferson.

"Bravo!" exclaimed Mr. Brand; "bravo, both of you!"

The two darkeys bowed their thanks, and while Monday grinned and showed his teeth with pleasure, Sunday swelled out his chest, and strutted like a bantam cock.

"What we want is prudence," said Harkaway. "The safety of the whole expedition is in your hands, it may be, and there must be no blundering the job."

"You may rely on me, Mr. Harkaway, sar," said Monday.

"I know it."

"And me, too," exclaimed Sunday, quickly.

"I believe you. Now, then, off with you. Your arms are all right?"

"Yes."

"Don't trust too much to your pistols; they make a noise."

"And miss fire occasionally," said Ben Hawser, stepping forward. "There's nothing like dropping them a good one on the nose—a peppery one, straight from the shoulder."

"I've a surer friend here," said Monday.

"Where?"

"Here—surer and quieter."

So saying, he drew his knife, a murderous-looking weapon, with a blade twelve inches long, and a hollowed handle that the hand fitted well into.

He was the wild Indian once more.

He looked, indeed, as though he had a foe under that knife.

"I pity the skunk who gets in the way of Monday's toothpick," said Mr. Jefferson in an undertone to Magog Brand.

"So do I."

*   *   *   *   *

They were gone.

Signals were arranged between the scouts and the main body, and every precaution taken, and then Jefferson, Harkaway, and Dick Harvey set about getting the whole body in order, to march through the ravine.

And now all was ready.

They only waited for the signals from above.

Presently they heard two distinct bird calls from the heights above, at not more than a minute's interval between them.

"Now."

"Stop, your honour," exclaimed Ben Hawser, running forward.

"What now?"

"Who is to serve as scout for the main body?"

"I don't understand you," was Jack's reply.

"Why, I can propose a scout—an advanced guard that'll beat all the darkeys in the world in discretion."

"Where is he?"

"Here."

He whistled shrilly two or three times, and then a little shaggy Scotch terrier came bounding up.

"Good Mike," said Ben, "brave Mike; look how fond he is of his old daddy."

The little dog seemed as though he could devour his master with gratitude at being taken notice of.

"Now, Mike," said Ben Hawser, holding the dog in his left arm and admonishing him with his right fore finger.

"Now you'll have to run on ahead and smell out anybody skulking about; do ye hear?"

The dog replied with a whine of intelligence.

"Now call him, your honour," said Ben.

"'HELP, TORO! HELP ME, FOR I AM SINKING.'"

"Come, Mike," said Jack.

Mike looked wistfully at his master.

"Go on, that's your cap'en now."

Off they started, Mike leading.

And so they pushed through the ravine.

* * * * *

In the meantime, Nero had scrambled up one of the heights after Monday.

The latter had, however, got such a start of Nero that he had some difficulty in finding him, and so he climbed into a tree; then he saw crouching beneath him a dark-visaged man, who was peering through the thickly-grown shrubs upon the party passing beneath.

Nero saw, too, that this man was nervously grasping a rifle which he was about to bring to his shoulder, his intended target being the heart of Jack Harkaway the elder.

CHAPTER VI.

PIONEER MIKE HEADS THE PARTY—MONDAY ON THE WAR-PATH—THE FIGHT IN THE THICKET.

MIKE strutted before the party with an air of dignity, as if conscious of the importance of his position.

He was not a majestic terrier, strictly speaking.

Yet now he evidently felt that he had the safety of the party upon his shoulders, and presently, when about half the distance of the passage through the ravine had been traversed, Mike stopped short, and pricked up his ears; and then he sniffed about uneasily, while a low ominous growl escaped him.

It was startling.

Not a word was spoken, but each member of the small party instinctively grasped his weapons. On guard.

Scarcely an inch of the ground was unwatched by those wary adventurers.

Not a word was spoken.

Suddenly there was a noise in the shrubs overhanging the right cliff, then a crash of breaking twigs and branches, and something whizzed through the air, and fell at the feet of Magog Brand.

It was a rifle.

The little man popped his foot upon it, and placing his own piece to his shoulder, he pointed it straight up at the spot whence the rifle had apparently fallen.

He was not alone in this movement.

A dozen rifles were pointed at the same spot in a trice.

"Forward!" exclaimed Jack Harkaway, promptly; "this may be an ambush; we mustn't be shot here like pigeons out of the traps. Bring on the rifle with you; forward!"

"One moment," said Magog Brand. "Mike has proved himself king of scouts; let him go ahead."

"Right."

"Good dog," said Jefferson; "clear the way, Mike, and you shall have the choicest bit of our first meal."

"I second that," cried Dick Harvey, laughing. "Bravo, Mike! good dog."

With ears erect, and mobile tail, Mike marched on, and so the procession passed safely through the ravine, and through the threatening danger.

* * * * *

We have stated that Nero followed Monday up the heights.

Now Monday's quick ear caught the sound of Nero clambering through the branches of the trees to his perch—for Nero was almost as big as a man—and not dreaming it was his monkey friend. Monday took out his long knife, and looked about him.

After listening intently, while he discovered the direction whence the sounds came, he made that way.

Creeping through the thicket with the greatest caution, he was suddenly brought to a standstill by receiving a smart crack on the head.

A cocoanut fell at his feet.

"Hullo!" thought Monday, "that's somebody pelting me with nuts, and he's almost cracked mine."

But he was silent.

He simply rubbed the damaged part of his head.

And then he looked sharply about him for another.

It was not long in coming.

But forewarned, forearmed.

Monday dodged it with considerable agility.

In getting out of harm's way his eye dropped upon Nero up aloft.

There he was, squatting on a branch, and gathering such missiles as were within reach.

One he had in his hand ready for another shy.

But Monday was surprised to find that he was not the target this time.

There was something almost immediately underneath that apparently excited his attention more than all else.

Monday crept forward on all fours, and there he perceived the body of a man stretched upon the ground.

He also perceived that this man was leaning over the edge of a precipice.

Holding his knife in his teeth by the blade, Monday crawled on.

The man in front, unsuspecting danger to himself, had just raised his rifle to his shoulder, pointed to Harkaway down the precipice.

Monday still crawled on, and then he heard the measured tramp of the party passing through the ravine.

A thousand dreadful fears flashed in an instant through his mind.

Not ten minutes before he had given the signal that all was safe for the march through the ravine.

All this was but the reflection of a moment.

Before he had even time to advance another foot, Nero dropped from his perch on to the next lower branch.

Then he dropped another step, and plumped upon the back of the man overhanging the precipice.

The man gave a yell, and dropped the rifle over the cliff.

The man, frightened at the noise, sprang up, and scrambled—slipped—fell over. Monday looked on surprised.

But soon recovering himself, he crawled up to the edge and looked over, expecting to see the body of the unlucky wretch writhing beneath.

But what was his surprise to discover that he had not fallen more than three feet?

Just beneath them was a wide ledge of land, upon which he had fallen, and contrived to stop himself from rolling further.

Now just as Monday looked over, the man had recovered his balance, and was scrambling into the thicket.

Monday watched his progress.

Then glancing over to the party below, he crawled back, and went in pursuit of the pirate who had had such a lucky escape.

"He hasn't seen me," said Monday to himself, "so I have all the advantage."

He crept on.

Softly he made his way after the other, full of hope of discovering something which would prove of use to his party.

The Prince of Limbi chuckled, when he thought how his success would give him a signal triumph over his African rival, Sunday.

Now barely had this fancy crossed him when he made a very unpleasant discovery.

He had lost the scent.

But he did not give it up yet.

Crawling on, he made his way with more speed than ever.

With more speed, in point of fact, than prudence.

But only for a while.

Then he pulled up and grew wiser.

He got clear of the thicket growth, and then he bent his head to the ground, peering about him like a bloodhound.

He had struck the trail.

He looked to his weapons and went on—on—on.

Soon he was within sight of an opening, from whence started three foot tracks through the dense growth of trees and shrubs, and at the point to which these tracks converged stood a ghastly object—a human head upon a pole stuck in the ground.

Monday paused.

The recollection of that awful sight made him feel uncomfortable, and he did not relish the thought of facing it again.

But in these things there is a fearful fascination, while they horrify, and he could not refrain from peering through the shrubs for a glance at the dreadful object.

And then judge of his surprise, when

he discovered that the opening was already occupied by another.

Yes!

There was the very man he sought.

The object of his pursuit.

And this man was in the act of venting his spleen upon that poor, helpless fragment of a man that had so very recently been full of life and vigour, the head of Spirillo.

Monday could not understand his words.

The pirate was expressing his contempt for Spirillo, and threatening him with all kinds of indignities.

The ruffian concluded a regular tirade of invectives by spitting upon the ghastly object on the pole.

"You shall pay for that," said Monday to himself.

And he set to work.

He crept round through the thick shrubs, and stealing a march thus upon the unscrupulous ruffian, who had not known how to respect a valiant enemy, he suddenly faced him.

"I have you now," said Monday; "and you shall die for this."

"Caramba!" ejaculated the man, thus discovered.

He stood facing Monday for a second or so, fixed to the spot with surprise.

While he was thus spellbound, Monday took his knife in his left hand, and with the other he whipped out the short axe that he had stuck handy in his belt.

The pirate fell back.

Then silently drew his knife.

Monday crept on, slowly, cautiously, and stealthily.

Crept as a cat does on a mouse.

The other retreated slowly—backwards—facing the foe.

Monday was sure of his victim, so he thought, and his face was illuminated with a vicious and triumphant smile.

Suddenly the pirate gave a strange cry, turned round, and plunged into the thicket.

He disappeared.

Yes, he was gone.

Monday gave a cry of utter rage and disgust.

Then he dashed after him.

Bursting his way through the thick undergrowth, he pushed on, literally carving himself a passage with his axe.

The man turned quickly, with knife in hand, but Monday, with his old Indian war shout, was upon him.

The next moment the man lay dead at his feet.

Monday stooped to look at his fallen foe, and was surprised to find he had killed, not the man he was in pursuit of, but one like him only in dress.

"Oh, oh!" thought Monday, "there are more pirates about than one."

Suddenly he stopped short.

Something had struck him in the back.

A treacherous blow it was, too, and it seemed to poor Monday as though his spine had been scared with a red-hot iron.

Not a cry, not a murmur, not a sound escaped him.

Quick as a tiger upon his prey, the Prince of Limbi was round with his face to the enemy.

It was the man he was after.

He had stolen a march upon poor Monday, doubled, and stabbed him in the back.

Then, having delivered the blow, he would have disappeared again, but before he could get quite out of harm's way, Monday hurled the axe at him with all his might.

A wild cry from the pirate told that it had taken effect.

Monday made a rush forward; but the other, in spite of his hurt, managed to dodge him.

In an instant he was gone again.

Monday followed a little way, and having recovered his axe, which was blood-stained, he began to think of turning back. A sickly feeling stole over him.

The wound in the back was beginning to tell, he knew.

"I must get to my party," thought the brave black, "or I shall be found, and decorate another pole beside poor Spirillo."

He turned faint, but he drove this feeling back with fierce resolution, and pushed on.

Suddenly an arm was thrust out of the thicket; a hand with a gleaming knife in it was upraised, and down it came.

Just shaved.

He had seen it, had Monday, and slightly jerking himself aside, avoided the blow.

He turned then, with his old Limbian war-cry, and fell on the hidden enemy, chopping with such desperation with his axe, that there was a regular shower of splinters from the shrubs.

A hollow groan told, too, that he had struck something more than the bushes.

A moment more and the enemy lay revealed, dead at his feet.

One doughty blow severed the unhappy wretch's head from his body.

"Now, sar, you are number two," said Monday, with a grim smile; "so me take down Spirillo, and put dis poll on de oder pole. Yah, yah!"

This worthy savage had dropped back half a lifetime in civilization, by simply returning to the instincts of his youth.

He was on the war path.

All was justifiable.

Dragging himself painfully along, and bearing the ghastly trophy with him, he reached the well-known opening to which converged the different paths through the thicket.

"Come down, Spirillo," said he tenderly; "come down, ole friend, and let me poke up in your place dis oder dam tief."

And then he grew fainter and fainter.

A film spread over his eyes.

"I'm a 'coon—gone 'coon," he faltered He sank upon the ground.

"My head will be dere after all," he murmured.

The thought gave him a moment's renewed strength.

So he jerked up, and whistled three times upon a small silver call he carried.

"Where dat nigger Sunday—why him not here now to help me?"

Then after a moment's pause—

"Massa Harkaway," he faltered; "Jack! Massa Dick! Come—help—I die."

And he sank back.

Then as he lost consciousness, two fierce eyes gleamed at him through the foliage, and a long, lank form crept stealthily out into the open.

CHAPTER VII.

ADVENTURES IN MAGIC ISLAND—A SAD BEGINNING—EXTRAORDINARY FESTIVITIES IN THE WOOD.

THEY heard poor Monday's signal below, but before they could render him any assistance, the chances were that his own prophecy would be realised—that his head would make the third ghastly trophy in that grim scene.

"Hark!" said Mr. Jefferson; "do you hear?"

"Yes; it is Monday."

"He is hurt."

"Or has long odds to meet," suggested Harvey.

"I should like to be in his place, then," said Mr. Mole, grandly.

"No doubt."

"No, gentlemen," said the American doctor, "the cry we heard sounded like someone in distress, and if we are to render any assistance to our faithful friend, we must be quick."

Harkaway blew an answer to Monday's signal.

"Hark!"

They listened for a reply.

But listened in vain.

After a minute or two's ominous silence, they began to look at each other, with long faces.

They said nothing, but they all felt that some fresh calamity was threatening.

They did not dare to speak their thoughts.

They feared that poor Monday had shared Spirillo's fate.

"Halt!" said Jack; "I will sound the signal once more."

No answer.

"This looks bad for poor Monday," said Harkaway; "we must be quick, gentlemen."

He then led the way up the heights, from the opposite side to that which Monday had started from.

They went up in skirmishing order, Mike being generally selected to lead the van.

Mike trudged on.

He knew he had serious work to do.

The grave faces of his friends and patrons impressed him deeply; for a most impressionable dog was Mike.

In skirmishing order they mounted the heights, until Mr. Mole was forced to pull up for assistance.

"Harvey," he groaned.

"What is it, Mr. Mole?" asked Dick.

"With my infirmity I can't make headway."

"Footway, you mean, sir," suggested Harvey, looking at Mole's legs.

Mr. Mole frowned at Dick, who, however, remained perfectly serious.

"I slip as I go on, Harvey," he said.

"One step forward and two back?" suggested Harvey.

"Yes."

"As if it was on a glacier?"

"Exactly."

"I know what you want, then, Mr. Mole."

"Indeed?"

"Yes; you want roughing."

"What?"

"Roughing, sir, about the feet, depend upon it," said Dick.

"Mr. Harvey, I must beg you to be more respectful in your manner."

"No disrespect, sir," said Harvey, "none whatever. Allow me."

And he stooped to lift up one of Mr. Mole's timber toes.

Dick was actually treating Mr. Mole as a farrier would a horse.

Mole would have resented the liberty thus taken with him, but Dick had him by the leg.

So, to save himself from falling, he had to clutch his tormentor round the shoulders for support.

Dick examined the bottom of the wooden limb with a critical air.

"Yes," he said, "a nail in each of those will convert Mr. Mole into a pair of perambulating alpenstocks."

"Think so, Harvey?"

"Yes. Happy thought. Keep steady, sir."

For the sake of the advantage to be gained, the tutor submitted to the operation, and soon Mr. Mole was firmer at each step than any member of the party, and all through that simple operation.

A nail was driven into the tip of each wooden leg, and the spikes dug in the ground, prevented him slipping.

And Isaac Mole smiled with gratification as he went, even condescending to approve, in a patronising manner, of Dick's small pleasantries at his expense.

*   *   *   *   *

What was that?

The dog Mike growled.

There was a general halt.

Every hand grasped a weapon with a nervous grip, as if in instant expectation of being called upon to use it.

Mike went on a few paces further, and then sniffed the ground and began to paw the earth.

They stooped to look at what excited the intelligent canine's attention.

The ground was moist in a round, hollow place, and when they approached to examine it closely, they discovered that the moisture was blood.

"See here!" exclaimed Harkaway; "there has been foul play."

"Yes, no doubt," said Harvey; "look, the blood extends along here."

"Blood."

"Blood!" echoed everyone, in one voice as it were.

"Is it Monday's?"

A shudder went through the whole assemblage.

Poor Monday.

Could they have only known of his piteous plight, and how close he was to them at that moment, what would they have done?

And yet poor Monday was close upon the spot.

They might have seen the luckless and faithful Prince of Limbi stretched upon the ground, scarcely any life to speak of in him.

They would have seen a dark-visaged Greek, hovering near, knife in hand, ready to take what life yet remained in that poor motionless body.

Twice had that murderous-looking Greek crept out to wreak his vengeance upon the hapless Monday.

Twice had he been startled by a strange noise, that he could by no means understand, but he now, with a firm step, ventured out, knife in hand.

It looked very bad for poor Monday now.

It seemed that no power could save him.

And the ruffian gloated at the prospect of revenge that was not at his command.

He knelt over the senseless Limbian, and felt his heart, and then tried various parts of his body for a pulse.

But he tried in vain.

There must have been very little—if any—life in poor, unlucky Monday by this time.

Then finding Monday as lifeless as he could wish, he bared his throat, and felt the edge of his knife.

He set to work now.

With his brutal left hand, he thrust back the destined victim's chin; with his right he brought the long ugly knife close to the throat.

"Your head," he said, looking with fierce eyes at Monday, "shall deck another pole."

"Ha, ha!"

A wild cry escaped him.

Some invisible foe had dragged him by the hair with such fierceness that it seemed as though his scalp was coming away.

He dropped his knife, and clapped his hand to the injured part.

"Ha, ha!"

He yelled again and again, and the harder he yelled, the harder did this unseen enemy drag.

He wrestled mightily with the foe, nevertheless, and suddenly wriggling himself round, he caught a glimpse of his assailant.

Now that glimpse filled his very soul with fear.

The Greek's only thought was that the evil one had come to claim his own at last.

So desperate did his struggles now become, that he actually tore himself away, leaving a good handful of his gory locks in the hands of the enemy, and as he got free, he turned to the thicket just at the very instant that a man—Magog Brand—appeared in the opening.

Magog cocked his rifle and blazed away after him.

The ruffian did not get altogether clear off.

The shot took effect in his left ham, but so far on the side, that it made a narrow fissure in his flesh, and passed on without resting in his body.

"Ha, ha!"

And he howled more than ever as he made his escape.

"Look, here is poor Monday," cried Brand.

They were right glad when they came up to poor Monday.

"What do you say, doctor?" asked Harkaway, eagerly. "Is he dangerously hurt?"

The doctor paused.

He looked grave for a minute, then said—

"He will live."

"Thank Heaven!" ejaculated Harkaway, fervently.

"Amen!" said Dick.

They had been through so many perils and troubles together, in many lands, that they felt the greatest affection for their dear old friend and companion, whose friendship they had made under circumstances of no ordinary danger.

"He has had a very ugly blow," said the American doctor, with a serious air, "and his recovery will certainly take a long while."

"We must get him back to the ship," said Harkaway.

"Shall we all go?"

"No need for that," said Jack Harkaway; "let four of the party be told off for the service, and two more serve as escort; this will be all that is necessary."

They set to work hurriedly to construct a litter, and then they bore the poor fellow tenderly away.

But while this was proceeding, Mr. Jefferson was looking about in anxious inquiry.

"What is it, Jefferson?" cried Harkaway.

"Where's Mole?"

"Mr. Mole!" Jack shouted.

Isaac Mole was somehow or other absent.

"Where was he last seen?"

"Who saw him last?"

There were plenty to put this question, but few were in a position to answer it.

"For Heaven's sake, speak, some of you," exclaimed Harkaway; "I fear this Greek ruffian has murdered him!"

At length one of the sailors volunteered a little information.

"Where did you see him, Ben?" asked Harkaway.

"Why, your honour," answered the honest tar, "he fell out to refresh."

"Refresh?"

"Yes."

"What, to drink?"

"Yes, sir."

"Well," ejaculated Jefferson, "that's a big joke, I reckon."

"Don't think he'll find it one," said Magog Brand.

"Poor old Mole," said Dick Harvey; "one or two of us ought to hark back and look about for him."

"Aye, aye!"

"Who'll go with me?"

"I will, your honour," said Ben Hawser, "if so be as it ain't agin the rules, for I shouldn't like to see the schoolmaster come to grief—damme!"

"Off with you then," said Harkaway. "But pray use every caution."

"Trust me."

"Be sure to give the signal in case of danger."

"I will."

"And now you return as quickly as you can to the ship, with all care for your patient."

"Yes."

And so they started off.

* * * * *

The disappointed ruffian, who had to beat a retreat, crawled through the thicket and got out of danger.

Moaning and groaning, he went on all fours.

He had got an ugly gash on the head, that he owed to Monday in their skirmish; he had lost a tuft of hair, and in addition to this, he had received a bullet wound in the haunch, which left him very unhappy indeed.

Chairs were scarce in Magic Island, but if they had had them in plenty, this unhappy wretch could not have ventured to have enjoyed one.

And as he crawled along, he came suddenly upon a remarkable object.

It was nothing less than a man squatting upon the ground and sucking ardent liquor from a bottle.

This man's face was flushed.

His nose was tipped with a very ruddy glow.

His eyes sparkled brilliantly, and he rocked to and fro as he sat.

Now when the wounded ruffian approached, the carouser looked up, and fixing his eyes upon him, said—

"Come and sit down, the pair of you, and don't get dancing round and round like that, you'll gid getty—that is, get giddy. Come, come, old fellow, and liquor up."

And then he burst out into a bacchanalian chant, which surprised the newcomer—

> "'Gaily now my moments roll,
> While I quaff the bowing fiowl,
> Care shall never touch Ike Mole,
> If he deeply, deeply drinks his grog.'

"He, he, he! my cheerful pal. Gently; don't waltz round like that, but come and have a pull. Sit down, both of you; this is a free an' easy, an' not a dance—he, he!"

CHAPTER VIII.

MR. MOLE IN HIS WAR-PAINT—HIS BRUSH WITH THE ENEMY.

THE Greek ruffian looked more alarmed at Mr. Mole than if the latter had shown fight.

The probability is, that he took the worthy man for a magician, and thought that his bacchanalian ditty was an incantation.

"Come and sit down, ole f'lar," said Mr. Mole, waving his hand; "chake a tair—thatish takes shair—'scuse my speeth—spe—speech—I've been shuffering so with toothache that it'sh quite affected my talking; it's made my head bad too—precious bad—must have it off—pah—ha! Come an' sit down an' make yourselves happy!"

Then he looked about him with tipsy gravity.

"Where'sh the other?"

No answer coming, he went on—

"Mo'stronary—can't make where'sh th'other. Come an' sit down—what'll you take?"

He made an effort to rise.

Thereupon the Greek drew his knife.

Now, far gone as he was, Isaac Mole knew what that meant.

So he felt for his revolver and cocked it.

But he might as well have cocked a champagne bottle.

His revolver was filled with whisky, which had leaked from a bottle in his pocket, and the weapon was of no use.

The ruffian, seeing the revolver, grew awfully frightened.

He dropped his knife on the ground, and bowed in the most extravagant token of submission.

"Quite sho," said Isaac Mole; "come sit down, you ugly ruffian, or I shall shoot you."

Apparently the Greek did not understand the words, but the gestures accompanying the speech were full of meaning.

So down he dropped immediately, facing Mr. Mole.

"Now take a pull at this, you vagabond," said the latter, handing him the cup off his flask full of liquor.

The other gave him a Greek "thank you," and took a good draught at the cup.

Then he coughed, and spluttered, and nearly choked, for it was over-proof whisky—neat, that Mr. Mole had been drinking.

The Greek had not tasted whisky before.

And when he recovered his breath, he got on his feet and seized his knife again.

His eyes were half starting out from their sockets, and his face was blood-red.

Some violent ejaculations in his own tongue burst from him, and he made a rush at the astonished Mr. Mole.

The latter would have been in a sorry predicament, but for a singular accident.

He lifted his right leg to ward off the assault, and as the Greek made a mad rush, he spiked himself on the nail that tipped the timber toe—Dick Harvey's roughing.

"Aha!" cried the Greek.

And down he dropped his knife, as the pain of his hurt from the nail doubled him up.

Mr. Mole valiantly lunged out again, and this time he caught the Greek upon the neck.

"What are you howling at?" said Mole; but he was partly sobered by what he had seen, for it was rather a startling job, and so, with commendable presence of mind, he followed his success sharply up.

He first secured the Greek's knife and his own revolver, and then he rushed at the enemy.

The latter, having received half an inch of rusty nail in his neck, had been knocked over, but scrambling to his feet, he made off just as Mr. Mole remorselessly prodded him behind with his right leg—and right nail.

"Aha! Oho! Hoha!" yelled the Greek.

And he rushed away shrieking with fear; for Mr. Mole had "landed him" upon a sore spot—the fissure in his ham that had been made by Magog Brand's bullet. At the very moment that he disappeared, Dick Harvey, guided by the noise, rushed up to Mole.

"Hullo!" cried Dick, anxiously, "are you safe?"

"And sound," said Mole.

"Thank Heaven for that," said Harvey. "You gave us a precious fright, but we thought we heard a noise."

Mr. Mole smiled.

"My dear Harvey," said Mr. Mole, "I like to take the field single-handed."

"What?"

"I have met the foe!"

"Never!"

"I have—and conquered," said Mr. Mole. "It is true," he added moodily, "they were not in force—there were, in fact, only five of them."

"Five?"

"Yes, only five."

"You met them single-handed?"

"Of course."

"And fought?"

"Very much fought, of course."

"And you beat them all off?"

"Still more of course."

"Well," said Harvey, "well, you are a brave man, sir."

" Did you ever know me to turn my back to the foe?"

" No."

" I thought not."

"Nor your face either," muttered Dick.

Yet he was puzzled, for he certainly had heard cries as he came up.

Some more of the party came up.

" I have fought and conquered," said Isaac Mole, with a flourish; " behold the spoils of victory."

And he showed the knife that the frightened brigand had left behind him in his flight.

" Well done, Mr. Mole," said Brand.

" The brave Mole was alone, single-handed," said Harvey.

" Where are your victims?" inquired Brand.

" I can't say; the whole seven of them fled, scattered like chaff before the wind, and by this mighty arm alone."

" Seven!" said Harvey.

" Seven," said Mr. Mole, with serious emphasis.

" You said five."

" Five," explained Mr. Mole, with considerable readiness, " five I fought;

the other two can scarcely have been said to fight."

" How so?"

" Five of the poor scared wretches cut up so miserably bad, that the other two were quite demoralized, so I let one off with a prod in the ribs from my leg."

" Very kind."

" But the other got one from my fist that made him swallow six of his teeth."

" Did you also make them eat their heads?" asked Brand.

" Oh, oh, oh!" groaned the party in chorus.

" The Greek might have swallowed his teeth," said Dick, " but Mr. Mole will never expect us to swallow his tale."

" Mr. Harvey!" said Mole in great indignation.

" In point of fact," said Dick, laughing, " Mr. Mole's peculiar romance suggests a riddle."

" A riddle?"

" Yes."

" Let's have it," said Magog Brand.

" It is this," said Harvey. " Why is a tooth like a lie?"

" Give it up."

" Because it's a Mole-ar."

CHAPTER IX.

THE TIGER'S LAIR — DOWN IN THE EARTH.

THE Greek pirate, whom Mr. Mole had vanquished, fled to the thickest part of the wood.

And when he had ascertained that he was free from pursuit, he made his way to a spot, where cleverly concealed in the shrubs from even a close scrutiny, was a large, flat slab of stone, with an iron ring sunk in it.

This he raised.

Beneath was a flight of roughly-cut steps that went down into the earth, at least twenty feet.

The Greek stepped down, and replaced the stone after him.

This done, he descended the steps, and passed along a narrow vaulted passage, dark and gloomy, and furnished with a miserable flickering lamp of bad oil at intervals of twenty yards.

At the end of this passage he came to a barred gateway of great solidity, where he knocked four times loudly.

The gate was opened by a thick-set man, of weird and savage aspect.

A man whose age it was not easy to guess at from his appearance.

This man addressed the new comer in Italian.

The new comer replied in the same language.

" Who's there?"

" It is I, Stavros; is Monastos within?"

" Yes."

" Good. Keep a strict watch here, and mind what you are about. There are enemies abroad," said Stavros, seriously.

" Enemies!" repeated the other, looking blank.

" Aye, enemies, and clever enemies, too, crafty, cunning enemies, that get up to tricks; enemies to avoid, enemies to fear."

" Fear !"

And then he aroused himself a bit and stared.

" Aye, fear."

He nodded with a deal of significance, and repeated Stavros's last words, as the latter pushed on his way along the low, vaulted passage.

This second passage was about thirty yards long, and was guarded by a second door more massive than the first.

Passing through this, he came to a low, vaulted cavern.

This opened out into a larger vault or cave.

In this cave there was a thick-set man, with an iron-grey beard and weather-beaten face, that told of exposure to wind, and rain, and sun for many a long year.

This man was slightly above the middle height, and appeared to be the principal person in the company present.

He was busily employed in super-intending the loading of pistols, and polishing of steel arms of various makes and descriptions, while the bulk of the work was being performed by two men.

Near them was a beautiful girl.

The two men were evidently of a very low type; but there was an unmistak-ably superior look about the girl.

The other man, he of the iron-grey beard, was between forty and fifty years of age.

His closely-knit frame spoke of great bodily strength.

To the left of the door by which Stavros had entered was a vaulted aperture, beyond which could be seen the daylight faintly glistening through a dense foliage.

At this entrance stood two armed sentries.

Silent. Motionless.

The table was prepared in the centre of the cavern, and was already creaking and groaning under a profusion of riches, that were in strange contrast with the wild and rugged appearance of the dwelling itself.

Rich wines and fruits were there in abundance, and in endless variety, and the service was of gold plate.

There was the finest table-linen, and. in fine, every luxury of civilization and wealth.

So extraordinary did it look in such a place that it would sorely have puzzled any of the Harkaway party, could they have pierced that jealously-guarded entrance.

What would they have thought it was like ?

It recalled, more than aught else, a scene in a pantomime opening, where the change from gay to grave, from banquet-ing halls of dazzling light to the haunts of demon miners, is performed in a slip-shod manner by the slow scene-shifters, and the festive board is left forgotten, long after the brilliant walls and flashing mirrors have given place to the dismal cavern " flat."

Stavros stared at the preparations for the feast, and his eyes glistened.

" Captain Monastos !" he said, or rather gasped—for he was nearly done up with his late exertions.

" Stavros, you here !"

The captain turned in surprise as the latter entered.

Stavros dropped upon a cushion that lay nearly at his feet.

But he rolled over with a cry of pain.

He had fallen upon the wound that he owed to Magog Brand's unerring rifle.

Monastos and the rest of the people gathered around him.

" What is it, Stavros ?" asked the Greek captain ; " are you hurt ?"

" I am."

" Badly ?"

" I fear so."

" Is it this cut you have in the neck and head ?"

" That is not the worst, captain," re-plied Stavros. " I am faint with loss of blood and fatigue."

" Faint !" said Monastos. " Give him some wine."

This was obeyed.

A large goblet of silver was filled to the brim with rich wine.

The parched Stavros drank it to the dregs. Monastos stooped and hastily exa-mined the hurt upon his head.

" This is a bad knock," said he, " but it is by no means dangerous."

" That is not all," said Stavros. " I'm shot !"

" Shot ?"

" Aye."

" Not in the chest or body?" said Monastos, anxiously.

" No," replied Stavros, hesitating.

And looking up at the girl who was looking down upon him, full of solicitude for him—

" I am shot—in the rear."

" This shall be seen to at once."

" Paquita !"

" Yes, father," said the girl.

" Go and prepare a bed for Stavros in the adjoining chamber, as soft a one as possible, my child."

" Yes, father."

" Now tell me, Stavros," said the pirate and brigand chief, eagerly, as his daughter disappeared, " are they in force?"

" Yes."

" How many ?"

" Thirty, at least."

Monastos burst out laughing at this.

" Thirty ?" he ejaculated. " Why, Stavros, we shall eat thirty in about an hour."

" Not thirty of this breed," replied Stavros, " for take my word for it, they are thirty devils."

CHAPTER X.

THE BANQUET HALL—PETRUS THE IDIOT AND HIS TWIN BLOODHOUNDS— HUNTING A MAN—ON THE SCENT.

" HA, ha, ha !" laughed the brigand chief. " Why, you are getting quite jocular, Stavros."

" Wait till you have heard all," replied the latter.

" If thirty devils should come to attack us, my word upon it, our brave, if small, force will soon put them to flight."

" Perhaps."

" Or provide them with graves," added the brigand chief, fiercely.

Then he continued—

" The information is, I admit, to a certain extent, serious, although not anything as serious as you would lead us to believe."

" Good."

And Stavros looked as savage as a bear.

He had been doing all the work and receiving all the hard knocks up to the present.

" Before you treat this matter lightly, captain," said Stavros, " you should be sure that you may not have cause to weep."

The captain frowned.

" You are growing rather daring, Stavros," he said.

Captain Monastos looked a bit serious now.

" Come, come," he said, " tell me all."

" Well, in the first place, they have got a monkey dressed like a man that fights for them."

" A monkey ?" ejaculated Monastos.

" Yes."

" But surely a monkey can't be a dangerous enemy. He is not one of the devils ?"

" I don't know that. He looks more like the evil one than any man could."

This made the brigand captain laugh.

" Well, you may be right there, Stavros," he said; " but why not knock this monkey on the head ?"

Stavros laughed now.

A wild, sardonic grin it was too.

" Easily said."

" Not so easily done?"

" Not quite. Why, you can't get near him; I couldn't so much as touch his tail."

" Then surely you could knock him over with a bullet?"

" He's bullet proof," said Stavros, with great gravity; " you will have an opportunity of judging for yourself before long, no doubt."

" We shall see."

" Besides this, they have a very dangerous help in the shape of a little dog; don't laugh yet, until you have heard why he is such a dangerous help. This dog is trained to nose out everything that his master wants him to find. We had them covered in the ravine with our rifles; we could have picked them off one after the other; not one would have got through the pass alive, or at least unhurt."

"Well, well?" exclaimed Monastos eagerly.

"The dog smelt us—hang him!—and warned them, and not one was scratched. Besides this, they have two negro scouts, who are as daring as forty devils."

The captain's face grew more serious.

"Scouts?"

"Yes."

"Then we must look after them; they shall have our first care."

There was a murderous significance in his manner as he said this.

"That is not all," said Stavros.

"What more can there be?"

"They have a dwarf that looks like an unnatural imp, and who shot me without aiming at me."

"Have they anything else to mention besides their regular men?" asked the pirate captain.

"Yes; they have a man who has no legs."

"No legs?"

"No."

"Well, then, he can't do much damage."

Stavros clapped his hands to his two wounded parts, yet smarting with the stabs that the inebriated Mole had inflicted upon him with his "roughing."

"You wouldn't say that if you had been in my place."

"How? Why, surely a legless man can't have done you any harm?"

"Legless," said Stavros, "in a manner of speaking. His legs are gone, it is true, but they are replaced by stilts of wood, and fitted into the ends are sharp blades. Now this man can hop as if his body were upon springs, hop wonderful distances, and use one of his legs like a lance, and a devilish ugly weapon it makes."

He groaned as he rubbed the wounded parts that were souvenirs of Isaac Mole's prowess.

Captain Monastos opened his eyes wide in wonder.

"Well, Stavros," he said, rather more seriously, "I confess that it does make a queer list, after all—a monkey, a dog, two negro scouts, a dwarf that shoots round the corner, and a springy man mounted upon lances."

"I thought you would say so."

"Indeed, I do."

"But wait until you have come in contact with them yourself."

"Yes, wait," said the captain, significantly; "I have already thought of the two negroes, and how to dispose of them to advantage."

"How?"

"We have two faithful friends who do not object to the taste of negro flesh."

"The taste?"

"Yes; Castor and Cyrus, you may remember."

"The bloodhounds?"

"Yes."

"One of the negroes is already beyond harm, unless I am very much mistaken."

"How?"

"I have seen to him."

"Have you met and fought with him?"

"I have. Listen, captain."

"Go on."

"Costantino met the first of their party, a traitor, who ventured here, lurked behind him upon the wooded heights, then pounced upon him, and chopped him down to his death."

"Good!" cried Monastos. "That's brave."

"Wait, captain. He was a brave fellow, Costantino, was he not?"

"He was."

"Well, Costantino killed the spy, and stuck his head upon a pole just on the spot where he fell."

"Bravo, bravo!" cried several of the brigands, gathering round as the wounded man's narrative increased in interest.

"Well. A warning to any who should dare to follow," said the chief.

"Yes."

"Costantino shall find that I know how to reward my brave followers," said Captain Monastos, with the air of a grand monarch.

"He has already met with his reward."

"How? Speak," Monastos ejaculated angrily. "Why mumble so in riddles? What reward can Costantino have met with already?"

"He met one of the negro scouts," answered Stavros; "met him upon the very spot where the head stood up as a warning."

"Say on."

"They fought!"

"Costantino killed his man?" said the chief.

"No. Costantino did not conquer."

"Confusion!" exclaimed Monastos; "then he——"

"Is dead; killed by the black scout."

A groan came from the pirates.

"His head now replaces that of the first man—the spy who had the temerity to venture into the tiger's den; and what's more, I believe two of our band are killed."

"Then, Stavros," said the brigand captain, with a stern air of determination, "the man had better be at the bottom of the sea than face my vengeance; for I swear——"

"I have already begun that task," said Stavros; "the murderer of Costantino has that which he will not forget, and, but that I was interrupted, I would have settled his account with life to-day."

"Good, Stavros," said the captain, gloomily. "My men shall be bitterly avenged. Go on. Tell me how you fared while encountering this African savage."

"I had his throat and head at my mercy, when that demon ape fell upon me."

"The ape?"

"Aye. He is as big as a man."

"And the black scout got off?"

"He did; but not before I had avenged poor Costantino. He was yet living when I left him, but to his grave he will carry my marks."

"Bravo!"

"That is something," said the brigand captain exultingly; "but you should have killed him outright, even had it cost you your life."

Stavros frowned.

"Of what nation were they?" asked the pirate chief.

"English," said Stavros.

The captain was silent.

It was a position of difficulty.

Stavros was quite right when he said that his captain had not seen the full danger of the position.

"I do not like the English," said Monastos; "we must look well to our arms, and see that they do not escape us."

The force under Jack Harkaway as

now composed was indeed a formidable array.

Craft, wit, strength, were all and each amply represented.

They possessed men of daring beyond anything that their enemies contemplated.

Of their enterprise and ability they had already given good proofs.

* * * * *

"Tell us, Stavros, which way are they marching now?" asked Monastos.

"By the ravine path, thence by the main route."

"Good."

"The negro, who is yet safe and sound, is, or was, lost in the wooded height on the right of the ravine."

The brigand captain jumped up at this.

"That's the idea then," he said; "let us cut them off in detail, kill them off one by one, these cursed English."

"Good."

"The first thing, then," said the brigand captain, "is to send the twin bloodhounds to me."

"What, Castor and Cyrus?"

"Yes."

"Huzzah!" cried Stavros, half rising from the ground, and waving his hand. "You fill me with hope; send the hounds hither that I may look upon them before they go."

The next minute, a deep baying sound was heard, and one of the brigands brought in a pair of immense bloodhounds leashed together.

The man who brought them in, was the big, sullen man who guarded the first gate by which Stavros had entered the brigand fastness.

The man with the tawny beard and unkempt hair, whose looks of intelligence were but transient, and whose expression was generally vacant.

A man whose mind was a blank, one who could happily forget the past at times, for his past was brimfull of painful recollections.

"Ah, Petrus," said Monastos, "bring them here."

Petrus led them up to the captain and let go.

The captain half drew his pistols.

"Keep them well in hand," said he; "they are not muzzled."

"Fear not."

"Nay, I don't fear them," said Monastos, with an uneasy look; "only they never seem to take kindly to me."

"There's no danger," said Petrus.

And without more ado he set them at liberty.

Immediately, one crawled to the brigand chief, and growled ominously.

The captain was no coward, and did not fear meeting in combat any two men, yet somehow those fierce bloodhounds made him unhappy.

He would sooner face three men in single combat, than one of these fierce hounds.

He made a movement as though to chastise the dog, when at once it crouched to spring.

There was no mistaking this action.

His tail moved uneasily from side to side, and he looked full of fire.

The strange man they called Petrus seemed to watch with joy the hostile movements of the bloodhounds against the pirate and brigand captain.

"Call them off," cried the captain, "quick!"

"Castor!" shouted Petrus, angrily. "Come here, sir."

The noble beast turned with a whine to his keeper.

"Come, come," said Petrus; "good dog. Kiss me."

Thereupon, the hound leaped into his arms, opened to receive him, and caressed him eagerly.

He must have been a powerful fellow, indeed, to stand the shock of this huge animal.

But it did not even shake him, to all appearance.

"Petrus."

"Hola."

"Fetch this other hound from me; the brute smells the blood, I am sure, and he looks as though he were ready to eat me."

It was Stavros.

Cyrus did, indeed, hover round the wounded brigand, as though he would have relished a meal off him.

The wounds of the poor wretch were full of fragrance for Cyrus, as you might perceive by the greedy way in which he licked his fangs.

"Now you, Cyrus," cried Petrus, and the second hound also came quickly to his side, licking his hands.

"Bring them something to eat," said Monastos.

No sooner said than done.

A large wooden dish filled with meat and bones was placed in the middle of the floor, and the two bloodhounds flew to it.

But not to touch a morsel.

"Here," cried Petrus in a voice of thunder.

The hounds slunk back, and crouching with deep humility, they dragged their bellies along the ground to their noble master.

The rest of the brigands looked on astounded.

"You have them well in hand. It is marvellous," said Monastos.

"There appears to be a sort of understanding between them," said the wounded man.

"Yes. There is a species of affinity between an Englishman and a dog," said the captain, frowning.

Yells of laughter greeted this witticism.

And while they laughed, the half savage Petrus looked up, his eyes flashing fire for an instant.

But the gleam was only momentary.

It faded away, and was soon replaced by the regular vacant stare.

"Quite right, Captain Monastos," he said, with a mad laugh. "Quite right. You are a brave man and a wit. I am only an Englishman."

"You English are all dogs," said Monastos.

"Yes," said Petrus, staring vacantly at the ground, "I suppose that I am the next thing to a dog myself, and that is why I took so readily to you."

"Silence, dog," said the captain, "and start your twin beauties on the hunt. A nigger is your quarry, my brave Castor, and my doughty Cyrus. Hunt him down. Tear him piecemeal, and you shall have a meal to your liking. Real nigger black pudding. Ha, ha!"

Off they started with the hounds.

Poor Sunday was in fearful jeopardy now.

Before the twin bloodhounds had been out half an hour, they were upon the scent, and following it eagerly, with their noses to the ground.

"The dogs are on the scent," said Petrus, "and the poor wretch will be torn in shreds."

"NERO ARRIVES JUST IN TIME."

CHAPTER XI.

NEWS ON BOARD—IN THE STILL NIGHT—"THUS BEGINS THE VENGEANCE OF MONASTOS."

On board the "Westward Ho!" they were anything but comfortable.

Hilda was full of uneasiness, little Emily was never tired of uttering her misgivings about young Jack, and Mrs. Harkaway felt her own spirits sink more and more.

After the lapse of a few hours, a party of men was seen approaching the ship, bearing the body of poor Monday on a litter.

Ada ran forward to greet her faithful Monday, and received his inanimate form with deep emotion.

"Oh, my poor Monday, my poor Monday!" she cried. "What can I do to help you through this trouble?"

The wounded Prince of Limbi opened his eyes.

"I am all right, Ada," said he; "only a little hurt."

"Only a little," she iterated. "Why, Monday!"

"I shan't leave you a widow yet, Ada," said the faithful fellow with a faint laugh.

Emily ran up.

Her face was pale.

She was no chicken-hearted woman.

She had been in too many stirring scenes of danger and trouble to feel alarmed now without ample cause.

"How are the others, my poor Monday?" asked Emily, eagerly.

"All right."

"No one hurt?"

"No one."

"Ah!" she sighed, in deep relief.

"No," said he, "only poor unlucky Monday knocked out of the fun. Just my luck," he continued, with a groan. "That nigger Sunday has it all to himself; he'll have the laugh at me."

Would he?

Sunday's position at that particular moment was far from being enviable.

Poor Sunday!

Little short of a miracle would it be if he chanced to get through it with life.

* * * * *

Monday's hurts happily proved to be of a far less serious nature than might have been supposed.

The consequence was that the faithful fellow made rapid progress, and so, before he had been many hours on board, he began to entertain hopes of soon rejoining Harkaway and his adventurous party.

* * * * *

It was night.

The watch was set.

This watch was shared by Ben Hawser and the two lads, Jack Harkaway the younger and Harry Girdwood.

They were chatting in a half sleepy manner forward, when young Jack turned suddenly round and ejaculated—

"Do you hear that?"

"What?"

"That scraping noise."

Harry listened for awhile, and then he said to his companion—

"You must be mistaken."

"I'm sure I was not. Hark!"

"I certainly heard something that time."

"What do you think it can be?" said young Jack.

"It sounds very like the cable being parted."

They listened in silence some considerable time, but the sounds were not renewed.

What could it mean?

Was there something wrong going forward?—more evil doers lurking there?—and had they been surprised spite of the vigilance of the watch?

To tell the honest truth, the awful and sudden end of poor Spirillo had in some degree startled the whole of the party.

Suddenly there was a strange creaking noise, and the ship gave a lurch.

A lurch that would be nothing in the open sea, but which was enough to fill them with the greatest alarm, taking place in that sheltered creek, that was still as a mill-pond, with scarcely a ripple on its surface.

"Hullo there," cried Ben Hawser.

"What now?" said Jack.

"What can it mean?" said Harry Girdwood, seriously.

The vessel groaned as she moved on apace.

"Why, stop my grog!" cried Ben Hawser, "if she arn't under way. There's something wrong here."

The two boys looked at each other.

There was no mistaking the fact now.

The "Westward Ho!" was moving, gliding slowly along the water.

"By Heaven! you were right, Harry!" exclaimed young Jack. "The cable has been parted!"

For a few seconds they were quite staggered with this discovery.

But the gallant old tar, Ben Hawser, was the first to recover his presence of mind.

"Damme!" he cried, "the enemy is up to divers' tricks."

"And sundry artifices," said young Jack, who had the true Harkaway relish for a joke.

Ben Hawser stepped over the bulwarks and slid down the rope to the water.

Then, grasping the ship's chains, he groped along round the vessel.

Nearly the whole of his body was submerged, but, like a veteran sea lion, he was prepared for any sudden emergency by contriving, in spite of difficulties, to keep his powder dry.

And this is how he did it.

He carried his revolver in a stout leathern case, the lid of which he held in his teeth, and groping along thus, he presently came in sight of a dark form swimming at the head of the ship.

Drawing nearer, he contrived to see that it was a man.

He appeared to be holding on to something attached to the keel, which was invisible to Ben.

Nearer and nearer he crept, and then he made this alarming discovery.

"Why, the swab has chopped our cable, fastened on a line, and blow my bags if they aren't towing of us out. I'll make sure of that shark anyhow."

And then Ben Hawser showed the prudence of keeping his powder dry.

Poising himself with his left hand upon the ship's chains, he took the revolver in his right hand out of the leather case.

He straightened his arm and took a deliberate aim.

"Take that, you son of a sea-cook," exclaimed honest Ben, as he pulled the trigger.

When the smoke of the shot cleared away, Ben Hawser's target had disappeared.

Simultaneously the "Westward Ho!" stopped in her mysterious passage.

It was very strange.

That one man could not be towing out the big ship single-handed.

Hercules himself could not have performed such a labour. No.

The only solution of this seeming mystery could be that Ben Hawser's shot had alarmed that man's accomplices, but Ben's attention was suddenly attracted above.

There was a great outcry upon the deck.

Back he scrambled, and clambered up the ship's side as nimbly as Nero himself could have done it.

Just as he reached the deck, he heard the sound of a girl's voice calling for help.

He ran across young Jack and Harry Girdwood.

They were rushing along the deck in the greatest excitement.

Consternation was depicted upon every countenance.

"It's all right, Master Jack," said Ben Hawser, "we put an end to their towing out."

He attributed all the commotion to the exciting scene that had taken place below, in which he had been the principal actor, but in this he was very speedily undeceived.

"Hark!" cried young Jack; "which way was that?"

The girl's shrieks before alluded to were again heard, but they were soon stifled, and a stentorian voice, that drowned every other sound, was heard to shout out in broken English—

"Beware of Monastos. Thus begins his vengeance!"

CHAPTER XII.

A MOTHER'S GRIEF—THE UNJUST TAUNTS—TO THE RESCUE OR TO DEATH.

"WHO is that?" asked the puzzled Ben. "What cries were those for help?"

"Little Emily has been carried off by the brigands."

Ben Hawser staggered back aghast at the news.

"But how?"

"While we were watching you for'ard, they scrambled up aft; little Emily had just run on deck, and was seized in a moment, burked and hauled overboard."

Poor girl!

It was too true.

Little Emily had been carried off by the Greek brigands.

Kidnapped, with the utmost audacity, from the deck of the "Westward Ho!"

Swiftly yet stealthily a burly ruffian had clambered up the ship's side, and met Harvey's daughter as she was running on deck, to ascertain the meaning of the strange commotion.

Before she could utter a word or cry out, a pair of brutal hands had seized her, and whisked her off with as little effort or ceremony as if she had been a doll.

Ready hands awaited the prize below.

And then, profiting by their knowledge of the locality, the kidnappers hustled their victim out of sight, and were soon lost in the adjacent intricacies that bordered Fairy Creek.

At first the folks on board the "Westward Ho!" were thunderstruck, stupefied. But speedily recovering themselves, they looked hurriedly to their arms, and rushed off in pursuit.

They had little to guide them.

The only indication that they had was the direction from whence came those two despairing cries of the hapless girl.

No matter.

On they rushed, scrambled up the steep banks, and with difficulty penetrated the thickly-grown shrubs.

But they failed—failed entirely—in finding Little Emily.

And after a fruitless search, they wended their way back to the ship, utterly crestfallen.

As young Jack gained the deck, he found himself face to face with Mrs. Harvey.

The poor mother's face was ashy pale as she asked, tremblingly, news of her child.

"Where is my Emily? Oh, Jack!" she exclaimed, "have you not found her?"

The boy hung his head.

"We shall find her yet, Mrs. Harvey," he said, falteringly.

"Find her!" echoed the grief-stricken mother. "Find her! You should never have returned without her."

Ben Hawser approached.

"Axing your pardon, ma'am," stammered the honest fellow, tugging at his forelock, "we have searched every p'int of the compass for Miss Emily, bless her heart!"

Mrs. Harvey wrung her hands, and moaned piteously.

"Had you done so," she exclaimed, with great bitterness, "my child would now be here."

Young Jack reddened to the roots of his hair at these words.

"Avast there, ma'am," exclaimed Ben Hawser seriously; "we've done all that mortal man could do, and as for Master Jack, why, he behaved with the pluck of a second Nelson."

Young Jack, recollecting himself, however, turned suddenly upon Hilda, and exclaimed—

"I'll rescue little Emily, or I'll leave my body in their hands."

And then, before anyone could divine his intention, he darted from the deck into the state saloon.

Here he eagerly searched the books and papers for Spirillo's famous chart.

He was lucky enough to drop his hand upon it almost immediately.

Tearing it eagerly open, he scanned it through until he came to a ground plan marked—

"*The prisoner's cavern.*"

"Now," said the boy, with fierce determination, "now we'll see, Mrs. Harvey, if you will taunt me with not finding Emily."

And then seizing a blank sheet of paper, he hurriedly made a sketch of the route and the plan, and a copy of the written indications.

This done, he turned to the cabin steps as Harry Girdwood came down and faced him.

"Where are you going, Jack?" demanded Harry eagerly.

"I am going to set little Emily free," returned young Jack resolutely, "or leave my body in the hands of the pirates."

"You know you are going to risk your life?" said his young comrade earnestly.

"I do."

"That you are going to almost certain death, Jack?"

"I know it," returned young Harkaway; "but Mrs. Harvey shall not taunt me with cowardice, right or wrong. I go. Good bye, Harry."

He held out his hand.

The other took it, but he did not release it at once.

"Do you think, Jack," said he, "that I would let you go——"

"Let me go!" began young Harkaway indignantly.

"Alone; never. We will face this danger together or not at all."

"Why should you run this risk for my sake?" said Jack, in a tone of remonstrance, but it was useless.

Harry Girdwood's manner showed that he would brook no denial.

"Enough, Jack. I go with you, or stay with you; we will face danger, it may be death, together."

Young Jack took his comrade's hand, and pressed it with deep emotion.

"Brave Harry," he said, in a broken voice, "you shall come, and we will share the danger together."

He ran up on deck, closely followed by Harry.

Here they met Ben Hawser.

"Avast there, young gentlemen," exclaimed the old salt; "whither away?"

"Ben," said young Jack, "we're going to find the pirates, and rescue Emily."

The old tar stared again at the speaker.

"Not wound up yet, Master Jack, at that 'ere tack?"

"No, nor do I intend to be until I have succeeded."

The old tar gave a long whistle.

"I'm afeard that'll take a precious long time," he said, dubiously.

"Maybe, Ben," said young Harkaway, "maybe, but I want you to bear the news to my mother as tenderly as you can."

"Here, I say, stow that," said Ben Hawser. "Why, I'd sooner face a broadside than have to go and tell that dear lady as how I had stood quietly by and let her boy parpetrate self-destruction; no, my hearty—axing your pardon—you shall tell her all about it yourself."

And then the wily old tar made one step to the grand cabin stairs.

"Mrs. Harkaway, ahoy!" shouted Ben Hawser.

He knew that he could not stop the boys himself, so he hoped to bring parental authority to bear upon Jack, but the latter was far too quick for old Ben.

With one bound the old tar was at the ship's side.

"Come on, Harry, old boy," he ejaculated; "follow me."

"I'm there."

And down the two boys dropped into the water.

Two minutes more and they had gained the shore.

At the self-same instant, Mrs. Harkaway reached the deck.

A hurried word of explanation sufficed to acquaint her with all that had occurred.

"That mad boy has rushed to his destruction," she exclaimed, in a frenzy of excitement. "Where is Ben Hawser?"

"Here, marm."

"Send up a rocket."

Ben started.

"A what?"

"A rocket. You know the signal that was to bring my husband back in case of danger? What danger could be more terrible than that which threatens us now—that my rash boy, alone, seeks the pirates' den?"

CHAPTER XIII.

YOUNG JACK AND HARRY GIRDWOOD SEEK ADVENTURES AND MEET WITH THEM; CHIEFLY AWKWARD.

As the two boys gained an open space, Harry Girdwood's attention was attracted to the whiz of the rocket on board the "Westward Ho!"

"Hark!"

"I hear," said Jack.

They turned round, and then they saw the rocket shooting heavenwards like a fiery meteor.

"Do you know what that signal means?" said Harry.

"I know that it is a rocket," answered young Harkaway; "what of that?"

"But you also remember that it was the signal agreed upon with your father to recall the party in case of danger."

Jack started.

The brave boy had not contemplated this.

"Oh, Harry, Harry," he exclaimed, "what have I done?"

"Upset the whole party."

Young Jack sighed.

"It is very difficult to define one's duty clearly."

"It is."

"And I could not bear Mrs. Harvey's reproaches. Moreover, think of poor little Emily."

"Poor girl!"

"Yes, yes, Harry," he said resolutely; "after all, we had but one course open to us."

"To go to the rescue."

"Yes, to the rescue of Emily."

And so the two boys went on.

Now, when they had got some distance, they began to hold a council of war.

Harry Girdwood was anxious to hear the plan of the campaign.

Young Jack's plan was of the simplest possible description.

It was this.

He proposed to follow out the paths indicated in the copy of Spirillo's chart, and lurk about the stronghold of the brigands.

Thither he felt sure the captive girl had been carried.

His idea was that she would be left comparatively free there.

If so, she would not be watched while she strolled up and down about the cavern and its vicinity, of which, thanks to Spirillo's many yarns on board the "Flowery Land," he possessed acute foreknowledge.

He was indeed as well acquainted with the place already as was possible for one who had never seen it.

"And when you have seen her," said Harry Girdwood, "what then, old boy?"

"I shall trust in Providence," said young Jack.

Harry smiled.

"I hope I am as good a believer as you, Jack," said he, "but I believe in the old saying that Providence helps those that help themselves."

"So do I."

"Well, we must be careful and see what we can do, but I don't think we shall do much good in the dark."

"Nor I."

"Then the best thing will be to camp for the night in some place snug and secure, and then when morning dawns——"

"It would be better to get nearer to the brigand's stronghold."

"If you like."

"Get a light then, and let us look over the chart."

This was done.

It was a precious piece of imprudence, for the reflection of the light was the most likely thing of all to betray them to the enemy.

They soon discovered their error, for just as their lantern flashed, there was a shrill bird-call close by that startled them both.

"Do you hear that, Jack?"

"I do."

"And do you know what it means?"

"Yes; I suppose some bird," replied Jack.

"Jack," replied Harry Girdwood, in a whisper, "it was no bird. That is the signal of the enemy. Depend upon it, our light has alarmed something more dangerous than a bird."

"I hope not."

"I am sure."

"What shall we do, old fellow?" said Jack.

"Camp for the night."

"What, here?"

"It is dangerous, I think, Jack, thanks to our lantern, but I vote that we roost up a tree."

"Good; but we must not let the pirates put a rope round our necks in the night."

The two boys did not take long to make up their minds.

They selected the nearest tree in which the foliage appeared to be thick.

The reason for this selection was obvious.

They wished their bodies to be completely shaded from view by the leaves and branches.

They soon hit upon a capital perch, where the thick, forked branches made them as secure a resting place as though they had been upon *terra firma.*

It was indeed much more secure and required far less training than sleeping in a hammock.

Young Jack thought that he would never close his eyes, so thoroughly was he agitated by the events of the day, but presently his fatigue prevailed over the agitation, and our youthful hero was slumbering peacefully, even before his less demonstrative comrade.

Sober Harry Girdwood poised himself upon his perch and leant round to look at Jack, whose extreme quietude rather alarmed him.

"Jack, Jack," he said, in a voice loud enough for young Harkaway to hear if he were awake, yet not sufficiently loud to arouse him if he slept.

No answer.

"Are you snug, old man?"

Snore.

"That means yes," said Harry to himself. "He's as snug as if he were tucked up in the family four-poster."

And the care of young Jack being off his mind, his trusty comrade squatted, nestled closer yet into the sheltering arms of the tree, and slept.

*   *   *   *   *

"Harry, old fellow."

"Jack."

"Goodness me! I was nearly over," said young Jack.

"So it appears. Why, Jack, you are half over the branch; hold on, or you will have an ugly fall, old man."

Harry Girdwood straightened himself upon the branch, and looked about him to take their bearings.

And then he discovered that their tree was upon the border of the thick wood.

They dropped from their perches, and gained the open.

The boys were deeply impressed.

The unvarying beauty of the climate would have been strange indeed to one fresh from our own foggy island, but our two youthful adventurers were veteran travellers.

Birds of gay plumage were in immense variety.

The vegetation was rich and varied—guavas, bananas, mangroves, bread-fruit, and palms were common enough.

Occasionally a tree-fern—one of the most graceful of plants—was met with; the long feathered leaves, which in their general character resemble the common fern leaves of our own hedges, grow in a mass upon the top of a stem thirty or forty feet high, and descend nearly to the ground.

The hills in Fairy Island assumed strange, fantastic shapes, and were feathered with wood to their summits.

The boys were not insensible to the beauties of the place, but their thoughts were taken up by serious matters just now.

Soon after daybreak they examined the chart carefully together, and having made up their minds as to the precise part of the brigands' stronghold that they should make for, they started forth.

But it was a serious understanding between them that they were only to use their fire-arms in a case of dire extremity, in other words, when their very lives depended upon it.

Their route, according to Spirillo's plan, lay for a certain distance across the open country, and through rich prairies, but they were forced, from motives of prudence, to alter their course a bit.

Naturally, they could not make as much headway when forcing a passage through the thickly-grown bushes and shrubs that garnished the endless hills.

It was a long journey, but their dogged perseverance met with its reward, and when they least expected it, they found themselves suddenly close upon the pirates' lair.

They recognised the spot by a tall palm tree, and other landmarks, marked down in Spirillo's chart, and then the discovery was so sudden that it startled them not a little.

From beyond the palm tree in question, some thirty or forty yards, there was a low range of hills, stretched right across their path.

There was the range of hills, sure enough, but where was the river?

"Before we go any further," said young Jack, "I'll climb the palm tree, and take observations. There may be pirates about."

"Good," said his wary comrade, "but be careful not to speak to me while you are up there "

Up went young Jack, and when he had reached a considerable altitude, he nodded excitedly to the expectant Harry.

"He sees the river," said Harry to himself.

Down came Jack.

They made now for the hills, choosing the part where there was the thickest growth of bush and shrub, and, as they had reached the crest of the hill, they suddenly found themselves upon the brink of a precipice.

At its base rippled the stream marked in the chart.

As they stood there, they heard the sound of voices close at hand.

The words being in Greek, were not understood; but they guessed their meaning, from the tone of command which was accompanied by the clinking of arms.

They were changing guard.

But where?

Then followed the regular marching sound as of drilled troops.

They thrust their heads further and further over the precipice, and peered down. The first object that caught young Jack's attention was the muzzle of a long gun barrel, pointed directly at him.

This was, to say the least, not a cheerful thing to contemplate; but it did not disturb young Harkaway at all, and for this simple reason—it was not presented at him; but it was carried over the shoulder of a sentry below.

This man walked up and down twice or thrice, and then he dropped his musket butt on to the ground and rested his arms upon the muzzle, striking unconsciously a most picturesque attitude.

Stretching over still further, young Jack now perceived the explanation of all that had puzzled him before in connection with this episode.

Immediately beneath them was the cavern of the redoubtable Monastos.

The sentry was mounting guard at its entrance.

"Harry, I could pop off that fellow; it would make one less of their party."

"And two less of ours," returned his companion in the same tone. "Remember our compact; not to fire till we are compelled."

Barely were the words uttered, ere they were seized from behind and made prisoners.

CHAPTER XIV.

YOUNG JACK IS DOOMED—AT THE CANNON'S MOUTH.

YOUNG Jack and Harry were cruelly handled, and bound with cords that were dragged at as though they were bales of woollen cloths for shipment to distant parts; and, added to this, their villanous captors heaped upon them the vilest threats and most abusive epithets in their vocabulary.

Upon second thoughts, this latter part of their indignities did not count for much, as neither of the English or American boys could understand a word.

The two boys were hurried down the mountain slope by a path hitherto unperceived by them, and in a few moments they were brought before Monastos, the pirate and brigand of Magic Island.

As soon as Monastos saw the two boys, he nodded and smiled pleasantly at them, to their intense surprise.

Looking round, Jack saw that they were in a cavern, the centre of which was supported by part of a broken ship's mast.

In other respects, too, the place was fitted up in a seafaring style.

"Dimitri," said he in English, which he spoke admirably, "why have you bound up these two children so, with huge thongs that eat into their flesh, when for all purposes traces of packthread would have done as well?"

The man addressed as Dimitri uttered some apology.

The thongs were severed, and the two lads stood free.

"Now, young gentlemen," said Monastos, "just tell me what you are doing, trespassing on my property."

The pirate never ceased to smile in the same friendly manner upon his young prisoners.

"Had we known that the island was the property of anyone in particular, we should not have ventured here," replied young Harkaway.

"Unless your people are curious, inquisitive, spying people," said Monastos, pleasantly, "scoundrels and jail-birds," he smiled more agreeably than ever; "which is, indeed, very probable, according to appearances."

Jack fired up at this.

"My father's friends and his servants are all honourable people," he said.

The pirate's eyes twinkled at this.

"Your father?"

"Yes."

"So he is at the head?"

"Yes."

"What is his name?"

"Jack, that is, I mean John Harkaway."

"Humph! John Harkaway; I shall remember that name."

Harry Girdwood noticed his manner, and he felt uneasy.

The chief's smile had a nameless terror in it.

And he judged aright, for a cold, cruel man was Monastos, who took a life as coolly and remorselessly as he would shoot a bird.

And it had as little effect upon him.

* * * * *

Jack was silent.

Had he said too much?

Harry feared it.

"Keep mum now, old boy," he whispered, so low that the chief could not catch a word; but although he could not hear, he could see pretty well by the boy's manner what it meant.

"Dimitri."

"Excellency."

"Take out that boy; he's too quiet and artful; leave me alone with the talkative one."

"Yes, sir."

Dimitri then tapped Harry Girdwood upon the shoulder and ushered him out.

Jack was about to follow too, when Monastos took him by the wrist, and detained him with gentle force.

"I want you."

Young Jack felt a little uncomfortable at this.

He was not afraid, but the separation from Harry Girdwood was an unpleasant reminder that for the time being they were not their own masters.

Monastos, never even appearing to notice the longing, lingering looks which young Jack cast after his comrade, motioned him to sit down on a pile of cushions.

Young Jack hesitated, and was inclined to refuse, but prudence bade him obey.

So down he sat.

"Now, my young friend," said Monastos, with a bland smile, "answer me one or two questions."

"What are they?"

"How many, then, has your father got at the back of him?"

"A great many," answered Jack.

"I suppose they are all well armed?"

"Yes, well armed."

"How did they gain their knowledge of this place?"

"That I cannot, will not tell," said young Jack.

"Oh, you had better tell all that you know, without making any difficulties, for"—and here he smiled more pleasantly than ever—"you would find the consequences most disagreeable, unless you tell all you possibly can."

"Even then," said young Jack, stoutly, "I will not tell."

"Impudent child," said the pirate chief. "Why refuse information, when, as you may guess, I already know as much as you can tell me?"

"Why then ask me?" said young Jack, quickly.

"To test your truth."

"That wants no testing," said young Jack; "I am like my father; if I speak at all, I speak the truth."

"I believe you. But now tell me how much the traitor Spirillo has been able to inform you of—for it was he who brought you here, and he has paid for his treachery with his life, the renegade."

Young Jack was silent.

"On passing through the ravine, between those lofty, wooded heights, which direction does your party take?"

Young Jack found his tongue at this.

"Well," he said, with a light laugh, "you surely don't expect me to tell you that."

"Oh, yes, I do," said Monastos; "indeed I do."

"Then, sir," said Jack, quietly, "you will be disappointed."

"Oh, no," said Monastos, with that peculiar smile again; "I shall know all that you can tell upon the matter, for sure."

"You mistake."

"Not I."

"Indeed you do, for nothing in the world should induce me to divulge my father's movements in his endeavour to capture you and your wicked band."

"Nothing, my young friend?" said the pirate.

"Nothing," replied Jack.

"We shall see."

Monastos turned and called one of his men, and upon the man making his appearance, he gave him some hurried instructions in his own native tongue.

This, it is needless to say, was "all Greek" to young Harkaway.

But the result of it soon appeared.

Through the wide opening a huge iron gun was wheeled into the cavern, and run up, seemingly with comparative ease, just behind where young Jack stood.

"Seize the boy, and bind him tight to the cannon's mouth," cried Monastos, and in an instant the unfortunate boy was strapped to the muzzle of the gun.

"Now bring the fuze."

This was obeyed promptly. and Monastos took it in his hand and made one step up to the gun.

"Now, Master Harkaway," said his majesty, still smiling, "where is the information that I ask you for?"

The boy was silent.

"My patience will not hold out long," said Monastos; "give me the information, or—" and here he flourished the fuze.

But young Jack was silent, and looked him boldly in the face.

We do not pretend to say that he felt unmoved at the alarming directions given by the pirate chief to his men.

"One last word," said Monastos; "I give you time to reflect and recant."

"I want no time," retorted young Jack. "You are a cold-blooded villain, and will meet your fate at the hands of my father."

"That remains to be seen. Your father, this cursed Englishman, shall yet be treated by me as you are. Now will you confess?"

"No. I am fully resolved as to what duty bids me do—do your worst at once; not a word shall you wring from me."

"Do you understand, boy, that as soon as I apply this fuze to the touch-hole, your body will be scattered in fragments?"

Young Jack closed his eyes, and a slight tremor of the lids showed that he was not insensible to the pirate's fatal menaces, but he was resolved to betray no emotion before them.

"Once more, boy," said Monastos, "I give you the chance of saving yourself; will you speak?"

"No."

"For the second time, will you answer my questions?"

"No."

"For the third time, I say, will you speak, and save your life?"

"From you, pirate? Never!"

"Then that is the last chance you have on this side of the grave. I am now placing the light to the touch-hole —die!"

"Monastos! Monastos! captain!" cried Dimitri, who here ran in and demanded eagerly of his chief if Paquita, his daughter, was there.

Monastos turned round with his fuze in his hand.

"My daughter here?" said the pirate chief. "What do you mean, fool? Begone, and do not interrupt me again on your life."

"I fear me," returned Dimitri, "that some accident has happened to her."

The brigand captain looked uneasy.

"What grounds have you for supposing that?" said he.

"Her voice was heard just now calling for assistance."

"There must be some mistake."

"No mistake; I fear she has been imprudent enough to venture forth, and has fallen into the hands of the enemy, to be held as a hostage?"

The pirate chief looked spitefully at Jack for a moment, then let fall the fuze from his hand.

His coolness deserted him; then suddenly rousing himself, he turned to Dimitri with a loud ejaculation.

"Have you sent out many in pursuit?" he asked.

"Not yet," said Dimitri.

"Then," said Monastos, "let it be done; scatter your men right and left—north and south immediately, for if they are about this part, we shall snare them yet."

"It shall be done," said Dimitri, "but until something more is learnt, I would give a word of advice."

"What is it?"

"Suspend punishment," he added, with a significant glance at Jack strapped to the cannon's muzzle; "for, my life on it, they would take bitter revenge."

"Boy," said the pirate chief, "your life for one short hour is spared; but think not to escape your doom."

Then the pirate hurried forth to give further directions to recover his lost child.

CHAPTER XV.

ON THE WAR-PATH—MAGOG BRAND'S PRISONER—THE ALARM—NERO PLAYS POSTMAN.

IT is time to return to the main body.

Before sundown, they were destined to learn that Monastos' army was far more important than they had been led to suppose; for the pirate had of late greatly increased his band.

But although his arrangements were pretty perfect, he was yet ill at ease.

He dreaded lest the very wind should waft out to sea the secrets of his treasure isle.

You can imagine, therefore, with what mingled sensations of rage he saw the ship "Westward Ho!" harboured in Fairy Creek, with daring Jack Harkaway and his fellow adventurers.

Diverging a bit from the exact line of route which Harkaway had laid down, the party found themselves under the necessity of fording a stream.

The opposite banks of this stream were bordered by a thick growth of shrub and bush.

"Stop, stop," said Magog Brand; "before any more is done, let scouts be sent out."

"Who will act as scout?"

"I'll scout," said Magog, who feared to be accused of making a proposal and shirking the consequences of it.

And then, before a word could be uttered in opposition, he started off.

He forded across, until it got too deep for him, and then he swam the rest of the way.

Clambering carefully up the steep heights, he reached the brow of the hill, where, suddenly, he dropped upon a man stretched on the ground.

The strength of Magog Brand's fingers was something prodigious.

They closed round the throat of the unfortunate brigand, and, with what seemed to be a gentle squeeze, it drove every gasp of breath out of his body.

"Say half a word," he hissed in his ear, "and I'll pin you to the ground, like a butterfly in a collector's case."

With this promise, it is needless to say that little Mr. Brand's prisoner preserved a dignified silence.

He looked about him while he held his prisoner on the ground, and seeing that all was safe, he signalled the rest of his party to follow on.

"Come, old man," said Jack Harkaway to Brand; "that's not so bad. We must turn this prisoner to account."

They made the unfortunate Greek struggle to his feet and trudge on.

He showed some considerable alacrity in obeying this last order.

If he contemplated making a bolt of it, he was doomed to a cruel disappointment.

At his elbow walked Jack Harkaway, the elder, armed with his death-dealing weapon.

The least show of treachery upon the unhappy man's part would have been immediately followed by the ramming of a pistol muzzle into his ear.

In the event of that contingency arising, the brigand's life with Harkaway and Company would be a short, but not a merry one.

"Speak English?" bawled Mr. Jefferson in his ear.

The prisoner, half deafened, shook his head.

"French?"

"No."

"Italian?"

The prisoner's eyes glistened intelligently.

"Italiano, si."

"That's your sort," said Jefferson; "now you can fire away at him, Harkaway."

"I want you," said Jack Harkaway, in Italian, "to take me by a safe route to the stronghold of Monastos, the pirate chief."

The prisoner made no reply, but stared stolidly before him.

"Do you hear?" said Harkaway. "*Havete intosso male?*"

"Yes," replied the brigand, doggedly; "but if I refuse?"

"That as you please," returned Harkaway in the same tongue; "if you do, we have but one resource."

"What is that?"

"To hang you."

And then, turning to his party, Harkaway added—

"Get a rope ready, tie a noose at the end, and throw it over a tree that will make the handiest gallows."

The significant look accompanying these words told them what was wanted.

So Jack Harkaway's order was carried out with a certain flourish with a view to making an impression upon the prisoner.

But the Greek stared straight before him in silence; apparently he was unmoved by it all.

"Takes no notice," said Jack Harkaway; "can't frighten him, I suppose."

"Wait a bit," said Jefferson; "we'll try."

Magog Brand's thoughts ran in the same direction, for seizing the rope, he cast the noose over the prisoner's head.

Now our Greek was by no means a coward, but as the rope came in contact with his flesh, a change came over his face.

"For the last time," said Jack Harkaway, "decide your own fate."

No reply.

The brigand's lips quivered, and he closed his eyes.

"For the last time of asking," said Harkaway, "answer our questions or hang."

He waited a second—perhaps two or three—and then waved his hand by way of signal.

"Let him hang till he is dead."

"Pull ahoy—ahoy," cried Magog Brand gleefully.

And he did pull, too, with a vengeance.

In a moment the unfortunate wretch was swinging in the air.

As his body was jerked up in the air, the victim threw his arms wildly about him.

"I will answer," he cried.

Down he came with a flop upon the ground, all in a heap, like a bundle of rags.

If his face had been pale before, it was black enough now.

They knelt down over him, and removing the rope, threw open his shirt.

"Hullo!" said Jefferson, "we have gone a little too far."

"Give him some water."

"Nonsense," said Magog Brand, "give him some whisky."

This advice was followed by one of the men.

The flask was thrust to his mouth, and a few drops of the fiery spirit poured down his throat.

Thereupon he blinked and winked and opened his eyes.

He coughed and spluttered and used some bad language, and scowled upon his captors.

"Well," said Harkaway, "have you made up your mind to listen to reason?"

"I am in your power," growled the Greek, "and cannot help myself."

"Glad, old man, you see things in their proper light," said Harkaway, cheerfully.

"But I consent on one condition only."

"Make no conditions with him," said Jefferson.

"But we may as well hear what the villain has to say," cried Brand.

"Speak."

"Supposing," said the brigand, "that your expedition should be successful, I want you to engage that my life shall be spared—that I shall not be handed over to the authorities. Else I should only be spared to serve your purpose now."

"What does he say?"

Jack briefly translated the brigand's speech.

"That's reasonable enough," said Jefferson; "consent then."

Jack Harkaway gave the required assurance, and the party prepared to start.

"Be true to us," said Harkaway, "and you'll not find us bad friends; we are better friends, in fact, than we are enemies, and it may be more to your profit to serve us than it has been to serve Monastos."

"You cannot expect too much good, Jack, from one who shows himself a traitor to start with."

"I know that," said Jack; "but be as true to us as you have shown yourself to Monastos, and we will ask no more. Monastos, I believe, is not too safe a man to work for."

"I serve him, but do not like him,' said the brigand.

Harkaway then explained that it was a much safer game to serve the "Westward Ho!" than to follow the treacherous Monastos.

They saw the influence of Harkaway's reasoning in the prisoner's altered manner, but they did not relax their vigilance.

It was pitchy dark, when suddenly a glare in the sky caught their attention.

"See there!" ejaculated Magog Brand; "what's that?"

"Look how it trails down," said Jefferson; "it's a rocket."

Just then a familiar voice was heard close at hand, signalling the party.

It was Harvey.

He had been reconnoitring at some little distance from the party for hours past, and now he had rejoined the main body upon seeing the rocket.

"Do you see that?" said he, in tones of alarm; "the danger signal from our ship, the "Westward Ho!"

The words thrilled everyone who heard them.

CHAPTER XVI.

HOW HARKAWAY AND MOLE SET FORTH IN COMPANY, AND WHAT CAME OF IT—YOUNG JACK AGAIN—THE SURPRISE—SIX TO ONE—A DESPERATE FIGHT.

JACK HARKAWAY held a hurried council of war, in which it was agreed that some should camp there for the night, while two of the party returned to the ship for information.

Some few slept, but they mostly passed the night in restless anxiety.

Towards daybreak the sentinel was heard to cock his rifle.

Slight as was the noise, it was heard by all.

They saw the vigilant guard bring his rifle up to his shoulder.

They also saw that he was aiming at some tall shaggy object.

And in a moment more, when he was about to pull the trigger, Magog Brand bounded forward.

Don't you see who it is?" said he to the sentry.

Just then the shaggy object came into the open, and who should it be but Nero?

"I knew it could be no enemy," said Magog, "because our friend Mike was so quiet."

Nero advanced with his familiar waddle, and carrying his tail under his right arm with a certain grace.

He shook hands with the party generally.

"Oh, Nero," said Harkaway, "why can't you talk?"

"He is too artful," said Jefferson, with a grin.

He had a string round his neck now, at which he tugged persistently until they were forced to see it.

"He has got a string necklace," said Magog.

They pulled at the necklace, and found that at the back of it was attached a piece of paper, upon which these words had been hastily scribbled—

"Jack and I have fallen into the power of Monastos, and are now in great danger. If you have any prisoners, offer exchange.—HARRY GIRDWOOD."

There was a postscript, which had been written even yet more hurriedly.

It read as follows—

"Miss Emily is here, I believe, but we have not yet been able to see her. Monastos is bloodthirsty, cruel, and revengeful. Be careful and take no lives. You may want prisoners to exchange."

"Well," said Jefferson, pulling a long breath, "what do you say to that?"

Harvey shook his head.

"I don't like it."

"It certainly looks very ugly," said Magog, who had an extraordinary degree of confidence in anything young Jack did, "but that boy will get out of it all right, I'll wager my life. Why, he has got the devil's luck and his own too."

Harkaway did not look very hopeful.

"A belief in luck is all very well in its way," said he, "but I have my presentiments too."

"You must not despond," said Jefferson.

"I don't."

"Despond," echoed little Magog; "desponding is all pickles. They talk of

a cat's nine lives; young Jack Harkaway has fifty lives. Why, I verily believe that if he were hanged, he would come to life——"

"Like Ambrose Gwinnette, who was hanged on the sands?"

"Yes."

"Perhaps."

"I'm sure of it. Moreover, I believe that the bullet is not cast, nor the hemp grown for the rope, that can take the life of young Jack Harkaway."

"I share that belief," said Jefferson.

"So do I."

"And I."

"And so do I," said Isaac Mole, with the air of a man who puts the finishing stroke to an argument; "and what is more, in the course of the next four-and-twenty hours I'll bring back my dear young Jack to you safe and sound."

"You?"

"Yes, I."

Mr. Mole struck an attitude in which modesty and boldness, diffidence and defiance, were judiciously mingled.

"Am I to understand, Mr. Mole," said Harvey, "that you mean to do this single-handed?"

Isaac Mole swelled out like a bantam cock as he replied—

"Such is my intention."

Jack Harkaway had grown very impatient.

He could wait no longer the return of the party from the ship.

Harkaway felt anxious to know the exact truth, for when he reflected that his brave boy was a prisoner in the hands of the enemy, it made him feel that Jack's danger was indeed great.

As may be supposed, Dick Harvey also felt not a little anxious.

But he prudently resolved to await the return of the party from the ship for confirmation of the bad tidings.

Jack Harkaway vowed that he would start off alone.

This was opposed by most of the party.

But the strongest opposition was made by no less a person than Isaac Mole.

If Harkaway went, the warrior Mole swore that he would go with him.

"Well, old friend," cried Jack, "you shall go with me; it will remind me of old times, for we have often been on desperate services together."

"Jack, my dear boy," said Mole, "it is very kind of you to speak so, and you shall find Mole, your old friend, has still his courage to fight for his old pupil, Jack Harkaway."

"Bravo, Mole," cried Harvey; "give us the old friendly grip of your hand, then off you go with Jack."

When they had covered about a mile of ground, Harkaway stopped suddenly, saying—

"I have made a discovery."

"Where, Jack?" cried Mole, taking out his revolver.

"Look there," said Jack, quickly. "A party of six armed men are marching along with a prisoner, whose arms are securely fastened behind him."

Now bold Jack's heart beat high when he saw them, for in spite of the distance that separated them, he recognised the prisoner at the first glance.

It was his son, young Jack.

"I see my son, Mr. Mole," said he, gleefully. "I see him. Look."

Mole saw young Jack looking as bold as ever.

"How shall we do, Harkaway?" said he; "steal round and fall upon them?"

Harkaway stared at the speaker.

But the latter meant it.

The thought of his young pupil's peril filled him with desire to be at the enemy.

"No, that will not do; leave me here; you can do me good service by seeking our friends."

"And leave you, Jack?" cried Mole.

"Yes, make all haste back," said Harkaway, "and get Jefferson, with someone else, to come back at the double."

"But they are marching," said Mr. Mole, "marching fast, and before we can get up, they will have cleared off."

"Leave that to me," said Harkaway; "I will undertake to keep them employed until you can come up with assistance."

"Off I go then," said Mole; "anything to serve you, Jack, and our dear boy."

Off he went.

He stumped over the ground at a great rate, and was very soon out of sight.

* * * * * *

Harkaway made for the party with all caution.

His object was to surprise the party.

Jack felt all his old courage mount to his heart, for fear was unknown to him.

He was a desperate man—for was not his only son in peril?

"Patience, patience, Jack," he said to himself, "or you will do your brave boy more harm than good by rashness."

At length, the party of Greeks with their prisoner were within pistol shot, and it became necessary to adopt some definite plan of action.

He eyed the advancing party keenly, from a snug spot where he himself was invisible to them.

Seven men!

"Seven Greek brigands to one Englishman," said Harkaway; "humph! long odds, but I must rescue my boy at any risk."

He did not fear for his own life, but what he did fear was to fail in his purpose.

If he should be beaten off, or perhaps killed, what would become of his dear boy?

He shuddered at the bare idea.

Death would not be the worst of it, in all probability, for Spirillo had told him such tales of the atrocities perpetrated by these villanous compounds of pirates and brigands, that it made his blood run cold.

The savage Indians were gentle by comparison.

Jack Harkaway had not long to consider about his plan of action.

They were close upon him.

Creeping up behind a thick tree, he prepared.

He loosened his cutlass in its fastenings, then looked to the priming of his pistols.

They were all ready for action, and so was our old friend Jack.

Carefully, yet hurriedly, he loosened them, so that no bungling at the critical moment might spoil his chance.

The brigands marched on, and now their steady, regular tramp sounded close at hand.

Harkaway gripped his cutlass nervously in his sinewy palm, and waited.

Seven stalwart fellows they were, too.

Men standing nearly six feet high, for the most part, all broad-shouldered and powerful fellows, as far as he could judge.

"I shall want all my old luck and pluck to back me up, or good-bye to me, and to my boy as well."

"IT IS YOUR LIFE OR MINE," SAID HUNSTON.

And now they were within a dozen paces.

"I will do no coward's trick, but face them boldly," cried Jack.

"Now for it!"

They were just passing the spot where he stood when he stepped forth, and with pistol in hand faced them.

"Stand, you ruffians!"

They did not understand the meaning of Jack's words, but there was no misunderstanding the gesture which accompanied them.

With a simultaneous cry of surprise, they started back.

Harkaway, who had all his presence of mind about him, dashed forward, a sword in one hand, a pistol in the other.

Now, when they fell back aghast at the courage of one man, he made a rush, not at them, but, to their intense surprise, at the prisoner.

"Jack, my boy!"

"Father."

His cutlass was as sharp as a razor, and two strokes at the cords which bound his arms set young Jack at liberty.

"Take this pistol, Jack, sharp."

"All right, father."

And in less time than it has taken to describe it, the odds were lessened by half.

They were two against seven instead of only one.

"Are you ready to fight for your life, Jack?" cried Harkaway.

"Aye, aye, sir," responded young Jack, quite gleefully.

The British tars are said to cheer as soon as they come in sight of the enemy, and so it was with our heroes the Harkaways.

They never thought much about odds.

These two bold spirits cheered now.

They looked upon the battle as their own already.

The Greeks, recovered from their first surprise, rallied, and turned to the Harkaways, but the pistols kept them at a respectful distance.

"Dare to raise your carbines and you are dead men," cried Jack, keeping his pistol well directed at their heads.

Suddenly, however, one of the Greeks swung round his carbine, and clapping the butt to his hip, cocked it.

It was pointed full at Harkaway senior.

Another moment, and a bullet would have, probably, put an end to the encounter, but before he could pull the trigger, a well-aimed shot from young Jack's pistol smashed his right arm, and the carbine fell from his grasp.

This was the signal for the fight to begin in earnest.

"Oh, if we had but old friend Dick here," cried Harkaway, "he would soon make short work of the villains."

Harkaway waved his cutlass round his head, and charged the whole party.

With one desperate blow, an enemy lay writhing at his feet.

A second stroke brought another to his knees, and he would have been further disabled had not the rest of the party, recovering from their first surprise, fallen upon Harkaway sword in hand.

Now Jack Harkaway was a splendid swordsman, but four to one are long odds, and soon he found himself very hard pressed.

Twice had he been wounded.

He was bleeding from two flesh wounds, that were not by any means serious, but were yet unpleasant reminders that one man at the best is no match for four.

Yet Harkaway was not discouraged; he felt sure of victory.

"Keep one of them engaged, Jack, my boy; this one will do," he cried, passing his sword quickly through one of the brigand's arms; "he can't do much now. I will soon settle the hash of the other three."

At that moment he heard the sound of hurried footsteps; he looked up, expecting to see his friends, but his disappointment was great, for instead of friends he saw two more Greek brigands, with swords in hand, dash forward.

Twice, then, was he beaten back, and one desperate downstroke had brought him to his knees, when he had a happy inspiration.

He bethought him of his old ventriloquial powers, and he managed to throw his voice to some little distance from the scene of the strife.

It sounded like a confused murmur of voices, and it succeeded in deceiving the brigands.

The Greeks fancied that their enemy was about to be rescued by his own party.

They started back a pace or two, expecting to see some of Jack's friends ready to rescue Harkaway and young Jack.

And in that moment of surprise, Jack Harkaway's chance was made.

"Be ready, boy," cried Harkaway to young Jack, "to do as I tell you."

"All right, dad," said young Jack; "we will make them remember we are English."

Harkaway then made another scramble forward, and attacking them vigorously, drove them further and further back.

At the same time Harkaway threw the sound of his voice in the wood, and it sounded like the hoarse words of menace that had before alarmed the Greeks.

What could they do?

A man and a boy faced them.

A whole crowd seemed to menace them in their rear.

Naturally they turned to see if the enemy was approaching from the wood.

It was but momentary, yet it was enough for Jack and his son to dart into the wood.

The Greeks now half guessed at the truth, for no sooner had the prisoners fled, than they rushed after them, unmindful for the time of that invisible, yet audible enemy, who had so startled them by their confused murmurs in the woods.

Now Harkaway anticipated this, however.

"Stop, Jack!" he cried to his son; "show fight again, like a true boy of England."

The boy was nothing loth.

Turning sharply round, they faced the enemy in their mad rush.

"Aim low, lad," said Harkaway. "Be steady."

"All right," said young Jack; "this little fellow will stop one."

And he cocked his pistol.

Barely were the words spoken, when a couple of shots did execution on the advancing enemy, and then the echo of the report had barely died away, when Harkaway cried—

"Ready again, lad."

Bang! bang!

The brigands stopped and knew not what to do.

Quick to take advantage of their momentary confusion, the two Harkaways plunged yet deeper into the wood, and soon they were hopelessly lost to the Greek brigands.

"Well done, Jack, my boy; we have given the brigands a lesson, that English pluck is more than a match for Greek brigands or pirates."

CHAPTER XVII.

HUNTED BY BLOODHOUNDS.

LET us leave Harkaway and his son for awhile, and take a brief glance at one whose fortunes we trust have your sympathies still.

Cæsar Hannibal Constantine Augustus Jex, or, as young Jack christened him—Sunday—was, as you may remember, in some considerable trouble.

Petrus, the half-daft brigand, had started with his twin bloodhounds, Castor and Cyrus, to hunt poor Sunday down, and consequently he was in deadly peril. Sunday was in great trouble through losing his way.

Vainly did he endeavour to get again into the beaten track—hopelessly did he wander in search of some familiar landmark.

Each tree and shrub seemed alike the twin brother of its neighbour.

"'Spose I'se gwine to die ob hunger like de blessed babbies in de wood," said poor Sunday to himself ruefully.

He sat down and thought.

He rose and acted.

He climbed up the tallest tree to reconnoitre.

He slid down to mother earth in despair.

He scratched his wool for an idea and looked as glum as possible.

At one time he was half inclined to give it up for a bad job.

"If I was to lay down," said he to himself, "and gib up de ghost, I wonder if any of dem cock sparrows would come and cober ober my blessed corpus with leaves and sich."

Then, after a moment's pause, he started off with a desperate resolution to recover the lost track.

And lo, soon came his reward.

Before he had been walking a quarter of an hour, he came upon a wide path, with roads abutting right and left, that evidently led to somewhere.

"Now," said he to himself, with a grin, "now I'se thar, haw, haw!"

This was holloaing before he was out of the wood with a vengeance.

But he had barely begun his grin, when he stopped short, and his expression changed suddenly.

Wherefore?

Why did his eyes open wider and wider, as though they would start from their sockets?

Why did he tremble and look fearfully around him then as if for protection?

A moment more, and the cause of his alarm was clear enough.

"Hark! what is that noise?"

The sound of the distant baying of dogs was heard.

Poor Jex had lived in the Southern States of America in his youth, and he had fallen into cruel hands there.

Goaded on to desperation, he had fled from his inhuman master, and he had been hunted down by bloodhounds.

His sable skin even then bore traces of that fearful conflict, in which he had by a mere chance escaped being torn piece-meal by the savage hounds.

Involuntarily he shuddered at the sound.

He looked to his weapons with some eagerness.

His pistols were ready for use.

His knife was loose in his sheath.

If the odds were not too great against him, he would prove an ugly customer to tackle.

This might be seen no less in his broad chest and muscular arms, than in the look of quiet resolution of his countenance.

He listened for a few moments intently.

Then his expression brightened again.

He felt relieved.

"Only two," he muttered. "Only two dogs; they shall have a bullet each, and as for those who are with the dogs,

let them beware; no mercy, no quarter, if I get within arm's length of them with this my good knife."

He meant it.

But it was not his intention to risk an encounter if he could avoid it.

No.

Fight he would if he were put to it, but he meant to try and escape first.

He fled along the winding road as fast as his legs would carry him.

Still he could hear the fierce dogs gaining upon him at every step.

They scented their prey from afar.

Now when Sunday had covered half a mile or rather more, the road he was taking ceased its serpentine career, and ran straight for nearly a mile, and being nearly level, you could see almost to the end of it.

Nearer and nearer sounded the baying of the bloodhounds.

Sunday turned as he ran to view his pursuers.

He did not stop for a moment for them, but rushed on at a greater pace than ever.

They sighted their prey now, and with a fierce bark of delight they flew on.

The race would have soon been over—the day would soon have been decided, but for one circumstance.

Castor and Cyrus were tied together, and consequently could not make the same progress that they would have made had they been more free in their movements.

Herein lay the flying negro's chance.

It was a poor one.

A few more strides they were close at his heels.

At this exciting juncture a voice was heard in the distance, and a man appeared flying in pursuit of the twin bloodhounds.

"Ho, Castor!" he shouted, "Cyrus, hey! ho! come here!"

The master of the dogs—for it was the mysterious brigand Petrus—called and shouted to his brutes until he was black in the face.

In vain.

They scented a victim.

They smelt blood.

Moreover, their master was barely within hearing.

"Brutes!" cried the exasperated brigand, "fiends; you shall not smell food for this for days to come. Hold, hold!"

But it was in vain.

The hounds yelped and bounded forward.

Another moment and poor Sunday felt them at his back.

The fight could not long be delayed.

He turned and faced them pistols in hand.

The hounds pulled up suddenly as the negro showed his face, and crouching, snarled and displayed their fangs.

"Not gwine to chaw up dis chile yet," said Sunday.

Now, while they crouched and watched, Petrus came on behind at a smart double.

Sunday could face the twin bloodhounds.

But this increased the odds considerably.

Was he a match for the hounds and their master?

"Come off," said Petrus approaching; "lie down, you brutes, or I'll be the death of you."

Sunday stared again,

This Greek's English was a good deal purer than his own.

It had well-nigh proved fatal to the poor negro's chance, for his attention was momentarily distracted, and no sooner did the watchful hounds perceive the enemy's glance wander than they sprang.

But they were not quick enough for the bold negro.

He left fly his left-hand pistol.

And then, without waiting to see the result of his shot, he turned and ran again.

The shot had brought the bloodhounds to a stand, and before Sunday had run very far, their master was kneeling before them.

"That's the reward for disobedience."

He looked after the flying negro as he spoke, and then he saw that Sunday was a very long way ahead.

"Hullo," he cried; "he'll drop into the river, if he doesn't watch it."

The words were barely uttered, when Sunday found himself floundering out of his depth in the water.

He had come so suddenly upon the river that he had not noticed it.

"If the poor fellow can't swim," said Petrus, "I shall have wrought his destruction all the same, although unintentionally."

Quick as thought he uncoupled the dogs, and ran at full speed to the river, followed by his fierce servitors.

But just as he got to the bank, he saw the negro breasting the water, and swimming like a fish.

He called and bawled after Sunday—

"I am a friend, I tell you; I wish you no harm; stop."

Sunday turned over on his back, shouting back—

"Not good enough for dis chile."

A few more strokes brought him to the opposite bank, up which he scrambled, panting and dripping.

"Licked yer, yah!" cried Sunday; "now take care of yourself, or dis chile give you something cold in shape of bullet."

"I tell you I'm a friend," cried Petrus across the water.

"Yah, yah!" laughed Sunday; "golly, a nice old friend, you dam tief——"

"I wish to speak with you," cried Petrus again; "to give you friendly advice."

"And to gib dem dam tykes a meal of dis chile, but dis chile gib dem toko instead—ah, yah! And I'll gib dere blessed master toko likewise, by golly."

He took out his pistol that was yet loaded, and aimed point blank at Petrus.

But the latter never flinched.

He feared not.

"I tell you I am your friend," again cried Petrus.

"You dam tief, you know dat," cried Sunday, and he made off as fast as his legs would carry him.

Petrus watched his retreating figure with disappointment.

Then he followed the course of the river some thirty or forty yards, until he came to a familiar spot, where he forded across, closely followed by his bloodhounds.

Once on the opposite bank, he shook the water from his garments, and followed Sunday.

Sunday soon got a glance of them in pursuit, and he redoubled his efforts, and very soon he managed to increase the distance which separated them.

As he ran, he presently came in sight of a large stone building that filled him with wonderment.

The stones were roughly hewn, and of

many forms and colours, and they were built up with an eye to solidity more than elegance.

In front of the first floor window was a wooden balcony of such massive construction, that the front wall must have been solid indeed to have been able to carry the weight of the huge beam upon which the verandah was built.

The sight of the house startled Sunday.

He looked in.

It was untenanted.

Bounding in, he swung to the massive door, and placed in position the thick bar of timber which fitted into grooves upon each side and kept it fast.

It was a tough job for one man to lift this huge plank.

The door itself was made of solid wood about six inches thick, and it would have taken ordnance to move it.

Having assured himself that this was secure, he ran to the back.

But there was no outlet there.

Then he mounted the stairs.

He was in some doubt before beginning his investigations here, for he made his way cautiously, knife in hand.

He had it all to himself.

The first floor consisted of four rooms, all lofty and spacious, and all furnished with windows, from which the country about could be seen.

Making with all speed for the front room, he threw open the shutters and looked out.

There was Petrus.

Yes, and there were the twin bloodhounds, Castor and Cyrus.

"Yah, yah!" cried Sunday. "Me dry my powder and have shot at you soon."

Petrus looked up.

"The rash fool!" cried Petrus aloud; "he's treed at last."

"Golly!" retorted Sunday; "you calls that treed, Massa Greek—I calls it saved."

CHAPTER XVIII.

HOW THE PIRATE'S DAUGHTER AIDED THE PRISONERS.

WE must not forget little Emily, or the daring manner in which her abduction had been effected by Monastos, the pirate chief himself.

If courage and daring should give a man pre-eminence amongst his fellows, then did Monastos earn the title of king of the island.

Poor little Emily would have again shrieked for help had not her cries been stifled and burked by the unceremonious treatment she experienced at the hands of her captors.

Twice—thrice did she cry out before they had completely stifled her voice.

Gagged and rendered absolutely helpless, she was forced to resign herself to her fate.

She knew that all the lamentation in the world could not help her now.

The myrmidons of Monastos hurried her along until they came to the cave by the river, where young Jack had been also a prisoner.

Here she had been seen by the daughter of Monastos, whose tender heart was touched by the girl's distress, and who interceded at once in her behalf.

There was nothing to be gained by opposing his daughter's wishes, and so Monastos gave over little Emily into her care.

The two girls could only converse by signs.

However, in spite of all difficulties, they soon contrived to establish between them a perfect understanding.

Little Emily explained her sad predicament, and the brigand's daughter fully condoled with her.

But while they were in the midst of their mutual confidence, a noise without attracted Paquita's attention.

She ran to ascertain the cause of it.

It is needless to say that it was the advent of Harry Girdwood.

Little did Emily dream who it was.

But great was her joy when the boy, escorted by two of the brigands, entered.

"Harry!"

"Emily!"

He was amazed, for he had never expected to meet her now, although the search for her had been the origin of their misadventure.

"You are not hurt, Emily?" he asked, anxiously.

"No."

"That is well. Why, they will be overjoyed to hear it, and as for Jack ——"

"Yes," interrupted Emily, with great eagerness; "he is not here, too?"

"Yes, he is," answered Harry, "worse luck!"

"How came you to be taken?"

"Seeking you."

"Are all safe but us?"

"Yes."

"Why is Jack not here?"

"The chief of these villains has kept him back for some purpose that I can't guess at."

Emily's countenance fell at these words.

Harry Girdwood stared at Paquita, and then at Emily.

"This is his daughter," said Emily.

"The pirate chief's?"

"Yes."

"She looks very kind and gentle," said Harry.

"And isn't she pretty?" exclaimed Emily, enthusiastically.

"Well, I think she is," said Harry, with the air of one who would not be led away rashly by female charms.

"Think! Why, you know she is lovely," said Emily.

And then to clinch the matter and settle it beyond further dispute, she seized the brigand's daughter and embraced her diligently.

Paquita returned her caresses with as much affection and warmth.

Already they were like old friends.

Paquita asked Emily in Greek who Harry was.

But as Emily could not understand her, she showed in pantomime what she meant to convey by pressing her hand to her heart, sighing deeply, and then kissing the tips of her fingers.

"No, no, no," said Emily.

Harry understood this likewise.

"No, no," said he; "he is there with your father."

Harry's words were to her as Greek was to him.

But she understood his gesture.

She gave them a nod and a smile of intelligence, and ran to the entrance of the adjoining cavern, where she learnt all that was going forward.

She heard the command given, and knowing the cruel, vindictive nature of her father, she trembled for the young prisoner.

She beckoned to Harry Girdwood.

He approached.

"Listen," she said, pointing to the other cavern.

He caught her meaning, and at the self-same instant he heard young Jack's voice indignantly refusing to betray his people.

He heard the bold boy scoffing at the King of Magic Island, hurling defiance in his very teeth.

Paquita saw the consternation in his face, and she was full of eagerness to aid young Jack, no less upon his friend's behalf than his own.

For about a minute she stood aloof buried in thought.

Then she looked up with a start and clapped her hands joyously.

She had hit upon a scheme.

"Come this way with me," she said, pointing to an aperture in the further end of the cavern. "Quick."

They followed her into the dark recess, where to their intense surprise they discovered a ladder leading to a large vaulted chamber above.

"Quick!" she exclaimed, excitedly. "*Andiamo.*"

"Hallo!" exclaimed Harry Girdwood, "that's not Greek. I shall be able to talk to her, if she can speak Italian."

He had learnt it from his friends, the Harkaways.

So diligently had he pursued his studies of that beautiful language, indeed, during the voyage of the "Westward Ho!" that he was tolerably proficient now.

"Where are we going?" he demanded in Italian.

"To save your friend," replied Paquita, eagerly. "You must be quick, or it will be too late. Up the ladder! Quick—quick!" she continued.

He ran up.

Emily followed.

Then went Paquita.

As soon as she was at the top, she pulled the ladder up after her, or more properly speaking, she essayed to do it, for it was so weighty that it required their united efforts to accomplish it.

When, however, it was safely there, Paquita suddenly startled the companions of her flight, by giving a succession of the most piercing shrieks.

"Help, help!" she cried. "Save me —oh, save me."

The brigands rushed into the cavern and looked about in all directions.

But not a trace could they discover of their chieftain's daughter.

One of the men, it is true, examined he recess beneath the aperture, where the fugitives stood watching, but seeing no ladder there, it never occurred to him that they had winged their flight in that direction.

One of the pirates then ran in to inform Monastos of the supposed fatal tidings, the capture of his daughter by the enemy, and for the time young Jack's life was spared.

* * * * *

Parties of armed men were sent out in every direction to seek for the daughter of King Monastos.

The most trusty scouts were sent to scour the woods and forests.

But in vain.

Not a trace of the lost Paquita could they find.

One of the men brought back the tidings that a whole army was advancing upon them.

"What army?" demanded the chief.

"Those cursed English have managed to get together a powerful force."

"Then call my men together. These bold intruders shall find a terrible foe when they meet me."

The brigand's fears had exaggerated the danger and tripled, at least in his fancy, the effective force of Harkaway's troops.

"You say they are marching in this direction?" said Monastos.

"Yes."

"And that their force presents how many men?"

The brigand, his informant, was taken at a nonplus here.

He was not very good at counting heads, and he had not expected to be called upon to knock off the precise quantity to such a fine point.

"I cannot estimate their number as to a dozen," said he, "but this I know, they are numerous enough to crush us by sheer force of numbers."

Monastos wore a troubled expression of countenance.

"Then," said the chief of the brigands, promptly, "we must make up in tact what we may lack in strength."

"This boy," resumed Monastos, indicating young Jack, "you will have taken under guard to the castle."

"Yes, captain."

"Away with you," said the chief, "and mind that you select those paths that the enemy has not yet advanced upon."

"It shall be done, captain."

"Once at the castle see to make everything secure, for we shall join you there as soon as we have got Paquita safely back."

"Good."

"Away!"

* * * * *

The orders of the autocratic chief were obeyed to the letter.

The armed escort of the young prisoner took a most secluded route—that is, the way that was the most remote from Fairy Creek.

But chance was against them, for during their march Jack Harkaway and Mr. Mole dropped across the party.

It is not necessary either to allude more closely to the fight in the woods between our old friend Jack and the brigands, or the boldness and dash which brought about the rescue of our youthful hero by his daring and adventurous father.

* * * * *

And now for Sunday.

CHAPTER XIX.

SUNDAY IN THE CASTLE—THE MOVABLE TRAP—A SNARE—A RARE BRIDGE—THE
SENTRY AND HIS HOUNDS—A SURPRISE—NEW HOPE!

THE stone building in the forest, in which our good friend Sunday had taken refuge, was the identical place to which the king of the brigands had ordered his young prisoners to be sent for security.

Now Sunday's first care was to fortify himself in his stronghold.

He had simply to protect himself against Petrus, the man of mystery, and the two bloodhounds.

Having made himself easy upon this point, he began to look about him to see if there was any water or food.

The upper rooms of the house bore signs of having been recently inhabited.

Upon the floors were thick Oriental carpets, that would have been of immense value in any of the European markets.

In two of the rooms, which may be styled the state apartments, there were beautiful crystal chandeliers, fitted with long wax candles.

In one of these rooms was a basket of lady's work—embroidery and knitting—and an open book of poems, which would tend to show that the place had been hastily vacated.

Having made this casual survey, he went to the verandah and peered cautiously out.

There sat Petrus and his ferocious pets, the two bloodhounds.

Sunday chuckled.

"You'll have to wait there some time, by golly," he said with a laugh; "you no put salt on this black bird's tail dis journey."

He went back into the room and dropped down on to one of the luxurious couches.

"Dis am bery nice bed; wish old Monday and Massa Jack was wid dis child."

Sunday then took out his pistols.

Both were wet.

First he carefully drew the charges.

Then he rubbed the two pistols as dry as he could upon one of the silk curtains.

This done, he examined his powder flask.

And now he had a bit of luck, for his powder was perfectly dry.

In order to make himself the more sure of his pistols, he looked about for the means of making a fire.

So after looking about, he ran downstairs and set to work to kindle a flame under some faggots that he found upon the stone hearth of one of the rooms.

Having got up a good blaze, he put his pistols close to it to dry, and—

"Hullo! What's dat?"

Something startled him.

Sunday did not turn pale, for that was physically impossible, but he showed unmistakable signs of alarm.

He turned towards the door and drew his knife.

A creaking noise was heard in the adjoining room, as though a door with rusty hinges had been cautiously opened.

Clutching his knife firmly, the negro stole forward.

Then as he came in sight of the room, he stood still, with his knife in his hand ready for action.

Another moment, and a trap in the floor was opened, and the figure of a girl appeared there.

Sunday stared, but held his knife still ready.

The girl mounted a ladder, which Sunday could not see, and reaching the floor, peered cautiously about her.

Then she called to someone below to come on.

"Now," thought Sunday, "now or never is my time."

With two steps, or rather jumps, he was beside the girl.

One vigorous kick sent the trapdoor down.

Then planting his foot firmly upon it, he dragged the girl over it, and flourished the knife before her eyes.

"Half a word," hissed Sunday in her face—"a breath—a wink, and I'll cut yer head right off, s'elp my golly!"

The girl said nothing.

She stared at her sable captor and gasped.

And then she lay like a log in his arms.

Sunday looked around him in sheer wonderment.

It had all taken place so suddenly that he could scarcely believe it was real.

So to test the truth of it, he prodded himself with his knife in the thigh.

"Ha—whoo!" he yelled; "dat's real enough—dat's flesh and blood—yes, by golly! and hyar's the blood."

And he nearly let his lovely burden drop.

* * * * *

Hark!

"Paquita!"

"Paquita!"

"Push the door open, Harry! something has happened," said a voice beneath the trap.

"I will, Emily, if you stand out of danger."

Sunday heard all this distinctly.

"Am dis chile awake," thought Sunday, "or am he dreaming?"

There was no mistaking that voice—in fact, those voices, for both were equally familiar to him.

He did not know what to do.

So first he moved his swooning burden carefully out of the way.

And then, knife in hand, to guard against all accidents, he gently raised the trapdoor and looked down.

Then two voices exclaimed simultaneously—

"Sunday!"

"Massa Harry! By golly! am dat you?"

"Yes, Sunday. I am glad to find you here. Lend me a hand," said Harry Girdwood.

"By golly! and Missie Emily too?"

"Yes, Sunday," returned little Emily; "it's me. But where's Paquita?"

"Hyar's de oder female gal," answered Sunday. "My pretty face has frightened all de breaf out of her body. If old Monday had been here, him ugly face hab frightened her to def, poor young critter."

Little Emily was already by Paquita's side, doing all she possibly could to restore her to her senses.

After a lapse of about a minute or so, she opened her eyes and looked about her.

Then her eyes dropping upon Sunday, she gave a shudder and shrank back.

"There is nothing to fear," said Harry Girdwood, in Italian, "this is only a faithful old friend of ours, though how he has got here quite bewilders me."

"Your friend?" said Paquita, in the same language; "why, he must be connected with the——"

"The what?"

"*Il Diavolo.*"

Harry Girdwood burst out laughing at this.

"What am *Diavolo*, Massa Harry?" asked Sunday.

"Why, the devil," whispered Harry.

Then continued—

"There's no danger. Sunday is quite harmless."

Paquita accepted their assurances with apparent good faith, and yet seemed to have some misgivings.

"If what they say is true," she said, to herself, "it is all very singular. How came this negro here?"

Had she been able to speak English, she would have understood just then the conversation that was going forward between Harry and Sunday.

A few words put him in possession of the whole of the facts.

And as soon as he knew all, he explained to Paquita.

He told her how poor Sunday had lost his way in the forest, and how he had been pursued by the twin bloodhounds of the pirate chief.

Sunday—to whom the Greek maiden was now completely reconciled—took her by the hand, and led her to the window.

"See dere, missie," said he.

She peeped cautiously out.

"There are the two beautiful dogs," she exclaimed in rapture.

"Booful dogs!" exclaimed Sunday; "cussed tykes, Missie Brigand, dat's what I calls 'em. Why, dey try to eat dis young and tender chile."

"Then they are not particular to a trifle," said Harry Girdwood, laughing; "for you must be precious tough, Sunday."

Paquita laughed, and seemed to take great interest in all that interested Harry Girdwood.

As she looked out, her face grew suddenly thoughtful.

"Petrus with his dogs will wait," she said to Harry.

"So it seems."

"Yes, he has been sent on by my father, who will come on after with his men, and then we shall be taken."

"But you have nothing to fear. It is our lives he will take. He would never harm you."

She shook her head, and taking Harry Girdwood by the hands, said, smiling—

"No; he loves me too much. My only fears are for you."

"You must not fear on my account."

"But I do. My father is good and gentle to me, but cruel to his foes."

"I believe that," said Harry; "but still, dear young lady, we do not know for sure that they are coming."

She shook her head.

"You don't know my father," she said; "he is all powerful here, and he is sure to have Petrus followed up, sure—look there."

"Where?"

"Petrus."

Harry looked out, and then it must be confessed he was a little startled.

Petrus had taken his dogs by the chain, and dragged them nearer to him, while he held their muzzles tightly to prevent them betraying him.

The two hounds were restless, and pawed the ground impatiently, anxious to be off.

At the same time Petrus' manner showed that he had heard someone coming, and moreover, that that person was an enemy.

Petrus looked stealthily out.

Then he withdrew into the covered part, right into the thicker growth of shrub and bush.

"Look !" said Harry Girdwood, excitedly; "two men are approaching."

"Where ?"

"There—see !"

"I see! I see! turning the corner of the path."

"Yes."

Little Emily peered eagerly out of the window.

"I see them! I see them!" she ejaculated.

And then she started and stared, while her face changed colour.

"Sunday."

"Yes, missie."

"Look !"

"Whar ?"

"Don't you see who those two are ?" asked Emily.

Sunday stared, and then he rubbed his eyes again.

"By golly!" he cried, in wonder, "dis chile tink him ought to know dem. Ho, golly! It am Massa Harkaway."

"Yes," returned little Emily joyously. "It is Mr. Harkaway and dear Jack."

CHAPTER XX.

FRIENDS OR FOES—A STRANGE ALLY—THE MAN OF MYSTERY SPEAKS OUT.

AND so it was.

Jack Harkaway and his gallant boy.

"Oh ! brave, good Jack," said Emily, " he will save us."

"Yes, by golly, Massa Jack chip of de old block; 'im fight like young giant."

As Harkaway appeared before the house, there was a commotion observed in the bushes, and then a low, ominous growl was heard.

"Steady ; what was that ?" ejaculated Harkaway.

"It sounded like a stifled growl."

"Right, boy," said Harkaway; "keep your eyes open."

"All right, dad," replied our young hero; "trust me."

"I do, Jack."

They looked to their arms carefully, and stood back to back upon the *qui vive*.

A formidable couple they were, too, this father and son.

The two Harkaways—father and son—scented danger.

Sunday, Harry Girdwood, and little Emily dare not interfere to help the Harkaways, for they ran the risk of exposing them to a surprise.

But their suspense did not last a very long time.

Suddenly the ferocious hounds broke from the care of their master, and bounded out into the open.

With three or four leaps they were upon the Harkaways, and had them upon the ground.

Emily shrieked.

Harry Girdwood dashed open the window to leap out, but before they could interfere, Petrus was there.

"Come here!" he cried in a voice of thunder. "Desist, brutes, desist, I say!"

And he accompanied each word with a succession of blows with his fist that sent them howling back.

"Rise, gentlemen," said he, courteously, as he turned to menace the fierce bloodhounds again.

They were more surprised at this than they had been at the attack, but they quickly recovered their weapons.

"You have no need to seek your pistols," said Petrus; "my dogs will not hurt you if you give me your hands in friendship."

These words, spoken in an English accent, caused Jack Harkaway to stare in utter amazement.

"You hear? Do you not understand? I say give me your hands to show signs of friendship, and then you will be quite safe from their fangs."

"Friendship?" echoed Harkaway in surprise. "But can we give our hands so to you?"

"Have I shown myself an enemy to you?"

"Why, no."

"Your hands then; you shall not regret it."

He held out his hands to them as he spoke, but as they hesitated to take them, he went on—

"Well, I cannot wonder at your refusal. You see me a degraded outcast, and one of a band of pirates. But reserve your judgment and give me your hand in outward sign of friendship, to guarantee you against the attacks of my dogs. They are faithful and sagacious to friends as they are ferocious to strangers and foes,

and once you seem to have my friendship you have nothing to fear from them."

Harkaway hesitated no longer.

Young Jack gave him a hearty grasp, and the strange brigand flushed with evident pleasure.

"Castor," he exclaimed. "Cyrus; hey, come here!"

The two fierce hounds crept slowly up.

"Nearer, sir," said Petrus, sternly; "now give this gentleman your paw."

Castor obeyed with wonderful promptitude.

"Now, sir, you."

The other followed his brother's example with great docility.

It was strange to see those great fierce brutes then, licking the hands, and fawning upon the enemies they would lately have devoured.

At this juncture the door was thrown open, and Sunday and Harry Girdwood appeared, rifle in hand.

They brought their guns to their shoulders, ready for action.

"Sunday?" ejaculated Harkaway.

"Harry," cried young Jack, in amazement.

The docility of the bloodhounds vanished on the instant.

They crouched, and prepared to spring upon the new comers.

"Are these friends of yours?" asked Petrus, pointing to the door.

"Yes."

"Good."

"Recover arms," called out Harkaway, "and come here."

They were about to obey, when Petrus interposed.

"If they are indeed your friends," said he, "and true men, let me first make sure of my dogs."

And then turning to the hounds, he bade them sternly to lie down.

Walking up to the old negro and Harry Girdwood, he extended a hand to each.

"Give me your hand," said he; "I am a friend to you."

Both obeyed.

"A very particular odd friend to dis chile," said Sunday.

"Why?"

"Because you chivy dis infant half over de blessed island wid your pups."

"You are mistaken," said Petrus. "I did not mean it."

"It looks most dam uncomfor'ble like it, by golly!"

"I merely sought to overtake you," said Petrus, "to come to that understanding which I hope to bring about now."

"This man is a friend," said Harkaway, who was thoroughly convinced by Petrus' manner of his honesty of purpose.

Sunday accepted this as an order from his master, and a general reconciliation was brought about.

"How came you here?" said Harkaway.

"How did you manage your escape?" demanded young Jack eagerly.

"Have you any news of Emily?" asked Harkaway.

"Is she still in the brigand's clutches?" asked young Jack.

Fast as they showered the questions upon them, Harry Girdwood found means of replying.

"No. Emily is safe, and here she comes to answer for herself."

"Jack!"

Young Jack flew to the door as Emily appeared, and catching her in his arms, he showed his joy at her escape by kissing her until her blushing cheeks recalled him to a sense of decorum.

"After you, Jack," said his father, taking Emily by the hand and kissing her.

"But who is this?" demanded young Jack, pointing to the door, where the brigand's daughter lingered as if unwilling to disturb the harmony of the scene.

"Paquita?"

"Yes," said Harry Girdwood, "it is Paquita, the daughter of the terrible Monastos. It is to her kindness we owe everything—perhaps our very lives."

Emily ran back to her new-found friend, and, placing her arm round her waist, led her gently forward.

"Jack," said Harry Girdwood, "she saved your life too."

"Mine?"

"Yes."

"How?"

"At the moment when Monastos had you bound to the gun, she led us out of his clutches and placed herself in our power, in order to frighten her tyrant father into sparing you."

And then followed a full explanation of what the reader already knows concerning the manner of their escape from the brigand's cavern by the river.

Young Jack was thoroughly overcome by the recital.

But his father, having discovered in what tongue they could understand each other, made her the warmest acknowledgments upon their joint behalf.

"Receive a father's heartfelt thanks, my dear young lady," said he, with deep emotion, "for saving the lives of my son and of our friends."

Paquita smiled her reply to Harkaway.

It was indeed a happy reunion to all the party.

* * * *

During the foregoing scene, Petrus, the man of mystery, looked sternly on.

He seemed like one in a dream.

"Why do you side with your father's enemies, young lady?" said he, advancing towards her.

"Because my father would have behaved cruelly to them."

"But do you know what the consequences of this will be?"

"My conscience acquits me of all blame," returned Paquita; "I should do the same again if the same opportunity offered itself."

A smile lighted up his countenance.

"Your conscience tells you right, young lady," said he.

"I know it."

"Follow its dictates ever; and some day I will impart an important secret to you."

Suddenly the conversation was rudely interrupted by Sunday.

"By golly! Massa Harry," he exclaimed, "s'pose some of dem fellers get up de chimbly too?"

"The chimney?"

"Yes, sar; de flue, sar."

"The flue?"

"Yes, sar."

The party looked at each other for an explanation.

"Why, didn't you all come up a hole in de floor?" said Sunday, indignantly.

Thereupon, Harry Girdwood burst out laughing.

"Oh! that's what you call the flue."

"Yes, sar."

"We did."

"S'pose den, Massa Harry, dat dem piratical beasts plays a lily game at follow my leader up de hole in de floor, and give dis chile bullet, he get de belly ache, by golly!"

"You are right, Sunday," cried Harkaway; "we must take precaution, and at once, or the pirates will take us all by surprise by forcing their way through the flue, as you call it."

Until Sunday's opportune but unpleasant suggestion cropped up, they had thought only of looking out for enemies from the woods.

Harry Girdwood led the way into the house.

Petrus, in the meanwhile, tethered Castor to the door-post while he brought the other dog in with him.

It was well he did so.

Following the party to the inner chamber, in which was the trap-door in the floor, he found that they had already passed through it, and were anxiously peering down.

"Well, can you hear any sounds below?"

"No."

"All is safe for the present."

"Good."

"But every precaution must certainly be taken now."

Petrus did not appear satisfied with their investigation; he preferred taking observations for himself.

"Hey, Cyrus, boy, come here! Stand you there on guard, good dog."

The dog obeyed.

"Listen there for anyone coming, and if you fail to warn us in due time of danger, I'll kill you."

The hound replied to his master's exhortation by an intelligent wag of the tail.

This settled, they went round the house to examine the various apartments, and in one of the upper rooms Petrus delighted the party by discovering a cupboard, concealed from the casual glance, which was amply stocked with wines and fruit, and some welcome eatables.

"You can sit and regale at your ease," said Petrus.

"We must not be surprised," said Harkaway.

Petrus smiled.

"No fear of that."

"Sure?"

"Quite; the sentinels I have posted will keep better guard than the most reliable soldiers we could ever have."

Thus reassured by Petrus, they partook of the various delicacies that the house afforded.

"Before we proceed farther, tell me," said Harkaway, "how came you, an Englishman, to be here with such miscreants as are Monastos and his gang of brigands?"

As Harkaway spoke, a sickly expression flitted across the other one's face.

"It would take too long at present," he replied, grimly, "to tell the whole tale of my woes, to relate the horrors that I have gone through during my captivity here; but as we are strangers, and as some particulars are due to you, if only in proof of my good faith, I will put my sad history into the briefest possible form."

"Did I understand you aright?" said Harkaway. "Did you say captivity?"

"Yes."

"Has it lasted long?"

"Five years."

"How have you lived it through?"

"By looking forward to this day," replied Petrus, with a flushed cheek and flashing eyes. "The hour that I have been praying for, sighing for, weeping for, has come at last, and my deliverance will be brought about exactly as I've seen it in my dreams."

"But why did you not rise up against your oppressors? You are an Englishman. I should have slain my tyrant, if my body had been hacked piecemeal next moment."

"I will tell you why," replied Petrus; "my vengeance could not be satisfied by his death. Had he a hundred lives, and could lose each by slow torture, it would not satisfy me. On this island is a treasure of fabulous wealth, that has been got together by this man monster, the labour of a life of crime."

"I know it," said Harkaway.

"Each ounce of gold," continued Petrus, "represents broken hearts, sighs, tears—aye, tears of blood; every imaginable crime. To lose this treasure would pain this monster far more than the thought of death, for he is physically brave. Now, it shall be my task to let him know he is losing it, to wring his heart, to let him drain the bitter cup to the very dregs, and then devote my whole life to making his end wretched, a horror, one long degradation as mine has been ; aye, a long death. I would——"

"Hark !"

" What was that ?"

" Listen. Did you not hear ?"

" Massa Harkaway," cried Sunday.

" What is it ? Danger ?"

" Yes, sar. The dog at the flue hears suffink."

It was true.

Cyrus had already given his note of warning.

A low growl.

" Come," said Petrus, moving towards the door, " we have work before us now. We may in a few moments be surrounded by the pirates of this island."

And they followed him in anxious expectancy to the chamber below.

CHAPTER XXI.

THE PIRATE CHIEF'S GRIEF—BOLD RESOLUTIONS—THE WARNING—A SURPRISE—AN OLD FRIEND IS FOUND FULL OF SPIRITS—MOLE IN A NEW CHARACTER; THAT OF TARGET.

THE pirate, or King Monastos, as he liked to be called, was in distress about Paquita.

Heartless ruffian as he was, this pirate had one soft place in his heart.

Paquita filled it.

It was most remarkable to see a girl brought up in the midst of cruelty, brutality, and vice, and yet preserve her purity of mind and her gentle, guileless nature.

Yet so it was.

And this, perhaps, it was that so made the despotic brigand's heart yearn towards her.

She was so utterly unlike anyone with whom he came in contact, that he looked upon her as a superior being altogether.

Her singular disappearance completely unmanned him.

Presently he would fall a-cursing the English adventurers.

" I'll kill them all—all ! To the last one they shall die !" he cried aloud, shaking his clenched fists in the intense bitterness of his wrath.

" Ho, there !" he shouted after awhile; " where is Dimitri ?"

" He is away."

" Where ?"

" Conducting the prisoner to the castle by your orders, captain."

A smile of fiendish triumph lit up the brigand's face.

" We must be up and doing," he exclaimed, arousing himself; " let the worst come to the worst, we will show our teeth, and then let them beware of Monastos, the king of the brigands."

" We have received no news yet, captain, of your daughter."

Monastos made a gesture of impatience.

" Oh, if I had those English devils in my power, I would grind their lives out by slow torture ; but my Paquita must not be lost to me."

*   *   *   *   *

" You have got the boy safe, captain ?' demanded one of the band.

" Yes, under a strong guard ; but we must be ready for action, or these English will escape."

A dozen chosen men were armed and got ready to sally out into the woods in search of the enemy.

Besides the dozen men there were three trusty scouts, who preceded the party a considerable distance, and with whom a series of signals was arranged.

In this way they proceeded a considerable distance, when they heard the sound of a parrot.

" That's Moustakos; he imitates a parrot perfectly," said one of the pirates.

These children of the forest and mountain side possessed wonderful powers of imitation.

The pirate's reply was the shrill call of a bird, which no one would have thought possible to have emanated from a human throat.

Then came the countersign from Moustakos.

Their code of signals was perfect.

"'YOUR HEAD,' SAID HE, LOOKING AT MONDAY, 'SHALL SURMOUNT ANOTHER POLE.'"

Monastos joined again his band.

"Let no sound be heard; all depends upon surprising the enemy."

They were passing along a sort of natural lane, with tall forest trees bordering it, beyond which was a large open of glade.

Suddenly Monastos stopped short.

"Hush!"

He held up his hand in warning, for close by they could hear the sound of voices.

"We have them now," said Monastos.

He made a sign to his followers to spread themselves out, and silently, noiselessly, they obeyed orders.

Each man took up his post behind a tree and slowly prepared arms.

Then they turned to their captain.

They wanted fresh orders.

But a faint noise in the thicket caused them to suspend operations for a moment.

Looking in the direction of the sound, they saw a neatly-turned piece of wood passed gently through the foliage.

This was surmounted by a trouser leg.

Then came a human frame, dragging after it a second wooden member, the exact counterpart of the first.

The brigands stared amazed at this strange figure, but the strange figure in question was all unconscious of the excitement his presence was creating.

In fact he hugged himself in the belief that he was quite alone.

First he looked over his shoulders, and then he gave a sort of comfortable sigh, as he drew from his pocket a black bottle, which had been his constant companion and trusty friend in many a distant clime.

Gently he withdrew the cork.

Then he wiped the neck of the bottle with the cuff of his coat, and took a gentle pull.

"How unpleasant it is to be surrounded by such a suspicious set of people. I verily believe that some of them would suspect their own mothers of taking strong waters on the sly."

He sucked again.

"It was a happy thought of mine," murmured this singular person, who was no other than our old friend Mole, "to offer to mount this guard, for I can keep careful watch, and take my drop of comfort at the same time."

He washed down this observation with another gentle pull at the black bottle.

"Come what will," said Mole, "I am determined that the success of this expedition shall be due to my courage and forethought."

He solaced himself once more with that little black bottle.

"Hullo! what noise is that?" and he hastily clapped the bottle in his breast-pocket, and looked up.

"Why," he gasped again, "what does all this mean?"

And well he might.

He found himself the target for twelve long-barrelled guns, and all the twelve so close to him that there was not the faintest hope of their missing their aim

Isaac Mole tried to cry out.

He could not.

He thought he was a dead man this time.

The brigands closed upon him until the tips of their musket barrels touched him.

The cold sweat poured down his back, for every instant he expected to receive the contents of those twelve gun barrels in his devoted carcase.

Suddenly he found his tongue, and at a moment that they certainly did not expect it.

Mole gave a loud yell, and then he fell forward flat on his face.

CHAPTER XXII.

GUERILLA WARFARE—THE ARKANSAS DUEL ON A LARGE SCALE—MOLE IN ANOTHER NEW PART; THAT OF MAIL ARMOUR!

WHAT ensued was gone through with wonderful rapidity.

"Hullo, there! is that you, Mole, yelling out for help?"

The next moment Jefferson made a rush forward.

And then a surprise awaited him.

The band of Monastos, with admirable precision, wheeled round at a sign from their chief, and turned their guns upon Jefferson.

The latter looked and stared as though suddenly bereft of his senses.

Seven of the guns were pointing at him.

"Treed, by gum!" exclaimed the American giant.

But he did not give in.

Suddenly he darted round, sprang back into the bushes, and rolling back, disappeared before they could say "Jack Robinson," or its equivalent in Greek.

"Take a tree, every mother's son of you," he cried to his friends, who were advancing, "or you'll be catawampously chawed up by the pirates."

They needed no second warning.

In the twinkling of an eye, Harkaway's party sought refuge behind trees.

"Be cautious, lads, and don't pop your heads out too soon," cried Jefferson.

And then began an Arkansas duel upon a very extensive scale.

Not another word was spoken for several minutes.

Then suddenly the silence was broken by the sharp crack of a rifle, and Yanni, the pirate chief's favourite, was dropped.

"That's a chalk to me, Jeff," said Magog Brand, complacently.

"Bravo, Magog!" returned Jefferson.

But as he spoke, he was busy fixing his own quarry, and before the echo of Magog's shot had died away, there was a second report, and down dropped another of the brigands.

This was warm work for the Greeks.

But Monastos was equal to the task.

He made a sudden grab at Mr. Mole's collar, and dragged him up, rested his own rifle over his prisoner's shoulder, and kept him as a shield in front of himself.

But Mole soon slipped down, and the consequence was that Monastos emptied both barrels upon the enemy, but missed ignominiously in both cases.

Dick Harvey made his presence felt then.

No sooner did he catch sight of the commanding figure of Monastos, than he marked him for his own.

"Now then, Mr. Mole," he shouted, as Monastos once more dragged Mole to his feet, "drop to the ground when I give the word. Now!"

Mole dropped, but it was not in obedience to Dick's order.

Fear seemed to have got possession of him to such an extent that it took all the power out of his body, and appeared actually to infect his wooden legs.

At that very instant, Dick pulled the trigger.

Monastos staggered back, clapping his hand to his shoulder.

"He's potted!" ejaculated Jefferson.

"A good shot, Harvey."

But the Greeks were not beaten, by any means; they set up a cry of alarm when they saw their leader hit, but they kept to their work.

A second shot from the English party whizzed unpleasantly close to Monastos' royal ear.

"Curses on you all!" he cried.

Then stooping down, he grasped poor Isaac Mole firmly by the shoulders, and without any very great difficulty, he lifted him up and trotted him, pig-a-back, across the open.

Mole yelled.

He struggled and kicked, and he galled his captor's legs with the spikes with which his wooden pins were tipped.

JACK HARKAWAY AND HIS SON'S ADVENTURES.

Captor and captive were suffering, after their fashion, at the same time.

Another shot was fired, and Mole gave a wild, unearthly yell.

Was he struck?

Evidently.

Else, why he did he kick and wriggle so wildly upon the back of his captor?

"Here," cried the chief to one of his men, throwing poor Mole on the ground, "pick up this wretched Englishman, and carry him to our cave."

A savage-looking brigand then threw Mole on his back, and commenced to trot away with him.

But Mole was not to be taken off so easily, for he began to probe the calves of the man's legs with his spikes.

"Keep still!" roared the brigand, as he trudged on.

"Oh! Aha!"

"Quiet, you English dog!"

"Aha—oh!" cried Mole.

"If you scratch my legs with your toe-nails, like that, I'll have your nails drawn with pincers," said the amiable brigand.

"Oh!"

"Be still."

"I can't."

"Then I shall have the pleasure of cutting your throat," said the brigand.

"Beast!" returned Mr. Mole, with great readiness; "you know I am wounded."

"Are you hit?"

"Yes."

"Where?"

"Where? In the rear; I can't stand in comfort on these timber pins, and now I shall never be able to sit down again."

"We shan't want you to," answered the brigand, trotting on.

"I shall, though," groaned Mole.

"Oh, no; we shall lay you down," said the man.

"Lay me down? Wh—wh—where? Don't jiggle, joggle so. Let me try and walk."

The brigand, who seemed in no way incommoded by his burden, made a goat-like skip, upon finding how much his prisoner was suffering—so gratified was he at the thought—and trotted on.

"Where shall we lay you down, my friend? I'll tell you," and he dropped into a sharp trot; "we shall find you a nice soft bit of earth, *caro mio*, and dig down, a good six or eight feet, English measurement, for your earthy bed, and then——"

Mole gasped.

"And then?"

"And then we shall drop you in, whether you are alive or dead."

"Oh—oh—oh!"

"Yes, my brave Englishman," said the brigand, "we shall find you a good deep grave, and cover you up with good solid earth; so let me advise you to die quickly before reaching your last bed-room—it will be better for you. Ha, ha!"

"Oh, Jerusalem!" cried Mole, "you don't mean to bury me alive. I say, old fellow, stop a bit, and take a little drop out of my bottle."

"Oh, no," said the brigand; "I intend to give you a drop, and that very soon, in your deep grave; I can then help my-self out of your bottle."

"You horrid vagabond," cried Mole, trying to wriggle himself out of the brigand's grasp, "let me go."

In this way poor Mole was trotted off to captivity. Poor Mole!

Bit by bit, leg by leg, he had been disappearing from the scene.

And now it looked sadly like a whole-sale vanishing of the rest of his tough old hide.

CHAPTER XXIII.

THE MYSTERIOUS RETREAT—CAMPING OUT—THE NIGHT WATCH—ASLEEP ON
HIS POST—MESSENGER MIKE.

HARKAWAY'S party waited in security behind the trees for some minutes.

Not a sound was heard—not even a whisper.

What could it mean?

After waiting for some few minutes, with every nerve in his body tingling with the subdued excitement, Magog Brand stole out.

"Hist! Magog, hist!" exclaimed Jefferson; "keep back, or you will be a dead man."

Magog Brand's reply was brief but expressive.

"Are you mad?" said Jefferson. "Come back, I say."

"No, I'll face the brigands."

He stepped out into the open as if there was nothing to fear, as though he had the utmost contempt for their adversaries, who were, truth to tell, anything but contemptible marksmen.

He walked forward with gun in hand, as though he bore a charmed life against rifle bullets.

"Silly fellow!" exclaimed poor Jefferson; "this will be the last appearance on any stage of Magog Brand."

But Magog was not to die yet.

His appearance beyond the shelter of the trees excited no attention on the part of the enemy.

He made direct for a wide-spreading tree, from which the hottest fire had come during the skirmish.

And then turning round, he shouted out to his companion—

"The skunks have gone!"

"What?"

"Bolted, by Jove!"

Jefferson could not credit the announcement thus briefly conveyed.

"Impossible!"

"Come and see; there is not a brigand in sight."

Although his words and manner implied a doubt, yet he showed pretty clearly that he accepted it in good faith by marching out into the open.

Then he ascertained the truth himself.

The brigands were indeed gone.

"Well!" cried Jefferson in amazement, "I thought to have potted a few more of the vagabonds."

"We are doubled on this time."

"So it seems."

"But what of poor old Mole?"

"Poor Mole!"

They were sincere in this, for, in spite of his drawbacks, Mole was a favourite with all, and now it seemed as though death, perhaps a cruel death, was about to snatch their old friend from them, for the brigands, they knew, would have no mercy on poor Mole.

"Poor old fellow," said Harvey sadly; "I fear that I shall never laugh over your tricks again."

Jefferson shook his head mournfully.

"I fear not."

"At any rate, there is this to be said, Mole as a prisoner will be no trifling incumbrance, and will so far impede their movements that I've no doubt we shall be able to come up with them."

"I hope so."

"In which direction do you think they can have gone?"

That was a question that required some thought, for the brigands had not left the faintest traces behind them, or the least indication that could aid the pursuers.

Amongst the latter were several experienced trappers and hunters, who were voted especially to the service of recovering the trail.

But their task was one of no ordinary difficulty, for the retreat of the brigands had been made through the woods.

For half-a-mile around their present camping place they searched diligently.

But in vain.

Not a trace or clue to help them!

Or stay, we were wrong in saying not the faintest clue, for they laboured under what may be described as the exactly opposite disadvantage.

There were too many traces—too many clues.

In other words, their examination of the ground convinced them that the party of brigands had broken up and scattered in all directions.

This was a puzzle.

They held a general consultation upon it.

"We have scattered them," said one of the party—a young American, called Hiram Lee; "there can be no two opinions about that, I should say."

"No."

"The victory is ours."

"Yes, it is a rout," added another enthusiast.

Harvey smiled.

"Not that," he said; "or else they would not have carried off their prisoners so easily."

"Poor Mole!"

"My opinion," said Jefferson, "is rather that they have scattered with the express purpose of throwing us off the scent, and have probably rejoined at a little distance off."

This was the most likely supposition.

All agreed to this.

Taking that for granted—

"Jefferson," said Dick Harvey, "the best thing for us to do is to keep our largest weather eye open, and look out for squalls."

"True."

"They will probably return in force and endeavour to surprise us."

"Probably."

"Well, then," said Magog Brand, "all I have to say is this. If, with that belief in our minds, we suffer ourselves to be surprised, we deserve the worst that can possibly befall us."

"Right."

"Agreed."

"Let us take every possible precaution to guard against it."

"We will."

"In the first place, let us take opinions about our next step."

"Good."

"You put the question, Harvey, for our consideration," said Jefferson.

"Hear, hear!"

"In the first place, then," said Dick, "what is to be done? Shall we camp here and fortify this position, or move on?"

"Camp here," cried several.

"Let us examine well the two questions before we decide," said Dick.

"Go on."

"If we remain here, there is this advantage; Harkaway will better be able to find us out."

"True, if he lives."

"Oh, he is safe enough," said Dick. "Jack and I have got through worse scrapes than this, I promise you."

"Doubtless; and I am no croaker of evil," said Jefferson; "but I confess that I would give a tall pile of dollars to shake hands with Jack Harkaway at this moment."

"Give me your hand, Jeff," said Dick, earnestly; "you're a good fellow—a true pal, and one of the luckiest days in my life was when I fell across you."

Jefferson returned his grasp warmly.

"On the contrary, my boy," he said, "you and brave Jack Harkaway have made life endurable for us—eh, Magog?"

"Rather," responded the dwarf quickly. "Why, Jefferson and I were dying of sloth—quietly humbugging each other with idleness and expiring of *ennui;* Harvey, my boy, you and Harkaway are our benefactors."

"Well, old fellow, I and Jack will never forget how you fought for us in the New York gaming house."

* * * *

"The disadvantage of staying here," said Hiram Lee, "is that the brigands, knowing the spot, will make their arrangements accordingly."

"True."

"March on, then."

"That is what I was coming to," said Dick.

"Let us examine the ground about," said one of the party, "and if we find any place more suitable, we can camp there, and yet keep a sharp look-out for friends or foes."

"Good."

A diligent search was made, and they selected a spot on high ground, yet sheltered by heavy timber, which commanded a view for some little distance.

This settled, Dick set to work, making secure arrangements for the coming night.

"I'll show you now," said he, "how I nd my old friend Jack used to fortify our position when attacked by Indians years ago."

This was watched with considerable curiosity.

Firstly, he set his friends and himself to work to chop off some branches of the nearest trees.

With these he had the ground strewn all round, covering a circumference, or rather the openings in it, of about a hundred feet.

Besides this, he fastened thin slips of willow from tree to tree, at about a foot from the ground, a very dangerous obstacle to men creeping on the ground in the dark.

By the time that this was done, it became necessary to post the sentries for the night.

Then they ate their cold supper, and washed it down with the contents of their ample flasks.

"Now," said Magog, "as my watch begins an hour hence, I'll take a snooze."

When he had snored gracefully for half an hour, he was awoke by something, soft and warm, brushing against his face.

Then there was something both cold and damp.

"Harvey!" he said, sitting bolt upright, "Dick! Jefferson!"

"Hullo!"

"What now?"

"Any alarm?"

"No."

They were already on their feet, rifles in hand, and upon the look-out.

"What is it?"

"Our friend come back," replied Magog with a chuckle.

"Surely not Harkaway?" gasped Harvey.

"No."

"I thought it was too good," he said.

"Yes; but we have our four-footed postman back with news."

"What, Mike?"

"Yes."

And then everyone had a kind word for that luckiest of lucky dogs.

They lit a lantern and took observations of Master Mike.

Around his neck was fastened a letter written by Mrs. Harkaway and by Mrs. Harvey.

It was brief and to the purpose.

"We hope you have got Emily safe with you by this time, and that our foolish boys have not been running risks in this dreadful place. We are all full of anxiety. Monday is nearly well. Unless you are soon back, he will start after you. As it is, we have all our work to do to restrain his impatience, and poor Ada is in a constant state of worry about him. That darling Mike is the prince of dogs. If he gets safely to you with this, he shall have a collar of gold and jewels, and feed upon all the dainties in the land, if once we escape from this desert. Oh, pray return at once."

*   *   *   *   *

Dick had but just finished the letter, when Mike was seen to prick up his ears and look sharply round.

Magog Brand watched him eagerly.

"That's my post," he said to himself.

So out he crept upon all fours towards the sentry whom he was to replace.

And the first thing he saw here filled him with wrath and indignation.

The solitude and the fatigue together had been too much for the sentry.

He was leaning upon the muzzle of his rifle, and in this position he was half dozing.

He was not strictly speaking asleep, but he had suffered the drowsiness so far to conquer him that he did not hear Magog Brand's approach.

Suddenly the dwarf was startled by a sound close beside him.

It was like the cocking of firearms—of a rifle or a pistol.

An alarming sound.

Magog did not wait to consider.

This was time for action—not thought.

To pause was to be lost.

He dropped his rifle and took out his bowie knife.

"This is like Paddy's shillelah," he said to himself. "It never misses fire."

Creeping through the brushwood, he suddenly saw before him the tall form of one of the Greek brigands watching the sleepy sentinel.

In his hands he carried a gun, that he was just upon the point of bringing to his shoulder.

He was a huge fellow, and he took a slow and deliberate aim.

The sentry was about to pay for his negligence.

He was doomed.

"Now!" said Magog to himself; "now is my time."

Gripping his long knife nervously, he stole forward in the direction of the brigand.

CHAPTER XXIV.

HOW MAGOG BRAND STOPPED AN INTRUDER—ADVENTURE ON THE MARCH—WAR'S ALARMS.

MAGOG BRAND was, figuratively speaking, all there.

He meant mischief.

You might see this by the vicious look about the corners of his mouth and the peculiar expression of his eyes.

It was not a long job for him, however.

Three or four strides brought him close to his man.

And then gathering up his strength for a big effort, he leapt upon the unsuspecting Greek from behind.

"Ugh!"

And that was about all the brigand said.

Magog was short, sharp, and decisive in his action.

Before the man could struggle much, that murderous long knife was buried up to the very hilt in his neck.

The windpipe was severed—it choked his utterance, and down he dropped upon the ground.

Two sharp strokes of the knife—right and then left—and what a few minutes before had been a huge muscular body, full of life and vigour, was now a hideous headless trunk.

Now this was accomplished without noise—and the sentry, whose life had been in danger, was actually unaware of what had taken place.

This truly horrible feat was barely accomplished when Magog was startled by the sound of someone advancing in that direction.

The stockade which Dick Harvey had suggested betrayed the approach, for the dried twigs were crushed beneath a heavy foot.

Magog glanced up, and catching sight of the outline of a tall figure, he felt that it was high time to beat a retreat.

But before going, he hit upon a novel defence.

Catching up the head of his victim, he hurled it with all his force in the direction of the new comer.

It was a good aim.

The reeking missile struck the man as he was coming on, and brought him to a sudden stop.

Then Magog snatched up the slaughtered brigand's gun and scampered back, just as the astonished sentry opened his sleepy eyes and gazed about him.

"On guard!" ejaculated the dwarf in a stage whisper.

"All right."

"It is now."

And back he scrambled to the camp.

Harvey and Jefferson were wide awake.

They had missed Magog, and were wondering what could have become of him; so that they saw him back again with considerable sensations of relief.

"Anything wrong?" demanded Jefferson.

"Not much."

"Are you hurt?"

"No."

"Why, what is that blood on you?—you are covered.

"So I am," replied the little man coolly; "but it is not mine."

"Whose then?"

"Another of the Greek brigands," was Magog's reply.

He thought no more of killing a brigand than he would of shooting a wolf.

"I was just in time," he explained; "our sentry was asleep on his post. I heard someone coming, so I crept and cut off one man's head and threw it at another. It saves powder and shot, you see."

His hearers stared.

And then when they got at the real truth of it, they shuddered at the recital.

Be that as it may, it saved the rest of the party.

For a craftily-planned surprise, the work of Monastos himself, was frustrated by Magog's courage; for when the gory head fell at the advancing brigand's feet, it filled him with horror and fear.

The man whom the desperate dwarf had thus cut down was one of the best and boldest of the brigands, and as soon as Monastos was told what had happened, he ordered the retreat to be sounded.

And then it was agreed that they must give it up for the night.

"We are discovered," said Monastos. "We are bunglers and growing unworthy of our names, when we cannot conduct an attack at night with more prudence than has been displayed this time."

The brigands slept very little that night.

The watches of Harkaway's party were doubled, and this left but three men unoccupied.

These three men were Dick Harvey, Jefferson, and Magog Brand.

* * * * *

Morning dawned.

The three sleepers woke up in a general state of alarm.

Their first impulse was to feel for their weapons.

"It's all right; no more brigands to decapitate."

They shook themselves together, and trotted about hither and thither to the various posts, for the purpose of shaking off their drowsiness and of ascertaining at the same time if their men were all safe.

Their cheeks were rather pale, and their eyes were rather bloodshot for want of rest.

In other respects all was as well as could be wished.

Magog Brand kindled the fire, and boiled some water, that they got from a neighbouring spring, in a tin pannikin which he carried in his knapsack, and with this he prepared some coffee.

And then a grand feast was held of cold meat, bread, and hot coffee.

They had been anxiously waiting for the reappearance of Harkaway, senior.

One and all of the party missed him sadly, and now at last they began to fear that something dreadful had happened to him.

"The skunks shall suffer for all that we suffer," said Jefferson bitterly.

"They shall, we swear!"

A general chorus of voices showed that they were all agreed upon this point.

If harm should have befallen Jack Harkaway or his boy, then woe betide the Greek brigand.

Here was a party of bold and desperate men, all meaning to protect each other; and if evil should happen to one or the other of them, the rest were pledged to fight with the avowed object of exterminating Monastos and his band of brigands.

They grew impatient of remaining inactive, and so they resolved to march on in search of Harkaway, and of adventure generally.

One of their advanced guards or beaters started a Greek scout just upon the skirts of a wood, and as soon as the Englishmen perceived him they gave the view halloo, and started off in pursuit, and when they had got about a hundred yards, they saw that the Greek was distancing them fast.

Run as fast as they could, the brigand lengthened the gap between them at every stride.

"He mustn't escape," said Jefferson.

"Not quite, Jeff," said his little friend.

They were of one mind upon this head.

Both men had stopped in the chase influenced by the same idea; they meant to put a stop to his flight by an ounce of lead.

Magog Brand, being loaded first, knelt, took a steady aim, and pulled the trigger.

They watched for the result of the shot with some anxiety.

But no use.

He was not touched.

On he ran faster than ever.

Jefferson knelt and had his turn now.

The big American was a crack shot with a rifle.

Jefferson pulled the trigger, and the fugitive bounded into the air.

"Hist!"

"Potted!"

"Spiked!"

Such were the ejaculations of the lookers-on.

They thought he was brought down for good; but although the unlucky man fell, evidently struck by Jefferson's bullet, yet he was not seriously damaged; not too seriously, that is, to prevent his resuming his flight.

He clapped his hand to his side—thus indicating his hurt—and flew on with as much speed and energy as before.

"Hullo!"

"Winged him only."

"He's badly hurt though," said Dick, "I can see, by his run."

"Then he is ours."

"Doubtless."

But they reckoned without their host for once.

By the time that they got another five minutes upon the way, the fugitive Greek, wounded as he was, had contrived to get clean off.

* * * * *

Suddenly they were startled by the sound of firearms.

First a single shot, then a straggling volley, and then followed a well-sustained though not very regular fire.

A very warm engagement was going forward close at hand.

"I can hear our rifles going it," said Dick Harvey. "I know the ring of them too well to be mistaken."

"You're right, Dick, there."

"We shall have some fighting now."

"Rather," exclaimed Magog Brand "and hang me if I am going to miss it."

"Nor I!"

"Nor I!"

"Forward, then. Look to your rifles and pistols all round, and let us get on to the fighting ground, wherever it is."

CHAPTER XXV.

TORTURING A PRISONER—MOLE BETRAYS HIS FRIENDS AFTER HIS OWN FASHION—THE POISONED WINE.

WE are compelled to leave the party on board the "Westward Ho!" for awhile longer and follow the changing fortunes of Mr. Mole.

We left that worthy gentleman hoisted upon the back of the muscular brigand, and while he served as a rampart, he received a wound in the rear from a bullet.

Poor Mole!

He was indeed unfortunate.

In spite of his kicking and struggling, poor Isaac Mole was carried away bodily from his friends by these desperate ruffians, who did with him pretty well as they liked, and when they began to find their burden grow heavy, they were out of range of fire, so they dropped him down to the ground.

He fell like a limp sack, and doubled up.

"Rise!" cried Monastos, who had followed the brigand who carried Mole. Then turning his band, he said—

"We must march quickly forward."

"Get up!" exclaimed the brigand to Mole, "and march."

But as Mr. Mole did not understand the meaning of the words "rise," or "get up," in *modern* Greek, he curled himself up with a hope that they were going to leave him to his own devices.

Vain hope.

His masters did not speak twce.

The brigand growled at him as if he were some wretched mongrel, and gave him a kick in the ribs.

"Ah, oh!"

It nearly took all the breath out of his body, but the brigand thought that there was something comical in the sound, so he dropped him another, playfully as before.

"Beast!" gasped Mole.

The precise meaning of this the brigand did not catch: but he shrewdly judged that it was abusive, and so he gently prodded Mr. Mole with the point of his stiletto.

"Oh!" shrieked poor old Mole; "murder! murder!"

Monastos was heading the party and marching in stern silence.

He turned sharply round at the noise.

"Who was that shrieking so loudly?" asked Monastos.

"The prisoner."

"Prisoner," said the chief of the brigands, in English, to Mole, "another such cry as that, and you will never utter another in this world."

Mole groaned, and said quietly to himself—

"Oh, you beast!"

The brutal brigand once more prodded Mole in his side with his stiletto.

"You had better slaughter me outright; have me stuck to death by inches, you ugly, dirty vagabond," cried poor Mole.

He had only received half an inch of the stiletto as yet.

"We shall not kill you," said Monastos, turning back, with lowering brow, and each word measured so as to fall like a death knell upon the hapless Mole's ears.

"That is very kind of you," muttered Mole; "perhaps you will tell me what you will do."

"We shall only cut your tongue out."

Mole turned faint.

There was a steady deliberation in the brigand's manner, which filled his very soul with terror.

The brigands who had charge of him bade him rise.

He winced as he received another playful prod, but he was mindful of the chief's words, and he bit his tongue to stifle the cry that rose to his lips.

Having got him upon the move, the two brigands in charge of him were merciless.

Not a step did he take without a reminder of their proximity, in the shape of a kick or cuff, or a dig with their stilettoes.

He was prodded all down his back, and it smarted and bled woefully, but he was in too great awe of the chief to breathe a sigh of complaint.

A mile or more was covered in this way, and Isaac Mole's sufferings grew intense.

At length he began to look about him in hopes of seeing some of his own party.

"Oh, Harkaway! Oh, Harvey! Why are you not here to help your old friend, Mole!"

Despair took possession of him.

Let him but see his tyrants beaten, tortured, killed.

Let him but see some retaliation for the indignities he had endured, and he would willingly risk his life.

But there was little hope of this.

As he glanced round, they seemed to anticipate his thoughts, to read his very heart.

The cold ring of a pistol barrel was pressed against his cheek, and a menacing hand motioned him to proceed.

"You blackguard!" groaned the injured Mole, inwardly, "if I had you by yourself, I would fight and show what Mole is made of."

Prod!

But never a word came from poor Mole.

Not a sound nor a groan escaped him.

Kick.

"Thief!" muttered Mr. Mole to himself; "dogs and scum of the earth! If Harkaway was here, how he would scatter you all."

Then came a gentle rap on the back of the head with the butt end of a pistol.

That is, a gentle rap according to the brigands' notions.

Luckily Mr. Mole's skull stood it bravely.

"I should like to have you pinned down to the earth naked," said Mr. Mole to himself, as he looked round at them, "and dance a fandango over you, with new spikes to my timber toes. Wouldn't I shuffle nimbly all over you?"

They camped for the night in a snug forest glade.

Mr. Mole watched most anxiously for any signs or movements upon the part of his captors by which he could profit.

But he had to labour against one great difficulty, and that was his ignorance of their language.

A scout came in, and conversed in an animated manner with the king.

The result of this was that a body of men were dispatched under the command of a huge fellow, whom the king addressed as Paradia, to make that memorable night attack.

Paradia boasted, and bragged, and swelled out his chest, as he swore to the king to bring him Harkaway's head or forfeit his own.

Result—he forfeited his own.

This was the fellow who fell at the hand of little Magog Brand, and had his head severed from his body by the knife of the little warrior.

The rest of the men came back to report to their chief the failure of their surprise.

Monastos grew more sullen and savage than ever.

Suddenly he ordered the prisoner to be brought before him.

"Do you—wretched English dog—know what has taken place?" said he to Mole, after staring at him for a while.

"No."

"Can you guess?"

As he put this question, he fixed Mole with a stern eye that appeared to go right through him.

"Answer me," he thundered.

"Well, yes, I can," responded Mole, with some hesitation.

"And you are pleased to think that we have failed? Do you hear me?"

"Yes."

"Then answer."

He turned abruptly off at this.

"You are right, too; for if my band had succeeded—if they had crushed the gang of thieves and intruders you belong to, your life would have paid the penalty as well."

Mr. Mole shuddered.

"As it is, we want you, and so you may live a little longer."

He breathed again.

"Your mission now is to give them up to us."

Mr. Mole stared.

"Mine?"

"Yes, yours."

"But how?" inquired Mole.

"You have to tell us how many there are, what arms they possess, and how they have planned their campaign; and how many men are left on board the ship to protect it in the absence of the rest of the party. Do you hear?"

Mole was silent.

"Speak!"

Not a word from Mole.

"Answer me, I say, or——"

One of the brigands prodded Mole as he had done before, and then he howled out wildly—

"Kill me—cut my tongue out, but I shan't utter a word. Do you expect me to betray my only friends? No; you may cut me to bits, and as you threaten, cut my tongue out, but I will be true to my dear old friends."

The king of the brigands smiled sardonically.

"We shall do neither the one nor the other," he said.

Whereupon Mr. Mole felt relieved.

"At present."

Mr. Mole had got relieved too quickly.

"Now, first in order, is the question of numbers," said the king of the brigands; "tell me what is their strength?"

Mole was silent.

"Do you hear me?"

Not a word.

The king frowned, and with a glance he beckoned two of his men to his side.

They were the two who had charge of Mr. Mole.

"The prisoner cannot find his tongue," said he significantly.

"Shall we assist him, your excellency?"

"Yes."

And they did, in this way.

One of them seized the prisoner's right hand and spread it open, while the other cut a thin swish from the nearest bush.

The swish was peeled and straightened, and then the man turned to the chief for further orders.

The pirate chief gravely inclined his head, as he said "fifty."

And then, while Mr. Mole was wondering what next was to take place, down came the swish upon his palm.

"Whoo!" he cried.

And he popped it under his left arm for solace, just as we have all done in our own schooldays.

"Confound their impudence!" thought he; "they are making a laughing-stock of me; they are showing their contempt of me by giving me cuts on the hands, as though I were a refractory boy at school."

The hand was dragged out again, and down came the second whack.

This time the unlucky tutor was better prepared, and he would not flinch.

"They shall find I am not to be cowed by a cut on the hand," he said, boldly.

Alas! poor Mole!

He little thought what this punishment could be worked up to in the hands of experienced torturers

But for his existing misfortunes, Mr. Mole would have begun by an introduction to the bastinado.

You probably know that the bastinado is a beating with canes on the soles of the naked feet.

But you may not know that it is one of the most horrible of refined cruelties.

Mole's punishment was the antithesis of the bastinado, and he soon discovered that it was no trifle.

At the tenth stroke the hand was swelling rapidly.

At the twelfth, he had bitten his tongue through to stifle his groans, and yet one burst from his very heart in spite of himself.

They expected he would give in then.

But no, the brave old man submitted to his torture; he knew well he was serving his old friends by remaining quiet.

He took his fifty strokes on the hand, and then he sank half fainting upon the ground.

His two torturers smiled upon him in derision, and Mole returned their glance with one of undying hatred.

"If I live," said he aloud, "it shall be my task to make sure of you two, and if I die, Harkaway shall have your disposal as my legacy."

Suffering actually invested the poor old gentleman, tippler and braggart though he was, with a sort of dignity.

"He holds out well," said the king of the brigands.

"He would not hold out long, sir," said one of the men, "if you gave me full power with him."

Monastos smiled, in a half condescending way.

"You are young and sanguine, Sarandi," he said.

Mole repeated the name.

"Sarandi, I shall not forget that."

"You would kill him before I had squeezed the information from him."

"No, captain. What I propose will not cause such pain as what he has but now received, but if he holds out against it, take my head."

The confident air of the ruffian caught the chief's attention.

"Speak, then," said he; "what have you to propose?"

The man drew near the pirate chief and whispered.

"Right," said the chief; "we will try the English hound"

The unfortunate prisoner was then bound hand and foot and stretched upon the ground, and then the brigand Sarandi lay down full length beside him.

The pirates looked on.

Mole was wondering what on earth was to come next, when he felt a sharp pricking sensation at the back of his head.

Sarandi had pulled out a single hair.

This is scarcely as painful as the prick of a pin, and Mr. Mole could only wonder what it was for.

He soon found out.

Hair after hair was drawn from his head, until the whole of his scalp was itching to the most painful degree.

The irritation increased every instant —his head was on fire with it.

He could not touch it with his hands, for he was bound.

The sensations communicated themselves to the rest of his body.

From head to legs he felt one mass of fiery irritation.

Indeed, he subsequently described his sensations as those of a man who has inadvertently swallowed a firework.

When this had gone on for ten minutes or so, poor Mole's sufferings quickened his inventive faculties.

"Why should I suffer so?" said he to himself; "why not give them a full account of all they ask, and betray my friends, after my own fashion? Yes, I will answer the wretches, but take care to deceive them."

Suddenly, as though he could no longer hold out, he cried—

"Enough. I'll tell."

"Hold!" said the king.

Sarandi turned to his chief.

"Shall I continue the torture?"

"Enough," said the chief of the brigands. "Set him loose."

This was done.

"Now answer my questions," said his majesty, "and your life shall be spared."

Mole bowed.

"How many men does the whole of your expedition muster?"

"All told?"

"Yes."

"On land and on board?"

"Yes."

Mole appeared to reflect for a moment two.

"Two hundred and fifty."

The pirate stared again at this, and his e grew grave.

"Are you sure that you don't over-estimate it?"

"Yes."

"I should recommend you to be very particular."

"I am," returned Mole, coolly; "I am not in the habit of saying what is not true."

"Who is the commander of the party?" inquired Monastos.

"I am the chief officer," responded Mole.

"You?"

"Yes."

The brigand chief looked dubiously at Mr. Mole.

"Beware; if you deceive me, you shall suffer more than death."

"I am a truthful man," said Mole.

"How many are on shore?" demanded the chief.

"I don't know to a man," replied Mole; "Perhaps a hundred."

"Where did you get your information of my treasure from?"

Mole thought awhile.

"There can be no harm in telling the truth there," said he to himself, "since poor Spirillo is dead and gone."

"Well?"

"It was Spirillo," answered Mole; "to him I owe all the information which led me to organise this expedition."

"I knew it," answered Monastos. "I put that question to test your truth."

Isaac Mole was smarting with the anguish of his wounds all over, but he could not repress an inward chuckle at this.

"Truthfulness, like honesty," he said to himself, "is its own reward."

Monastos, thinking he had gained his purpose, ordered one of the men to give the prisoner some wine.

He drank and made a very wry face.

"Good Heaven!" he suddenly ejaculated; "they think they have got all the information they want, and have poisoned me now. They half threatened it."

CHAPTER XXVI.

THE SCOUT—ON FOR THE CASTLE—THE FACE AT THE WINDOW—"HURRAH! HURRAH!"

MONASTOS thought long and earnestly over the important revelation which the prisoner had made.

If his estimate of the numbers of the enemy should be anything at all near the mark, their position was critical.

He was no coward.

He never for a single moment thought of flight.

No; he would fight it out to the bitter end, and, let the worst come, he would die upon the spot, guarding the treasure he had spent his life to obtain.

Such was the resolution of this bold, bad man.

The brigand monarch passed a sleepless night, brooding dismally over the camp fire, while poor old Mole slumbered peacefully, in spite of his bruised hand and aching head, his throbbing back and pricking side, dreaming that he was slaughtering the brigands wholesale by the side of Harkaway and his son.

With morning came a scout, bearing news of the most interesting nature.

The man was not a Greek, and he addressed the chief in Italian, which Mole could follow pretty easily.

"Some of the enemy have got possession of the castle," he said, "and they hold there as their prisoner your daughter, the Signorina Paquita."

"Are you sure? Whence do you gain your information? Answer."

"From the indisputable testimony of my own eyes."

The pirate chief thought for awhile in silence, and then he gave his orders.

The scout who had last arrived was a man to trust, so he was started off to the cavern home, with instructions to procure ladders, and proceed by the subterranean passage to the castle.

Then the march was resumed.

At length they came in sight of the castle.

"Who can be there?" said Mr. Mole to himself. "Who of our friends can be there? It would cheer me more than all the whisky I ever drank, if I could only look upon Harkaway or his friends' faces."

His wish was granted; his prayer answered. A face did appear at the window over the verandah.

A dusky countenance, illumined by two glistening big eyes and a set of pearly white teeth!

Mr. Mole stared again.

Could he believe his own eyes?

Yes, surely! There could be no mistake in this. It was the faithful negro, with whom he had had so many a passage at arms in happier days, and under more pleasant auspices.

"Sunday!" ejaculated Mr. Mole.

And as he looked, there appeared another countenance beside Sunday's woolly poll—a face that made Mr. Mole absolutely cry out with joy.

"Jack! Jack! my poor boy! my own Jack! Oh, where is your father?"

If Harkaway were near his troubles would be over. Such was his confidence in young Jack's father.

Another figure appeared on the balcony, and then Mole startled all the brigands out of their stolid, calm exterior by shrieking at the top of his voice—

"There he is! There he is! Hurrah, hurrah, hurrah for Harkaway!—and a little one in!"

CHAPTER XXVII.

TORO AND HUNSTON ARE RESCUED—THE LAZARETTO—HUNSTON'S FATE—THE FUNERAL TAKES PLACE AT MIDNIGHT.

WE left Toro and Hunston adrift on the ocean in an open boat.

It seemed as if their sufferings were about to be ended by violence.

But fate had ordered it otherwise.

Hunston slipped and fell back into the bottom of the boat, while Toro, quick to profit by the accident, strode across him with his dagger uplifted.

It was a narrow squeak for Hunston then.

Toro raised his knife.

It gleamed in the air—it descended.

But not on Hunston.

The latter wriggled his body out of harm's way, and only just in time, for the knife struck the seat upon which his left side had rested, and went more than an inch into the wood, where it stood quivering like a young sapling freshly planted.

The giant Italian seized it again and jerked it out of the seat, his rage not yet expended, and the next stroke would probably have settled the strife.

But it was not to be.

Just at this critical juncture, a sound reached his ears which caused him to look up in some surprise.

It was the sound of a gun.

It was a distant sound; it came ever so far across the sea, and Toro's sight was so dimmed with fasting and suffering that he could not perceive anything for awhile.

But presently he contrived to make out a ship.

It was a long way off.

Toro started up.

In an instant his enmity to Hunston was forgotten.

All he could think of was the coming vessel, and his chance of rescue.

Frantically he waved a handkerchief, being the only bunting they could muster on board that frail craft.

But no change in the ship's course showed that they were observed.

Toro shouted with all his strength, and again waved the handkerchief.

A Beautiful Companion Picture to our last, entitled "THINKING," will be given with our next Number.

"'COME ON HARRY,' CRIED JACK, 'FOLLOW ME!'—AND THEY LEAPED INTO THE WATER."

Presently they were answered.

A signal gun was fired, and then a boat was lowered and manned, and it pulled towards them.

The boat's crew saluted them, as it drew near, but they spoke in a language which Toro could not understand.

Toro shook his head.

Then he tried them in several languages, until he contrived to make himself understood.

Then he explained—

"We were wrecked," said he. "Our vessel went down, and all on board, with the exception of ourselves, perished. We got away in a boat, as you see, and have lived in daily and nightly dread ever since——"

"Of what?"

"Of being starved," was Toro's reply, "or of dying of thirst. I am choking now; my comrade is as badly off."

Hunston groaned.

"Here," said a sailor, "try this," and he held out a small flask.

Both put forth their hands for it, seeking to snatch it from the sailor who held it.

"Gently, gently," said the coxswain of the boat; "you must not drink much of it."

They were brought up to the ship, and helped on board.

The vessel on which they now found themselves was the "Constantine," and bound for a Greek port, whence, as the captain informed them, they could find a vessel for England.

The British consul would, of course, help them to that end.

This was because Toro volunteered information that the vessel from which they had escaped was bound for Liverpool.

Hunston's sufferings told severely on him, and for a long time he lingered between life and death.

The joint to which the mechanical arm was fixed grew worse from day to day, and the ship's surgeon feared that mortification might ensue.

But constant care and attention alone prevented this.

At length, when they reached their destination, and cast anchor, the first thing that was done was to bear off Hunston and his comrade to the nearest hospital.

The place they were taken to bore the ugly-sounding name of the Lazaretto.

"Toro," said Hunston, as he was carried in, "I think it is all over with me."

"Why?" demanded Toro. "You must not think that."

"I feel it is sure."

Hunston rose on the litter on which he was being carried, as they passed the gates of the Lazaretto, and pointed out to Toro, who walked beside him, a low, flat-roofed building, that stood away from the hospital.

"That's the dead house," replied one of the litter bearers to Toro.

"That's where I shall be, Toro," he said, "before many days are over."

Toro shuddered in spite of himself.

"You are low-spirited," he said, "and you get strange fancies into your head."

Hunston shook his head.

"You don't believe in presentiments?" he said.

"No."

"Do you remember Emmerson?" demanded Hunston, in a low, grave voice.

Toro felt uneasy.

He tried his best to change the topic.

But Hunston would not be denied.

"Emmerson knew that his end was near," said Hunston; "he felt sure of it, I know. I often think of it; and I feel sure that Emmerson felt then just as I feel now—as I feel now."

As he repeated the last phrase, his voice died away, and his head sank back.

A strange, unpleasant feeling crept over Toro.

Day by day Hunston sank.

Upon the fifth day one of the doctors stood beside Toro, when a messenger came to speak to him of a patient who had just died.

"Very curious case that, signor," said the doctor.

"Indeed."

"Yes: a man with a very wonderful mechanical arm."

Toro opened his ears.

"Yes."

"The arm has got out of order, and the symptoms that the shoulder just showed have altogether baffled us. We contemplated amputating it at the shoulder. But it almost seems as if there had been some subtle poison in the secret springs of the arm, which had been injected into one of the veins as the arm got out of order."

Toro listened in awe-struck silence at these words.

He thought of Hunston's last despairing speech.

He thought of Emmerson's dying words.

"Do you think you will have to amputate it?"

The doctor stared.

"No," he answered curtly.

"I'm glad of that."

"And I, too," responded the young doctor, flippantly, "for if we had amputated the shoulder joint, it would have put the poor devil to an unnecessary amount of suffering."

"Is he progressing now, then?" demanded Toro.

"He's dead."

"Dead!"

A shiver shook the ex-brigand's big frame.

The young doctor nodded and smiled quite pleasantly.

"Yes, dead. The porter was sent to ask if he should be taken to the dissecting room or to the dead house."

"Yes, and you——"

"Said the dead house. My opinion is that mortification had set in, and so we shall not be able to keep him long. He must be buried to-night."

Toro shuddered.

It was but too true.

Hunston was at that moment in the dead house of the Lazaretto, in the narrow, long box, made of the roughest unplaned deal.

"The man you speak of I knew well."

"Were you related?" asked the doctor.

"No; only comrades."

"Would you like to see him before——"

"If I could—yet—no—no," he added with a shiver.

"No," he decided, "he would not go to that awful dead house."

"Very good. It as well not. Only you would have to go now, or not at all. No one is allowed there after noon—at midnight he will be buried."

*　　*　　*　　*　　*

Now towards nightfall, Toro remembered that Hunston had got sewn up in the lining of his waistcoat certain valuables which they had agreed to keep as a reserve store.

The valuables consisted of diamonds and other precious stones, the fruits of crime.

Hunston dead, these belonged to Toro.

They represented, in fact, all his worldly wealth

"What is done with the clothes of those who die here?" he asked one of the nurses.

"Unless they have relatives, they are buried with them."

"In the coffin?"

The sister of mercy bowed her head gravely.

"A strange custom."

"It is," she responded.

Toro made no reply to this.

He felt uncomfortable about it.

He dared not mention the fact of the valuables existing, for the possession of such trinkets by two sailors would have excited grave suspicions.

Yet he could not lose them.

"No!" he exclaimed aloud. "Never, never; I'll have the diamonds if I have to snatch them from the grave itself."

CHAPTER XXVIII.

THE SIEGE OF THE CASTLE—HOW THE LITTLE GARRISON RESISTED AN ARMY!—
BATTERING RAMS!—SUNDAY'S WORK IN THE FIGHT—A NEW DANGER.

BACK we return to the castle, and take up the adventures of the inmates at the moment that the bloodhound Castor, who was posted over the trap-door in the floor, warned them of someone's approach.

"Silence all!" exclaimed Petrus. "Not a word now."

He raised the trap, and listened intently.

"They are coming in some force," he said, to Harkaway.

"What shall we do?"

"Let me think."

"S'pose I pick 'em off as dey come up?" said Sunday. "I'se quite ready, by golly!" and he looked like it.

His sleeves were tucked up to the muscles of his arms, and in his right hand he brandished his long, ugly bowie knife.

And, as he spoke, he dropped upon one knee over the opening, ready for the first man who should appear.

But Harkaway deemed it imprudent to leave the trap open.

In this Petrus fully concurred.

And he gave his reason for having that opinion.

"We are not strong enough in numbers to seek hostilities," he said. "Bad enough when we are forced to fight."

"True," said the elder Harkaway. "Right, Petrus."

"We must fasten the trap. Quick as you can. Gently—no noise; so."

The trap was replaced.

Then Petrus beckoned them to a yard or outhouse at the back, where they found a huge flat stone, that required their united strength to move.

By dint of much labour and perseverance, they contrived to roll this huge stone across the room and on to the trap.

This held it firmly.

Young Jack now brought the two bloodhounds in, and the main entrance was securely barricaded.

And when this was done, it was like a regular fortress.

Nothing short of cannon could reduce it.

When all their precautions were taken, they went upstairs again, leaving only two sentries below.

Castor and Cyrus.

The twin bloodhounds were posted, one at the trap and the other at the door, so that they might give warning of anyone's approach.

Young Jack and Harry Girdwood were charged with the examination of the firearms, while Harkaway and Petrus mounted to the upper rooms.

"How came you a prisoner in the power of Monastos?" suddenly asked Harkaway.

"How?" reiterated Petrus, bitterly; "How came I——"

Harkaway saw his strange glance and paused.

"Do not let us trouble you with any questions if they call up recollections that are painful."

"They are painful," answered the outcast; "bitter and painful beyond measure. Yet I like to brood, else I might forget what I live for——"

"Forget?"

"Aye."

"And what is it that you live for?" said Harkaway.

"Vengeance!"

The glare of the speaker's eye caused Harkaway to shudder.

He began to ask himself whether this strange Englishman was not mad.

"He has got a very mad eye;" thought Harkaway. "It is very likely that his wrongs may have turned his brain."

Petrus presently looked up, and said abruptly—

"My story can be told in a very few words; I am not a gifted speaker. Had I ever possessed the gift of eloquence, I should have lost it during my captivity here."

"Captivity!" replied Harkaway. "But surely you have had plenty of opportunities of escaping."

"Plenty, as you say—but too late to avail myself of them. When I could have escaped, I had no longer the will or inclination. I had a mission to fulfil. I had to wait for it. I have waited long years, and now the time has come, and you are the chosen instrument."

"I don't quite understand," said Harkaway.

"You will some day. You asked how I came here once—would you like to know?"

"Yes."

"I will tell you," said Petrus. "Monastos was cruising about in the neighbouring seas, when ill-luck brought him across the vessel in which I was travelling with my young wife and child. They varied brigandage with piracy. Well, our crew walked the plank—the passengers mostly followed them, and I was destined to follow, and in an evil hour their accursed chief cast his eyes upon my wife. She pleaded on her knees for my life—and he granted her prayer—the villain!—the devilish fiend! Ask me not to enter into particulars more closely than that—to describe in detail my own everlasting shame. I became the slave, the wretched, ill-used tool of that villanous monster, and my poor, martyred wife died after a twelve-month's life of horror upon this island. My mind went, I believe, for a time, but I survived for a purpose that is fast approaching consummation after all these years."

And then, overcome by the recollection, he buried his face in his hands and was silent.

Harkaway respected the strong man's grief.

It touched him to the heart to see a man so moved.

"Did you never rebel?"

Petrus shook his head.

"It is marvellous how you stood it; I never could have done so—my blood would have been up forty times an hour."

Petrus smiled.

"You don't know what adversity can move you to." he said, sadly. "When my life was clouded by this inhuman beast, the sorrow came so suddenly upon it that we were dazed; looking back, I can scarcely account for what occurred; I appear foggy, misty, about it. My spirit was cowed. We were absolutely at their mercy, and I feared for my poor darling's life. I lost my calm one day, however."

"How? What was the occasion?" asked Jack.

"I saw Monastos strike my poor wife to his feet, in my presence. My reason fled. Then I fell upon the evil doer and should have destroyed him in my fury— for he was taken completely by surprise. But I was torn away. Maimed and bleeding, I lay awaiting my doom."

"Death would surely have been a boon," said Harkaway.

"Aye, had she, my wife, been dead first. I could not bear to die and leave her to their tender mercies. Your thoughts came upon me then, and I prayed aloud that my darling might die before me."

"Well."

"The prayer was barely uttered ere it was heard. And it was responded to— oh, how fearfully! I was fetched by one of the men to her side. She was dying. Ill usage had done its work. She breathed her last in my arms, poor angel! As I laid her down, there came over me a fearful change. The iron entered my soul! From that moment my thoughts turned to one thing. I could only reflect upon one subject; on all else my thoughts refused to centre. So that it is not altogether without reason that they regarded me as an idiot. A man of one thought is practically an idiot. I had but one; day and night, sleeping or waking, it was ever with me—vengeance!"

Jack shuddered.

The bitter intensity of the wretched man filled Harkaway with horror.

"Well, well," said he, "I marvel that you supported it as you did."

"What would you have done?" then asked Petrus.

"I should have slain him a hundred times over," said Harkaway.

"What?" iterated Petrus, "you would kill Monastos?"

"Had I suffered as you have—yes; decidedly."

"Why, had Monastos a life for every hair of his head, and could I take them all with suffering for him, it would not satisfy my vengeance. Death," he added, "a boon, a gift for him, a reward for the righteous! No; Monastos must live. Life is torture; Death is oblivion—sleep, rest. Monastos must live. He shall be punished in his affections, by her he thinks his daughter; punished in his greed for money, for he shall, please Heaven, lose all, and know it but too well; punished in his pride, for he has despised me more than the meanest mongrel that ever crawled, and, if Heaven be just, he shall become my slave; my abject slave and tool! Unless I am utterly mad, my dreams will now be realised, and I shall have what I have waited for so patiently! What I have prayed and sighed for—for, ah, how many weary, weary years!"

* * * * *

At this point, one of the party came with the tidings that a number of men could be seen lurking among the trees, and evidently meaning to surround the building.

"Ha!" said Harkaway, "the work is beginning. Look to your rifles; load them all, and let us lie snug until they are close up."

The story of the poor Englishman's wrongs had almost unnerved him, and he welcomed the desperate tidings as a positive relief.

Harkaway now proceeded to post his party in the best positions for the business before them.

Young Jack and Harry Girdwood were sent to the top of the house with the two girls.

Sunday was placed at the window at the back of the house.

Harkaway himself, with Petrus, took the chief position, the window at the verandah.

Here, with rifles loaded and cocked, they waited the first demonstration of the foe.

Waited; waited.

"I wish dey'd come," said Sunday. "so as to have one pop at de ugly varmints."

"What are they doing?" said Harkaway.

"They are planning a surprise," said Petrus.

"The villains," returned Harkaway; "they don't like close quarters."

"They can fight well enough when they are put to it," returned Petrus, "if they are three to one. But look, they are coming!"

The brigands were now seen advancing in strong force.

They had advanced half-way to the house when Harkaway gave the word to fire.

The volley was answered by another, and a shout from the brigands, who, with Monastos at their head, now pressed on, but not until they had received a second discharge from Harkaway's little band and the brigands had fired in return.

Harkaway's trick told, for the brigands imagined their force to be much larger than it really was.

Monastos now ordered his men to spread themselves in a semicircle in front of the verandah and keep up a continuous fire.

This was returned by Harkaway's party for nearly an hour.

It was now getting dark.

Monastos and one of his men left the rest to continue the attack, while they glided towards the house to examine the door and lower windows.

There appeared little chance of forcing an entrance.

But it immediately occurred to them that under the verandah their men would not be exposed, and that they might fire through the floor of it upon those above.

Monastos hastened away, and returned with about half the men, leaving the others to continue the attack as before.

The advantage of his manœuvre was soon evident.

The musket balls of the brigand soon pierced the planks.

This startled Harkaway, and he ordered them all to retreat from the windows for a few minutes.

The brigands were quiet, as if preparing for another move.

Presently there was a slight crackling noise, and then a flame rose before the window.

They had fired the verandah, and the wood being very dry, it burnt up in a very few seconds.

"What shall we do now?" asked Harkaway.

"Well, they cannot set fire to the house, it being of solid stone," returned Petrus.

"Hist! they are trying the door."

"They may try," said Petrus; "they'll try a very long time; they should have arranged that matter before they burnt the verandah; that might have sheltered them "

"Will you go above," said Harkaway, "and give them a shot or two? Sunday and I will give them a few; we may keep them off for awhile, and at least we shall be gaining time."

But Sunday had a trick worth two of them.

While the rest of the party were absorbed in their various ideas for repulsing the attack, he mounted on to the roof, and with the point of his dagger set to work loosening some of the heavier pieces of masonry near the parapet.

A few minutes accomplished this work.

He lent all his strength to the task, and loosened the stone in its socket.

It rocked—it shook.

Just then he was startled by cries of triumph coming from below.

The brigands had made a large battering ram by felling a tree and lopping off its branches. With this they were charging the door, and the power they thus brought into play was something prodigious.

The door bulged in at the second charge.

At the third it fell in with an ominous crash.

On they pressed, shouting wildly; and above all the din was heard the voice of the king calling his men together, and giving orders as coolly as though commanding a troop of regular soldiers on parade.

The door no sooner gave way than a smart volley was poured in upon them from inside the house.

Twenty shots in rapid succession, and every bullet had its billet.

All their pistols were loaded, and amongst the defending party they mustered four revolvers and all their rifles.

The rifles were first discharged, then the revolvers came into play; and while the brigands imagined that twenty men at least were in front of them, the volley had taken them so completely by surprise that they never thought of firing in return. It cowed them.

Back they dropped, slowly, step by step, leaving several men upon the ground.

Monastos now showed his mettle.

"Cowards!" he cried in a voice of thunder, "flying from a mere handful of savages! Back—back, I say?"

He struck at one man with the flat of his sword.

This served, strangely enough, to rally them all, for the men stopped and turned.

Back to the charge they went.

They were steadied by a well-directed volley that met them upon the very threshold of the door.

"A hundred lire," cried Monastos, "to the first man in the house."

"Hurrah!" shouted several of them in response.

And there was a regular scramble for the doorway.

At this juncture a wild and unearthly cry was heard from above.

The very house seemed to shake.

Down fell the large block of stone upon the struggling mass.

And beneath were crushed three of the brigands, while several were maimed.

Sunday had contributed his portion to the work.

"Yah, yah, yah!" laughed the darkey. "Dat'll gib you toko, Massa Brigand— yah, yah!"

For awhile this awful incident paralysed the efforts of the attacking party.

"Back!" cried Monastos, with considerable readiness. "Retreat and reform. Look to your rifles."

His men struggled back.

"Their position is stronger than we supposed," said Monastos, hurriedly. "Fortune has played into their hands so far; but if we are quick, we shall take them all, and then they shall pay for the blood of my brave men with a slow torture!"

A cry—a yell of fierce glee from the pirates greeted these words.

CHAPTER XXIX.

CAUGHT IN THE REAR—THE HOLE IN THE WALL—CASTOR PINS HIS MAN—THE RELIEF OF THE GARRISON—HAND TO HAND, MAN TO MAN—THE TRAP AND THE MINE SPRING.

MONASTOS was speaking to gain time for thought.

More than half his men were *hors de combat.*

As for the enemy, he had no reason to suppose that anybody was so much as scathed.

"Keep to this part," he said, addressing one of his confidential men. "I will take six or seven good hands to the back of the place, and try what can be done there, while you engage their attention here."

"Good, captain."

Scarcely was it said, when a bullet whistled so close to Monastos' eye as to make him wink.

"That's a novice," said the king of the brigands, coolly.

"Now, men, follow me."

Round they went.

And now danger threatened our friends in the house, for the brigands knew too well where the weak part of the defences lay.

"I wish they would keep the fight up," said Harkaway. "While we are engaged in fair fight, I look upon two Englishmen as a match for a mob of these vermin. What I don't like is this dodging about."

"They are contemplating some different tactics," said Petrus.

"That big fellow is the master spirit in it all," said Harkaway, pointing.

"That is Monastos," was Petrus' reply.

"That!"

"Yes."

"Then, by Heaven!" ejaculated Harkaway, "I will soon end this."

"How?"

Harkaway, in reply, tapped his rifle significantly.

The pirate chief's life was in jeopardy for an instant only, fc~ at the moment that Jack pulled the trigger, the rifle was knocked up by Petrus.

Harkaway turned round indignantly.

"Petrus!"

"His life is mine," returned the man of mystery. "When his end comes, it must be my work, none other's, or I should not rest in my grave!"

Harkaway forbore to express his anger.

He remembered the wretched man's wrongs.

While they stood by their window, watching in great anxiety the movements of the enemy, young Jack was called to the rear premises by his friend Harry Girdwood.

The latter had been put upon the alert by their faithful though fierce ally, Castor.

His twin brother, Cyrus, was on guard, we should mention, at the broken entrance, where Petrus had placed him, carefully out of rifle reach, but so as to be able to pin any of the brigands who might venture to creep on all fours under the wall.

On reaching the rear of the house, Jack made a serious discovery.

The brigands were making a breach by displacing the stones of the wall.

Now, instead of calling for assistance, these two brave boys were of one mind.

They thrust their rifles into the breach and fired together.

A cry from without told them that one, at least, of their shots had taken effect.

"Hurrah! hurrah!" yelled young Jack desperately.

But barely was the triumph thus made known when a storm of bullets rattled into the place through the breach.

It was a fearful sound.

The room seemed alive with bullets

And young Jack was surprised to find himself untouched.

But alas! for poor Harry Girdwood.

He stepped back and sank against the wall on one knee, stretching out his hand for something to support himself by.

"Jack, old boy."

"Harry."

"I am hurt, Jack."

"No, I hope not, old fellow."

"I am, Jack; hurt in the thigh; give me a hand; the bone is broken, I think; I—I——"

Young Jack flew to his side, and caught him up by the waist belt, while poor Harry's head sank upon his shoulder.

It was imperative to remove him from that room.

"Castor, good boy," said Jack to the bloodhound, "eat the first man that comes in through that hole."

The bloodhound replied with a look of intelligence.

He had appetite enough for several brigands.

Young Jack raised his poor friend, Harry, and bore him tenderly away.

A third attack from the brigands sent the masonry flying, as he staggered out of the room.

"Jack," said Harry Girdwood faintly, "I think it is all over."

"Don't talk so, old fellow."

"If I die, promise me you will protect her."

"Who? Emily? Of course I shall."

"No; I mean Paquita, the pirate's child."

And then he fainted.

Young Jack staggered into the room under his heavy burthen, just in time for Petrus to catch him in his arms.

"Is he hurt?"

"Yes."

"Why, Jack," exclaimed his father, "you have been to the windows, and after my—my orders——"

"No, no, no, no," cried his son hurriedly, "they attacked the back of the house, and the wall has given way."

"Good Heaven! then we are lost."

"No," said Petrus, with great self-possession; "call your negro."

"Sunday."

"Yes, sar," replied the darkey.

"Keep guard here."

"Yes, sar."

Harkaway the elder, accompanied by Petrus, ran to the back of the house, where the breach was by this time considerably enlarged.

"Look at Castor," ejaculated young Jack.

There was something to look at here, indeed.

The huge bloodhound crouched over the lifeless brigand, whom he held by the throat.

He had obeyed young Jack's orders to the very letter.

Petrus called the hound off, and the man fell heavily to the ground.

"He is dead."

Castor had done his work but too well, for the wretched man's windpipe was severed, and he had not suffered long.

*   *   *   *   *

What surprised them most was the sudden silence without.

"Hurrah! Massa Jack," cried Sunday. "Massa Harkaway! Massa Petrus! Hurrah!"

"What now?" said Harkaway.

"Rescue, rescue!" cried the negro; "hyar's Massa Jeff. They have come, sar, to the rescue. Hark at dat moosic! be golly, it's j'yful, j'yful moosic, sar. Won't dem cuss pirates hab toko now!"

The music to which Sunday alluded was the rattle of rifle shots, that could now be heard plainly enough.

The new comers were divided into two parties.

One was headed by Jefferson, the other by Harvey.

They came on at a double; and when within easy range they delivered their fire and charged.

The brigands were in great measure taken by surprise, but they fought bravely.

Shots were heard, mingled with the clashing of swords, fierce oaths, and cries of the wounded.

It was a fearsome sight to see.

Obstinately was every inch of ground contested.

Desperately did they fight on every side.

And so resolute were they, that the issue appeared long doubtful.

"Now's our time," said Harkaway, sword and pistol in hand.

"Hurrah!"

"Down with the brigands!"

"Death to Monastos!"

"No!" thundered Petrus; "Monastos mine! Forward!"

And then from out the castle sallied Harkaway, closely followed by Petrus, by young Jack, and by Sunday.

These four took the enemy in the rear, and the result of the movement soon made itself manifest.

Sunday was armed only with a huge bar of iron, but he wielded the instrument with considerable ease and dexterity.

The stoutest swords essayed in vain to parry the fearful blows it dealt.

Every time it descended, it cracked a skull.

The carnage was most fearful to behold.

Dead and dying strewed the ground thickly.

Jack Harkaway, his arm bare to the shoulder, was covered with blood, and yet he wielded his heavy cutlass as though it had been a willow twig, and all unconscious of his hurts.

The men went down before him like wheat before the reaper's sickle, until the boldest hearts were cowed.

And involuntarily they retreated before him or opened out a passage to his desperate advance.

Petrus also fought bravely. He had an object in view.

Monastos.

No less an adversary than the redoubtable king of the brigands would satisfy our bold hero's thirst for glory.

The bloodstained king of the brigands saw Petrus approach, and he passed through the fray to face and kill his slave.

"Ha!" exclaimed Petrus. "At last we meet!"

Monastos brought down his trusty blade with a fearful clash, hoping to decide the combat at once with a single stroke.

But Petrus' sword was there to meet it.

The swords shot forth a shower of sparks, and it was a wonder that they did not break.

But they stood out boldly against the shock.

"Stand back!" cried Petrus, seeing his friends pressing in. "Let us alone; let no one interfere."

And then reluctantly they gathered round, while the two champions contested.

It was but a brief fight, for they feinted and finessed but little.

Their blows notched their weapons every stroke, and they were of a force to bring down an ox.

But the fourth blow that Monastos delivered was of such violence that he nearly over-balanced as Petrus simply leaped aside to avoid it.

And then, quickly as he recovered himself, Petrus put in a stroke that disarmed him, and sent his weapon spinning out of his hand.

In less time than it takes to record the fact, Petrus toppled him over, and planting his right foot firmly upon his chest, he pressed the point of his sword against the vanquished king's throat.

"Beg your life," he cried.

"Never, slave, from you!" cried the pirate chief.

Then, to the surprise of all, Petrus shouted—

"Long live Monastos! his life belongs to me, remember!"

But before another word could be uttered, the brigands, rallying, dragged their leader up.

"To the treasure cave!" he shouted, as he vanished from sight.

The rest of his party responded by shouts, and a general retreat began.

At least a dozen men got off to the woods, and once there, pursuit became a very difficult job.

"Petrus, you have let the villain escape," exclaimed Harkaway.

"Fear not; follow me," returned Petrus; "only, remember this—Monastos must not die! He must be my prisoner only."

"Agreed!"

"Agreed!"

"Do you hear, all?" cried Petrus. "Monastos' life is to be spared, for it belongs to me."

"Yes."

"Follow me, then."

He led them through the forest by a

series of short cuts known only to himself, and soon they came upon the range of caverns wherein was situated the treasure of the crime-stained chief of the brigands.

* * * * *

Meanwhile, Monastos and his followers gained the caves.

But, to their dismay, when they arrived upon the spot, they found that parts of the cave were already occupied by the enemy.

"Now," said Monastos, "we will exterminate them to a man!"

"We will," responded the bulk of them, as if in one voice.

"Stop!"

"Who speaks?" eagerly demanded Monastos.

"I—Stavros."

"What have you to say, Stavros?" demanded the chief.

"What reward are we to get for this service? It is dangerous work, and remember, two-thirds of our men have fallen in this fight."

"I know but too well brave men have fallen in fighting with these cursed English, and I give you my word you shall have half my treasures; in fact, more wealth than you can take away with you."

The pirates' eyes sparkled with ferocious glee.

"You promise!" cried the band of pirates.

"Good! brave lads!" he said, "you have my word—my promise—the promise of Monastos."

"Hurrah!" cried Stavros.

His cry was caught up by all, and they rushed precipitately after their brave leader.

As soon as they were gone a smile of devilish triumph lit up the chief's face, and shaking his clenched hands after the retreating forms, he turned and vanished in the opposite direction.

At the corner of the cavern in which the foregoing scene had taken place, was a massive wooden door in the wall, which none of the band of Monastos had ever seen removed.

One or two of the more inquisitive spirits had essayed to remove it, but its massive make resisted violence, and they were ignorant of the secret which rendered its removal a task of comparative ease.

Monastos, however, showed it to be a trifling job.

First stooping down, he scraped away a little of the earth upon the ground, disclosing an iron handle.

This he tugged heavily at, and the massive door swung back.

Monastos pushed it open and entered hastily.

Within there was a vault more spacious than any that the lair of the redoubtable brigand could boast.

It was filled with a motley collection of bowls filled with gold pieces, bags of leather gorged with precious stones and metals, coffers of iron and of wood, huge chests of valuable plunder of every description.

In the centre of the cavern were five small barrels piled up.

Monastos paused a moment or so to glance about him.

He smiled grimly as he noted each particular store of the vast riches contained in the vault.

There was no irresolution in his glance, for his mind was already irrevocably made up.

"Farewell!" said he, addressing his riches, "farewell to all for a time, but I may yet live to scrape you together again. And now for the punishment of traitors, and a glorious revenge on these savage English; for all shall perish at one fell blow."

While he thus spoke, he proceeded to drive a hole in the head of one of the casks.

This done, he tilted it, and out rolled a stream of black powder.

The quantity he abstracted was about two quarts.

With this he made a long train leading to the entrance of the cavern which was at once his treasury and his powder magazine.

He drew a pistol from his belt and got ready.

"I hear them above, shooting, stabbing, cutting each other's throats," he said to himself; "and now the moment is come for my stroke."

He knelt and presented a pistol to the train of powder.

Led by Petrus, the Harkaway party gained the cavern above the magazine.

"Hark!" said Petrus, "I hear the sound of the brigands' footsteps."

"I can now show you how to strengthen our position."

"How?"

"At the entrance that mass of rock is placed upon a kind of pivot, in such a way that it can be wheeled into its place by one man."

"Ha! I see."

"But how about the exit?" asked Jefferson.

"There is a huge boulder there, the same," responded Petrus.

"I begin to see."

"Once outside, we move the rock into its place, and then, as they pass in, we close the other side upon them, and we hold them at our mercy."

"Good, good."

"Bravo!" cried Magog; "that is splendidly thought of."

"Come, then," said Petrus; "let us not waste time in words."

Out they trooped, and when the last man had passed out, they watched Petrus, in some curiosity, bend to the massive rock and push against it with all his immense strength. Slowly it yielded.

Sluggishly, lazily, it rolled over, blocking up the egress from the cavern.

"Now for the other."

Petrus glided round as nimbly as Nero himself could have gone.

But he had barely time to secrete himself behind the huge rock, that stood like a sentry at the entrance to the cavern, when the brigands approached.

The decimated band of Monastos mustered now, perhaps, fifteen men; and of the fifteen not one had escaped scatheless

Some had but trifling hurts, yet all had wounds of greater or less gravity.

"I do not hear them," said one of the brigands.

Stavros placed his forefinger upon his lips, and, silently drawing his sword, he beckoned them to follow him.

He crept on, his men following close at his heels.

"There is no one here."

"They have fled!"

"Come along, follow."

Stavros only turned to beckon them, and then he made for the exit at the further end of the cavern.

Finding it closed, he turned to his men with a cry of wonderment; but ere the sounds died away upon his lips, the entrance through which they had just passed was barred up in a similar manner.

They were caught.

"Ha, ha!" laughed Petrus wildly, "we have them all now."

"All?"

"Monastos as well?" demanded Harkaway.

Petrus started.

"No, by thunder! I did not see him amongst the number; but so much the better. I shall trap him alone; and then my revenge——"

Why did he pause?

What caused his speech to falter?

What could it be?

The earth trembled violently beneath him.

Then, as they were one and all thrown down by this alarming earthquake, there was a terrific crash, and the whole of the cavern, not twenty yards away, was blown into the air.

*   *   *   *   *

Monastos had done his fatal work.

The king of the brigands had destroyed the remnant of his band at one dire stroke.

But his worst foes, Harkaway and the party, yet lived.

His worst foes?

Had he no worse enemy than them?

Yes; surely.

Petrus, the Englishman, his deadly foe, still lived.

And in Petrus he had yet to discover the worst enemy that mortal man ever knew.

CHAPTER XXX.

MR. MOLE IS RESCUED BY NERO—NERO GOES A-NUTTING—FIG FORAGING—ONE FOR HIS NOB—THE CASTLE AGAIN—MOLE IS AGAIN SERENADED—THE INVISIBLE SINGER.

WHEN the brigands made their formidable attack upon the castle, they were greatly embarrassed by their wooden-legged prisoner.

So they tied him up and put him in a snug part of the wood.

And here poor old Mole lay *perdu*, unable to stir a peg.

While the battle progressed, he trembled all over.

He would not have been able to render any particular service himself, yet he would have liked to watch the fray.

"They are sure to get their jackets dusted," said he to himself, "and that is some consolation. Torture a gentleman, will they?—pull the few remaining hairs out of his head, will they?—a landed proprietor like me."

Poor old Mole had suffered much, and he really felt exhausted.

To add to his mental sufferings, he remembered that he still carried in his breast pocket a flask of spirits, that in his present condition would only have proved too welcome a restorative could he have got at it.

But alas! that was impossible.

"I hope they'll die of thirst, some of them," groaned poor old Mole.

And then he began to vent his feelings in bad language—in reviling his captors in no measured words.

But as he grew more and more noisy in his speech, he reflected that it was very imprudent thus to let his feelings carry him away, inasmuch as the Greeks might return and vent their spite upon him.

While the firing was at its briskest, and the din of battle drowned all else, Mole was suddenly startled by the flitting of something in the trees above his head.

And down dropped a huge hairy figure.

"Nero."

Nero it was, too.

Young Jack's friend stood surveying Mole with an air of mingled curiosity and surprise.

Mr. Mole saw and appreciated Nero's wonder.

"Yes, Nero," he said, nodding in a patronising way, "it is me, your old friend Mole; don't go away; lend a poor old friend a hand—I mean a paw."

How he contrived to make the monkey understand it is beyond our power to say, but certain it is that Nero fell to biting the cords which bound Mr. Mole, and soon the prisoner was free.

Mole stretched himself out and got on his timber.

"Nero," said he, "you are a splendid fellow, and I hope to do you a good turn some day."

Nero appeared to understand.

He nodded, and then he took a sight at Mr. Mole in the quaintest manner in the world, a trick his young master had taught him with infinite pains, and then he had a brisk flea hunt upon his ribs.

The liberated prisoner took his flask out, had a good stiff pull at it, and passed it on to his liberator.

Nero took it, stared at Mr. Mole, and drank.

But the hot spirit half choked him, and so he spat it out and threw the bottle at its owner, who caught it with considerable dexterity.

"The monkey's an ass," said Mr. Mole with dignity, "to try and waste good liquor like that."

But a rattling fusilade from the castle put an end to their discussion.

Crack, bang, bang.

Nero hopped about like the proverbial parched pea in a fire shovel.

At every shot he capered along or bounced in the air on all fours.

"Warm work this, Nero," said Isaac

Mole. "You haven't learnt to stand fire with the coolness and equanimity of your old friend Mole.   Oh !"

His valiant speech was cut short by the crashing of a stray bullet through the trees and shrubs, that passed within two inches of his nose.

And as the last word of brag died away on his lips, he dropped upon the ground flat on his face.   Nero evidently thought that Mr. Mole was doing this for his special amusement.

And so while the old fellow lay thus quiet, Nero examined him all over until he came to the wooden legs.

Now Nero could not understand Mole being got up like a kitchen table, and convinced doubtless that therein lay some occult matter, which it was his duty, in the interest of monkeydom generally, to fathom, he tried to pull them off.

"Oh, oh !" cried Mole.

"Queek, queek !" responded Nero, capering away.

"Let my timber alone, you brute," cried Mole, and he arose and examined the fastenings of his wooden legs.

They were quite safe.

He then looked out for a snug corner where the bullets of the contending parties could not reach.

For this it was necessary to penetrate more deeply into the forest, where Nero was very glad to follow him.

Mr. Mole perched himself up in a tree, and having gone through considerable fatigue, he soon fell fast asleep.

Mr. Mole slept.

His head sank upon his breast, and he snored.

He dreamt of battles, and wars, and rumours of wars.

His soul was filled with thirst for martial glory in that dream.

He burned with a fierce desire to "seek the bubble reputation," even in the cannon's mouth.

He fancied that his aspirations were granted, and that he was leading the Harkaway party to battle against overwhelming odds.

He fancied that Monastos headed the brigands in the field; but that his— Mole's—presence inspired them with feelings of awe.

He headed the charges, and the enemy fell before him.

Just then there was a shot.

He was struck !

He felt the wound so plainly.

This part of his dream was so fearfully vivid that when he dreamed that he was struck by a rifle bullet, he woke up:

"Only a dream," he said, aloud, "and yet—ha !"

A missile hurled by an unseen hand struck him in the eye.

The object was soft, and it smashed there, completely bunging up Mr. Mole's optic.

"Good gracious me," he exclaimed, "what can it be ?"

And then Mole scooped gracefully out of his eye the remains of a ripe fig, when down came another shot, and landed him a regular stinger upon his proboscis.

This was another fig.

But this time it was beyond ripeness, and it spread across his face, making him look like a portrait in oils with a jar of paint upset over it !

"Good gracious me !" ejaculated Mole. "I never——"

A third one shaved his ear, and smashed on the bark of a tree, and then he caught sight of Nero making ready for another shot.

Mole dodged it with great dexterity.

"Ha, ha !"

And the next time he lunged sharply out and caught the fig.

They were wild figs which Nero had raked up, and not at all bad eating for a fasting man.

So he had a meal.

While this went on the firing ceased, and after allowing a certain time to elapse to make sure, he ventured from his perch.

Mole crept out of the wood, until he gained the clearing in which the castle was built.

Not a man was in sight.

"Where have they all gone to ?" asked Mole aloud.

"Queek !" replied Nero.

"Hold your tongue," whispered Mr. Mole; "if those beasts of brigands are anywhere near, you'll bring 'em down about our ears."

Cautiously he stepped forward, and made towards the deserted castle.

Deserted castle ! Was it deserted, though ?—he asked himself, with some anxiety.

He saw the splintered ruin.

"They have been going it here," he thought. "I hope our good friends are all safe and sound."

Followed closely by Nero, he crept up to the door.

"All gone," he said. "Ugh!—no! there's one there still."

One of the brigands, stiff and stark.

A huge fellow, whose face wore the hideous pallor of death, and whose features were distorted by the agony of his last moments.

In his hand he clutched a long dagger-knife, and the position of his arm, now rigid in death, showed that he was about to strike when he received the wound.

"Poor wretch!" murmured Mr. Mole. "I think I have had enough adventures for one while, and once I get safely home again to my old friends all, I'll make up my mind to get quite domesticated with Mrs. M. Still, the sight of this dead-house is anything but inspiring; it is grievous to see, and it's anything but pleasant to be in a lone place, with no company but dead bodies, and——"

He stopped short; and why?

He heard a voice—close at hand, too.

His colour fled from his cheeks, and his wooden legs threatened to give way beneath him.

A minute more, and the voice grew familiar.

Not only was the voice familiar, but it breathed—or, let us use a poetical figure, and say warbled—an air which Isaac Mole had heard under happier conditions.

The words were the very opposite of poetry; in fact, both words and music were decidedly jiggy.

We leave the readers to fit their own music, which they will probably do without any great difficulty.

> "Ole daddy Mole
> Was a Band of Hope soul,
>   Teetottlin' soul was he;
> Whisky and gin
> He regarded as sin;
>   A evil sperrit he vowed was brandie."

"Ha, ha!" ejaculated old Mole, with a theatrical start. "Surely—yet hark!"

Again the voice shouted—

> "Ole Ikey Mole
> Had no wool on his poll,
> An' no teef in his 'ead for to munch;
>   He'd two timber toes,
>   An' a grog blossom nose,
> Though it didn't insiniwate punch."

Mr. Mole jumped.

"Damme!" he cried, "it's that Sunday; the imp of darkness, I'll throttle him."

"Yah, yah!" laughed the invisible minstrel.

"Sunday."

"Yes, sar."

"Where are you?"

"Up here."

"I'll come, I'll come," cried Mole, trotting to the foot of the stairs.

He turned to call Nero.

But that erratic ape had disappeared.

So up Mole went alone.

Great was his surprise when he found himself in a gorgeous apartment, which we have already described.

And so great was his surprise that he did not notice the occupants of the chamber until a faint voice called him by name.

"Mr. Mole."

"Hullo!"

He turned round, and discovered a youth reclining upon a low ottoman.

The poor lad was badly hurt, and his cheek was ghastly pale.

Beside him knelt two young and lovely girls, both flushed with deep concern for the patient.

Is it necessary to give the names of the three?

Perhaps.

The suffering youth was poor Harry Girdwood.

The two gentle nurses were pretty little Emily and her new-found friend the lovely Paquita.

"Mr. Mole," said Harry, "I'm so glad to see you safe back."

These kind words showed such consideration from one suffering as the poor boy did, that Mr. Mole was melted.

"Are you much hurt, my dear Harry?" he asked in a broken voice, for the pallor of the lad's cheek alarmed him.

"No."

"He is," said little Emily, looking up into Mole's face; "but he is so brave that he will not let us know his pain."

Poor Paquita! Her eyes were bent upon the patient's face, and she followed his varying expressions with an eagerness that pierced his very thoughts.

"Who is that?" demanded Mr. Mole, pointing to her.

"'FOR THE THIRD TIME WILL YOU SPEAK OR DIE?' SAID THE PIRATE."

"Paquita."

At hearing her name mentioned, the girl looked up, and smiling a welcome at Mr. Mole, turned again to the patient.

His pain was less when the sunshine of her pure eyes rested upon him.

There was a magic in her glance which seemed to drive suffering back.

Did thirst assail him, her hand was there with the glass at his lips.

If the fever scorched his brow, she had a damp cloth ready to cool it; and when more than once he grew faint from loss of blood, and felt as though he were vanishing from the world, she was ready there to press his hand in hers and bring him back to life.

Who would not be wounded for such care?

Mr. Mole learnt all about Paquita, and very much surprised he was.

"But where," said Mr. Mole, looking about him, "where is Sunday?"

"Yah, yah!"

His voice sounded close by.

And then the faithful negro made his appearance.

Grinning all over his face, he ran up to Mr. Mole, and threw his arms around him in unaffected pleasure at seeing him again.

"Glad to see you, brudder Mole," he exclaimed; "puffectly considerable dam glad to meet you, ole brudder Mole."

"Keep off, you nigger," said Mr. Mole, with dignity.

He repulsed Sunday rather unceremoniously.

"You'se a ignorant ole pump after all," said the darkey; "you s'pose 'case a nigger fellar's skin is black, dat his heart can't be white as yourn. Sunday's a biled owl to wish you back, you cantankerous ole—ole—ole rhinoceros!"

"I don't care a fig, Sunday," Mole answered, "about a man's colour, only I don't like to be made a fool and a laughing-stock of by anybody, black or white, and——"

"Dat's dis infant's fault, den, brudder Mole; I'se berry much infernal confounded sorry; but 'tain't me so much as youself, brudder Mole; but I'm awful pleased you'se back so safe."

"I can see you are, Sunday," said Mr. Mole; "give me your fist."

And the brothers-in-law shook hands heartily, to the infinite pleasure of all.

CHAPTER XXXI.

MONASTOS PLAYS HIS LAST CARD—IT FAILS—THE FIGHT IN THE WATER AND DEATH OF GALLANT OLD BEN HAWSER.

WHEN Harry Girdwood came to be tended more closely, and his hurts examined, it was found that, come what would, it was not possible to move him.

Paquita saw this.

"But, my dear," said Mr. Mole, "don't you see that if he remains here, there is great danger?"

"No," replied the bold girl, "he is not in danger while I am here."

"I don't see that," replied Mr. Mole; "you are not, for they would not touch you, I suppose, but it is a very different matter with him, poor fellow."

"Do you think I would let them harm him?" exclaimed Paquita, with flashing eyes; "never, never, while I live!"

"I am safe with Paquita for a protector, Mr. Mole," said Harry.

Little Emily would have stayed to share Paquita's watch, but the others would not hear of it.

Mr. Mole, Sunday, and little Emily, therefore, started out in search of their party.

As they made their way through the intricacies of the wood, they were suddenly startled by a terrific explosion, which shook the earth as though by some awful volcanic eruption.

The remnant of the band of Monastos had been blown into eternity by the evil hand of the king of the brigands.

* * * * *

Monastos knew well the awful nature of the destruction he had wrought.

"Now," he cried, "before I escape from this island I will have my revenge on

Harkaway's friends left on board their ship."

And as he ran he conceived a devilish scheme for scuttling the "Westward Ho!" with its living freight.

The pirate chief was soon lurking in a small boat that was made fast to the ship's chains, and busying himself there, preparing to take his revenge on Emily and Hilda.

And he might have been sadly successful in what he sought but for an accident.

Young Jack was there before him, he having been sent forward to see if all on board were safe, for young Jack dearly longed to see his mother, and as soon as they had got through a rapturous greeting, Mrs. Harkaway sent him flying off to his berth to change his garments.

The consequence was that, while engaged in this hasty toilet, his attention was attracted by certain scraping sounds.

"Hullo!" thought Jack, "I must find out what that means."

So up he got, and was quickly on deck; then, looking over the side of the ship, he saw Monastos busy at his work of destruction.

Young Jack was dumbfounded at what he saw.

But he did not pause to reflect.

"Hullo! ugly mug!" he shouted, "what's your game?"

The brigand chief started, and with great presence of mind drew a pistol from his belt, and straightening his arm, he pulled the trigger.

Click!

Nothing more.

Monastos had forgotten that he had discharged his pistol some time back.

With a muttered imprecation he leapt over into the water and dived.

"You don't get off like that, you land shark," cried young Jack.

And before anyone could divine his intention, much less prevent him, the fearless boy went over head first after the pirate.

He had made a long dive, and as he rose to the surface he faced the redoubtable Monastos.

"What!" cried the king of the brigands, in mixed surprise and exultation; "is it you? You spawn of Satan, you shall soon be put out of harm's way."

Young Jack made one stroke and grappled boldly with the speaker.

"Yield, thou brutal pirate!" said the boy.

Monastos replied by a loud mocking laugh.

"Yield to you, young cub? Never! Your life I will have here; in this water."

As he spoke, his right hand groped about his belt for his knife.

He then grasped young Jack by the throat, and the unlucky boy was about to pay for his temerity with his life.

The huge brigand chief, by sheer weight alone, bore the struggling lad under water.

Had he been able to get out his knife, it would soon have ended young Jack's history; but before he could get hold of it fairly, there was someone else upon the scene.

A loud and manly voice was heard shouting—

"Hold on there, lad! I'm with you, Jack, my boy."

The next moment Monastos was seized roughly by the shoulder.

And then a burly voice bawled words of defiance in his ear.

"Why, you black-muzzled swab, let the boy go, or I'll precious soon make small biscuits of you, as sure as my name is Ben Hawser!"

Monastos had to make a hurried choice.

Either he must let Jack go, or go under himself.

Jack was released, and Monastos, knife in hand, turned upon bold Ben Hawser.

"Strike out for shore, lad, and leave this skunk to me," cried old Ben to Jack.

And now began a short, sharp, and decisive struggle in the water.

So quickly did it all take place, that by the time that young Jack had filled his lungs again with air, after his long immersion, he could not see either old Ben or Monastos.

Old Ben was tough and wiry, but his adversary was a man of immense power, and his weight alone told fatally in that brief contest which now ensued.

Ben seized Monastos by the throat, and twisting his horny hands in his neckcloth, pressed so hardly upon his windpipe that the brigand chief was in deadly peril;

but disengaging one hand, Monastos turned upon his opponent, and grappling fiercely, both went under.

A moment or so elapsed, and then young Jack saw only one rise to the surface eight or ten feet away.

It was Monastos.

"Ha! ha! ha!" he laughed demoniacally, as he struck out for shore; "one of my foes gone."

Before the echo of his laugh had died away, Ben rose too, and as he breasted the water, young Jack perceived, to his infinite horror, a poignard buried up to the very hilt in the old sailor's side.

"Master Jack, are you safe?" gasped the old man, as he shook the water from his face.

And then he was about to sink again, when young Jack made one vigorous strike to his side, and helped to support him.

"Where is the pirate?" faltered Ben.

"Gone; but are you hurt, Ben?"

"No, not much; are you, my boy?"

"No."

"Thank God," returned old Ben fervently; "but the swab has done for me."

Young Jack by now had hold of the edge of the boat, and somehow or other he contrived to scramble up, without releasing his hold of Ben Hawser.

And then he assisted his preserver up too.

As soon as they were in the boat, poor Ben sank back exhausted.

Panting, gasping, sighing his brave old life away.

"My poor Ben, are you so badly hurt?" asked young Jack, eagerly.

"Yes, dear boy, so badly," faltered the old man, "that I shan't want much of the sort before—before I'm food for fishes."

"Don't, Ben, don't."

"Now, Master Jack, don't you take on," said Ben, growing fainter every moment and at every word; "this battered old hull has done its sarvice, and I'm content; the lubberly shark has left his prodder sticking in me. He struck deep, wither him!—precious deep—deep——"

"Jack, Jack!" cried Mrs. Harkaway at this moment from the ship.

"All right, mother."

"Are you hurt, Jack?"

"No, ma'am," answered Ben, looking up with a cheery smile, although his face and lips were livid; "our boy's right and tight enough, but I'm waterlogged."

"No, no, Ben; I cannot part with you. Do not say you are dying; you will get over it."

"No, my boy, I'm wanted above; my time's up, and I must depart. God bless you, Jack! Don't forget Nero, and don't forget old Ben. Good-bye, lad; remember me to——"

And even as he spoke, the gallant old tar gave up the ghost.

"Ha! ha! ha!" rang out Monastos.

Glancing towards the shore, they saw the brigand chief climb up the bank.

A moment he stood to shake the water from his garments.

Then he plunged into the forest and was lost to sight.

CHAPTER XXXII.

THE PIRATE'S DESPAIR—ONE LAST MOVE—THE OUTCAST ENGLISHMAN FACES HIM—DESPERATE ENCOUNTER!—PETRUS TRIUMPHS—THE "WESTWARD HO!" SAILS FROM MAGIC ISLAND—THE LAST VIEW OF THE CHIEF OF THE PIRATES AND PETRUS THE OUTCAST.

MONASTOS paused to reflect only when in the depths of the forest.

Here he was safe from pursuit.

"I am alone now, and could I but find means of reaching Athens, I should be safe; my old comrades and allies are still flourishing. Yes, I could escape but for Paquita. How to get hold of her, that's the puzzle."

He hurriedly matured a plan of action. It was this.

In a creek on the coast of the island he had a sailing boat whose existence the Harkaway party utterly ignored.

This boat was ready to take to sea at a moment's notice.

True, it would want some working single-handed; but this difficulty could be got over.

But his great trouble was to get Paquita.

Now he was in league with a powerful tribe of brigands who infested the country round about Athens, and so ardently did his soul burn for revenge upon the adventurous owners of the "Westward Ho!" that he made up his mind to sacrifice the half of the treasure remaining to him in bribing the Athens band to help him to his dear vengeance.

"The bulk of my hard-earned store of wealth is scattered to the winds with the carrion of my traitor followers and the accursed Harkaways," mused the king of the brigands; "but I have yet a store of which they never dreamt, a rich coffer that Spirillo himself knew not of; with this I can buy the life of everyone on that ship. I'll have them, too, if I spend my last ducat in it."

But he reckoned without his host again.

A footstep was heard, and Petrus stood before him.

Monastos started again as one in a dream upon beholding the half-witted Englishman.

How could he have escaped the explosion?

However, the first surprise over, Monastos made himself easy about Petrus.

The wretched outcast alone was too contemptible an object to occasion a moment's fear.

"Petrus!" exclaimed the brigand chief, "why did you attack me with Harkaway's gang? But you have repented, I expect, and have now come to ask pardon and give me your help."

Petrus made no reply.

With folded arms he stood contemplating the Greek pirate, while his face wore a stolid look, that defied the keenest observer to read what was passing in his mind.

"Speak," said the Greek, "and tell me how you escaped from the rest."

"What rest?" demanded Petrus.

"The rest of our comrades," answered the brigand, "and with our accursed enemies."

"The English?"

"Yes."

"They are no enemies of mine."

"I see," answered the king, with a bitter smile, "being your countrymen. I ask your pardon."

"It is too late."

The king laughed boisterously at this, yet in spite of himself there was a strange sound in the outcast's voice which jarred upon his ear.

"Oho, Master Petrus," said he, "so you didn't like to see so many Englishmen blown to the devil. But now answer me why you drew your sword on me, and speak truly, or your life shall answer for it."

Petrus stared sternly into the brigand's eyes, and Monastos, for the first time in his life, felt under a species of magnetic influence.

Petrus advanced as if to strike the chief.

"Hah, you dare——"

"No, not yet; first know that the Englishmen and Americans all escaped.'

"All?"

"All."

A change came over the brigand's face; it was a desperate blow to him, and already his punishment was beginning to be sore indeed.

His brain was fired with a rush of confused thoughts which could not take shape.

"Where is Paquita?" he asked; "where is my daughter? Do you know?"

"Yes, I know where Paquita is now—at this moment."

"Where?"

"Lost to you."

"Lost? Cudgel your addled brain for a moment, idiot, and answer if you can. Where is she?"

"You will never see her again."

"Never?"

The brigand stared in agony.

"The terrors of what he has witnessed have driven away what little wit remained to him," said Monastos wonderingly.

Petrus shook his head.

"No," he said, in the same emotionless strain, "I am just recovering; I am shaking off an incubus that has been pressing upon my poor brain for a life time."

Monastos felt a strange sensation of uneasiness stealing over him.

"What do you mean?" he said.

"I mean that you have, by your own hand, hastened the end for which I so long have sighed——"

The chief of the pirates interrupted him with a cry of impatience.

"Silence your ravings," he said, imperiously, "and begone! And, mark you, bring back my daughter within three hours to this spot, or you shall suffer. I'll have you bastinadoed for hours—until you shall cry aloud for death to end your sufferings!"

Petrus smiled.

"Beware, monster, for now my revenge is near."

Monastos was goaded beyond endurance at this; he rushed at the outcast with uplifted hand, but, ere he could strike, Petrus caught him dexterously by one wrist, and gave it a twist that caused the brigand to spin round with a half-uttered cry of pain.

"Thunder and furies!" ejaculated the Greek, "your life shall answer for that."

"Oh, no," responded Petrus, coolly; "not my life—nor yours either."

Monastos had by this drawn his sword, and he made a desperate cut at Petrus; the latter parried it coolly enough, and retreated a step on guard.

Monastos followed him up quickly, and put in another powerful stroke, with the same result as before.

The brigand king was cunning of fence, and he soon perceived, to his no little surprise, that he had before him an adversary worthy of his sword.

So he feinted, and endeavoured to draw the other out. But the Englishman observed the same tactics, always acting strongly upon the defensive.

Ten minutes' foiling left the Englishman untouched, and with the same provoking coolness, the same composed exterior as before.

"He has carte and tierce at his fingers' ends," said the Greek to himself; "whoever would have suspected it? He is dangerous and must be destroyed."

His reflections were brusquely interrupted; a dexterous twist nearly sent his sword flying from his grasp.

"Hah!"

Monastos quickly recovered himself, and sprang back a pace or two, on guard; but he need have had no fear.

The outcast did not seek to follow up the advantage thus gained; he only remained as before—upon the defensive.

"I must end this," said the king of the brigands, with suppressed passion; and so saying, he made a desperate onslaught.

A terrific downstroke was caught by the Englishman close up to his sword-hilt, and the blade was shivered to atoms; at the same time the violence of the stroke brought him down upon one knee.

"Ha, ha!" cried the brigand chief in triumph, "at last!"

As the word was dying away on his lips, Petrus had shot in under his sword-arm, and seized him in a deathly clutch; one hand gripped the right wrist, the other was upon his neck.

As the fingers closed upon the wrist, it seemed as though a steel vice were being screwed down tighter and tighter; the sinews were pressed—benumbed, under that terrible hand, and the sword fell to the earth.

The snake-like fingers twined around the brigand's neck-cloth, and he fell.

Once upon the ground, a fearful struggle ensued; but the strength of the Greek availed him not.

The outcast used no jerks—profited by no knowledge of wrestling—but he bore his enemy to earth by sheer force; and, having him there, he held him—pinned him, as one might pin a noxious reptile.

And marvellous to relate, the Englishman preserved throughout the struggle his same stolid look.

The desperate fight even had not appeared to spend his breath.

"Curse you!" gasped the panting brigand, "the chance is yours. But ere you strike, tell me, is my daughter safe?"

Petrus stared into his face in a cold expressionless way.

"I do not mean to kill you," he said. "You must live — live — long — long—long!"

Involuntarily Monastos shuddered and closed his eyes.

His life was preserved him, and yet he felt that those icy tones, and that fixed, corpse-like stare meant something to which even death was preferable.

While Petrus knelt upon his prostrate adversary, he drew from his pocket a thick knotted rope in which a slip noose had been run.

Holding this between his teeth, he placed both hands upon the prostrate Greek, whom, with a sudden jerk, he dragged over on his face.

The pirate and murderer, Monastos, struggled desperately, but the outcast held him beneath his knee while he dragged back his arms with a wrench that seemed to force the joints from their sockets.

The rope was now brought into use.

The noose was slipped over the brigand's wrists and tightened until the cord cut into his flesh.

The other end of the rope was used to make fast his ancles.

This done, he rolled the helpless Greek over again, and he saw to his satisfaction that already the torture was telling.

The brigand had bitten the turf in his agony to stifle his groans.

Petrus smiled.

"This is as it should be," he said, with a hollow laugh. "Now listen to me, Monastos, monarch of the isle, while I wring your soul with terror."

"Madman, you may make me drain the cup of humiliation at being defeated by such a miserable wretch as you, but it is beyond your power to make me fear."

"Wait," said the Englishman, nodding his head gravely.

"I may wait till the crack of doom," returned Monastos boldly, "and yet not fear you."

"You will want patience more than I have shown, and I have been patient, as you know, for all these years. Why, I lived upon hope."

"Hope?"

"Yes."

"Of what?"

"Of seeing this day—this is balm to my bruised heart. It cannot bring her back to life, but it is solace to know you suffer. Every instant of agony you pass through is an hour of pleasure for me."

An awful dread crept over the brigand as he listened.

Till now he thought that his abject slave had turned upon him when in adversity, or perhaps because he knew that he was doomed with the rest to be blown to atoms;

but now he saw that he was suffering for the crimes of many years past.

He saw that the wretched outcast, the miserable slave who had been the sport and butt of the band, throughout had been living upon the hope of the day of deadly vengeance.

The reckoning was at hand, and in an agony of fear, which he would have died before admitting, he awaited to learn the nature of the punishment to which his once slave, now master, doomed him.

"Since when have you conceived this hatred for me?" asked Monastos.

"Since her death," answered the Englishman.

"Hers? Whose?"

"My murdered wife's," returned the outcast. "Ah! you can't provoke me into killing you. I have practised self-control under the bitterest conditions."

The captured brigand closed his eyes, and as he lay thus, in the power of the injured Englishman, an awful fear possessed him.

"Tell me," Monastos faltered hoarsely. "Your vengeance is upon my—my innocent child——"

And here he broke down.

"Ha, ha!" laughed the outcast.

"Beast!" cried the wretched captive, writhing until the blood trickled from the parts of his limbs where the cruel bonds cut into his flesh. "Monster! devil! a child—an angel like her, my Paquita!"

The ineffable tenderness with which he breathed that name brought a reply from Petrus.

"I must in spite of myself," he said, "ease your mind upon that head. Paquita is safe."

"And shall be protected?" demanded the king of the brigands, eagerly.

"And shall be protected," responded the other gravely.

"Good, good!" said the prisoner; "now you may do with me as you will."

Petrus eyed him with a grim smile of satisfaction.

"Aye, make yourself happy on that score, that your wretchedness may be the more complete when I have said what remains to be told."

Monastos was silent.

What new terror could this dreadful being have in store for him?

"You love Paquita?"

"More than my life," cried the pirate. "She is my only child."

"No!" thundered the Englishman. "Paquita is no child of yours; the girl you have been so tenderly caring for these long years is——"

He paused.

"Whose?"

"Mine."

"Liar and slave!" the captive brigand shouted.

"Ho, ho!" laughed the Englishman quietly; "I will convince you in spite of yourself. When you held me at your mercy, eleven—twelve—thirteen years ago—I have almost lost count—it pleased you to condemn me for some freak of resistance to your commands, to slay my own child. Do you remember?"

"Perdition seize you!" yelled Monastos, as, with herculean force, he burst his bonds.

But it was of little use. Petrus again had his heavy foot on the brigand's breast, holding him down with a giant's power.

"No," he cried, pointing a sword at his breast; "you escape not thus!"

And once again he proceeded to bind him more securely. The Englishman continued—

"I thought that as you showed some fondness for your own babe, which was of the same age, you might have spared mine. But no; you ordered me to kill my child under pain of death to myself and wife. I fled to where the two children lay, yours and mine. Your assassins followed close upon my heels, and I, inspired by the very terror you had called up, seized your child in my arms, intending to have life for life if your cruel commands should be obeyed. Your murderers entered, and seeing your child in my arms, thought it was mine—that I had taken it to protect it. They dragged it from me, and butchered the innocent babe before my eyes."

A hollow groan from his prisoner recalled him to himself, and he looked up with a fiendish smile.

"You lie!" cried Monastos, "you lie —foully lie; it was your child they killed!"

"No, no! You know that I speak the truth; you feel that now my vengeance began ere my sufferings had reached their climax. You feel that the child you nurtured and had so carefully tended was mine."

The brigand chief was silent awhile.

"Slave, if what you state is true, does Paquita know of it?" he demanded presently.

"Yes, she knows now how you were steeped to the very soul in blood, that you slew her mother, she knows all this, and loathes you. I have taught her to shudder at the very mention of your name."

The colour fled from the captive's cheek.

His bloodless lips quivered, and he trembled with the unutterable anguish he endured.

"Why, now," exclaimed the outcast, "this is prime. This is something like vengeance, and it was worth waiting for— aye, waiting for even for a lifetime. It is a feast fit for the gods, I swear!"

And then, as the prisoner groaned and bit his lips in the bitterness of his anguish, his master threw up his legs and danced in a wild savage manner around him.

"You have defeated your own object," said Monastos in a strangely altered voice.

"Indeed; how?"

"I have nothing left to care for in life. I want to die."

"Not so much as you will," replied the Englishman promptly; "there is to come a time when day and night you shall pray for death, and yet you shall live. I will see that you live—live—live for my own special enjoyment; my life is henceforth devoted to you. My child shall leave the island with our new friends. I shall remain here; you will try to starve; I shall not allow it; I shall force your mouth open and thrust food down your throat. For you must live to make my vengeance complete."

Who shall describe the depth of bitterness that fell upon the wretched brigand?

What pen shall describe the unutterable despair that filled the pirate's heart?

"You see this stone," said Petrus, pointing to a large boulder beside his prisoner; "that is to be the foundation stone of the kennel that I am going to build for you. You are to labour in it too."

Then he dragged the prisoner over, and forced him to kneel.

The stone in question he lifted, and

placed in the prisoner's hands, which were fastened, as we have said, by the wrists, behind his back.

If he let it fall, its weight would crush his legs.

"Now move," said his master; "shuffle forward on your knees, quicker."

And down came a rope's end upon the captive's shoulders.

He shuffled slowly, painfully forward, and then he let the stone fall.

"I'll not do it," he cried resolutely. "I'll die first."

"Oh, no, you shall not die," retorted Petrus, with a smile; "you shall live, I say. Crawl on now, or——"

"Never!"

"Then I'll bring the Englishmen to see you."

"I care not."

"I'll make Paquita come and spurn the murderer of her mother."

"No, no, no!" cried Monastos, imploringly, "not that; I'll obey."

"Crawl on, then."

And on he crawled, while his master, from time to time, whipped him with the end of a rope as though he had been one of the inferior animals.

Suddenly a familiar voice was heard, and glancing up, Petrus saw the Harkaway party marching along on the heights above.

Several of them had been silent witnesses of the scene, and they revolted at the horrible thoughts it conjured up.

They were not to say scrupulous, and had Petrus slain his cruel oppressor in cold blood, even after vanquishing him, it would not have surprised them.

But this was a refinement of vengeance which horrified them, and they began to murmur.

"Let no one come between me and my revenge," said Petrus sternly. "He, the murderer of my wife, belongs to me; he is my lawful property. I claim no other share of the plunder you will find here; take all."

"He is right," said Jefferson, "quite right. We have no jurisdiction here. This man has suffered no common wrongs. We may disapprove of the feelings which inspire him, but we have no right to interfere."

"Before we go, Petrus," said Harkaway, "one word—I call you Petrus."

"I would be known by none other," returned the outcast. "It is a constant reminder to me of my duty. They gave me the name of Petrus when I came here; let me be Petrus to my life's end. I feel it was fitting that I should be renamed, for here I began a new life."

"I was about to say," resumed Jack Harkaway, "that what money we take hence is not for ourselves. Our crew and those of our party who are needy will be provided for; the residue will be disposed of in various charities, and may the blood-stained gold carry no taint with it. Paquita shall be protected by all."

"Amen!"

They passed on, leaving the Englishman and Greek pirate, master and man—victor and vanquished—alone together.

*   *   *   *   *

Two days later, the "Westward Ho!" sailed from Magic Island.

They were anxious to be gone from the scene of so much strife and bloodshed, and had resolved to rub off many ugly recollections by a change of scene.

The gallant vessel glided gracefully out of Fairy Creek, and as they passed along the coast, young Jack had assisted Monday and Harry Girdwood up on to the poop to take a last look of the island.

"Look—look there!" exclaimed Harry Girdwood, as they glided along.

"Where?"

"There, don't you see—there's the Englishman—he's whipping a man who is crawling along the ground—see! It must be the pirate chief."

They looked, and recognised the man who knelt.

They were not a hundred feet from the shore, and the group was visible enough.

Petrus the outcast, whip in hand, stood over his victim, the latter being harnessed to a low cart or trolly laden with stones, and dragging it along over the rugged, uneven ground with much difficulty.

At every step, down came the whip, scourging the wretched prisoner's back and shoulders.

Such was the last view they caught of the once powerful chief of the pirates, as the "Westward Ho!" glided through the waters.

This, too, was the last they saw of the Magic Island.

CHAPTER XXXIII.

HOW JACK HARKAWAY VISITED HUNSTON AND TORO, BUT RECOGNISED NEITHER.

HUNSTON and Toro had been just eight days in the lazaretto, when Harkaway and his friends disembarked from the good ship "Westward Ho!" at the Greek port.

They sought out a residence where they could be away from the world in some degree, for they formed a pretty large circle of society of their own immediate friends, and the scenes which they had recently passed through were sufficiently exciting to satiate them with adventures for a long while to come.

To some of us it is given to pass through life in a slow and uninteresting manner, with no adventure to break the monotony of peaceful existence.

To others, it seems as though an unceasing round of excitement must of necessity be kept up, even if the excitement be unsought for.

So it was with Jack Harkaway and his son; and so it was in consequence with the friends who had been attracted into their circle by the enticing charm of their company.

Adventures appeared to crop up every instant.

Excitements were offered them with a regularity and a persistence which was almost unpleasant.

They joined jovial Jack and his son, and Dick Harvey, because those worthies had earned for themselves a not unmerited reputation for being about the most daredevil rovers and adventurers that the age had produced.

If their object was to get into danger, their object was fully achieved beyond all manner of doubt.

They were sure to get their bellyfull of danger as long as they kept near to Jack Harkaway, Dick Harvey, or to Jefferson either, for the matter of that.

Well, Jack Harkaway bought a villa, situated upon the skirts of Tripolitza, where he had room enough to accommodate the choicest spirits of their party.

And from these head quarters they made daily excursions to explore the neighbourhood and visit the lions of that part of the country.

Now one of the only facts worth recording here, is that two days after their arrival they visited the lazaretto, for the purpose of making a gift to that excellent charity of a portion of their booty from Magic Island.

It was in accordance with the programme they had traced themselves out.

This must be fresh in the reader's mind.

The heads of the hospital showed them about the place with the utmost politeness —the riches and generosity of the visitors had been communicated to them in advance.

Now, as Harvey and Jack Harkaway were going through one of the wards, their attention was drawn to one of the beds which was covered with a long sheet.

Beneath the sheet they could plainly see the outline of a man.

Rigid, stiff—stark!

The sheet looked like a shroud, they thought, and it made them feel just a bit uncomfortable.

Harkaway turned to the head surgeon, who accompanied them upon their tour of inspection.

"Is that——"

The doctor nodded in anticipation of the question.

"Yes."

"But surely," said Dick, "you don't keep the quick and the dead all in one room like this?"

"No," returned the doctor; "he is only just dead."

"Only just——"

"Within the past two hours. In the course of half an hour, he will be removed to the dead house."

"And you bury them soon?"

"Within twenty-four hours," was the reply; "in this case it will be much less."

"Why?"

"Because the nature of the death leads us to believe that mortification has set in."

"Indeed!"

"Yes, he died in very great suffering, apparently," said the surgeon, with the air of one commenting upon a matter in which a fellow creature's sufferings were of the smallest moment, "and indeed it was a most curious case."

"How curious?"

"The patient had a mechanical arm," returned the surgeon, "with a curious secret about some of the springs that almost baffled us. We were half inclined to think the arm was poisoned."

"Poisoned!" echoed his hearers in some surprise.

"Yes."

"Were the symptoms of a description to make you think so?"

"Yes."

"And could you come to no decision before he died?"

The doctor shook his head.

"None."

"Strange."

"Strange indeed. But we have many strange things occur here. By the way, gentlemen," he added, "from the interest you show in the case, I should judge that you have some knowledge of surgery."

"We have—an elementary knowledge only."

"You are at liberty, then, to make a close inspection of this case, if you feel interested."

And as he spoke, the surgeon was about to draw back the sheet which covered the body.

But they stopped him.

"Take no notice of the trouble," he said; "I am entirely at your service. I don't seek to weary you; only do here as you will."

Such is the power of gold.

Had a poor visitor presented himself, he might have asked in vain for half the privileges they were eager to offer the wealthy Englishmen.

"By the way, gentlemen," said the doctor, as an inducement to rouse their curiosity still further, "the patient was an Englishman, I believe."

"Indeed!"

"How strange."

Strange indeed, could they but have known that the object of their conversation was none other than their old enemy, Hunston.

They passed on to another patient, and then to the next ward.

And when they came to the ward in which Toro, the Italian, lay, the latter was fast asleep and his head was half concealed beneath the bedclothes.

So that they actually passed him by unnoticed.

Toro had weighty business on hand, and knowing that it would require all his strength, nerve, and presence of mind, he had wisely sought preparation in the arms of Morpheus.

To this accident alone was due the fact of his escaping the notice of the privileged visitors.

It was an unfortunate accident for them. But of this more anon.

Having made a handsome donation to the funds of the lazaretto, Jack Harkaway and Dick Harvey left the place and returned to the villa.

CHAPTER XXXIV.

THE TWO GREEK GENTLEMEN.

ONE day Jack Harkaway senior and his friend Dick Harvey were strolling in the vicinity of Tripolitza.

The town lay far behind them, and they were standing on an eminence, looking across to where the blue waters of the Mediterranean glittered in the sunlight.

"Lovely climate, this," remarked Jack, at length, enthusiastically, as the western breeze fanned his forehead.

"Very," replied his companion. "No

wonder it produces such fine grapes and olives."

" And poets; remember Greece is celebrated for her poets."

" Ah, yes, we mustn't forget the poets. A fellow can hardly live in a country like this without growing poetical."

" Have you got a touch of that complaint yet?" asked Jack with a laugh.

" I really think I have, but only slightly. I was attacked with slight symptoms yesterday morning."

" And have you produced a poem yet?"

" I've begun one," returned Dick, dryly, " and that's something."

" Decidedly. How many lines have you written?"

" Only two."

" Two; ha, ha! you'll never make a poet."

" I'm of the same opinion. I've made several attempts, and I find I always stick fast at the third line."

" For want of rhyme, eh?"

" Yes."

A slight laugh attracted the attention of the speakers.

Looking round, they saw two gentlemen standing at a short distance from them.

The strangers were Greeks, and well dressed.

Their features, though dark, were rather pleasant in their expression than otherwise.

They had evidently been listening to the foregoing conversation, and one of them remarked—

" There is something more than rhyme wanted to make good poetry."

" Reason, I suppose you mean?" said Jack, laughing in his turn.

" Precisely," returned the gentleman, as he advanced.

" You will pardon our intrusion, Mr. Harkaway," he continued, " since, though strangers to you, you are not entirely unknown to us."

" Indeed!" Jack replied. " I do not member having had the pleasure of eeting either of you before."

" We have seen you several times in the inn where you are staying."

This was perfectly true; they had been watching them for several days past—why will shortly appear.

" We are both especially fond of the frank, bold, English character, and on that account anxious to be introduced to you."

" No better opportunity then than the present," said Jack, as he raised his hat with gentlemanly courtesy. " My friend, Mr. Harvey," he added, as he pointed to Dick.

The strangers shook hands with remarkable cordiality.

" My name is Zavella," continued the gentleman, as the introduction concluded; " that of my companion, Carjani."

" Very happy to make your acquaintance," returned Jack and Dick.

The conversation now flowed freely.

" You like our country then?" said Zavella.

" Extremely," answered Jack Harkaway; " it is impossible to dislike it."

" Have you seen any of its noted places as yet?" asked Carjani.

" Oh, yes, my friend Harvey and I have a knack of seeing pretty well everything there is to be seen."

" And hearing everything that is to be heard—eh?"

This seemed rather a strange remark, and Jack looked at the gentleman who had made it inquiringly.

" I see my question puzzles you," he said with a smile; " but I was alluding to a wonderful echo that we have here."

" Echo! where is it to be heard?" asked Jack.

" In the Mount Calviero," returned Carjani.

" The name of the mountain is familiar to me—rather unpleasantly so," Jack replied.

" Indeed; how, may I ask?"

" As being the haunt of fierce banditti."

" Oh!" laughed the Greeks, carelessly; " that is only a traveller's tale; there are no brigands there now."

" What, then, has the government exterminated them?" inquired Dick Harvey.

" Not entirely; only driven them to another quarter."

" I see. But this echo—it is so very extraordinary?" asked Jack, whose curiosity was excited.

" Most marvellous," answered Zavella; " there is one particular spot in the mountain where it repeats a shout or the report of a pistol twenty times distinctly "

Jack and Dick looked at each other in astonishment.

"That is the most extensive echo I ever heard of," said the former at length.

"It is a fact, I assure you. And few visit this locality without going to hear it."

"I should like to hear it very much myself," exclaimed Jack eagerly.

"So should I," said Dick Harvey; "is it far from here?"

"About a league," replied Carjani.

"In what direction does it lie?"

"Northward," Zavella explained, as he pointed across the country. "But if you and your friend feel disposed to visit the mount, we shall be most happy to accompany you and show you the way."

"You are very kind. What say you, Dick?"

"I should like nothing better—but ——"

"But what?"

"I was thinking of dinner; we ordered it at——"

"Oh, never mind that; it can wait."

"Yes, but I can't. The air has given me a most tremendous appetite," said Dick, caressing his stomach in a soothing manner.

"I am happy to say that I can give you something to appease your craving."

As he spoke, he unstrung from his shoulder a leather bag such as a travelling pedestrian might carry. This he quickly opened.

"Eat!" he said, as he opened a packet of sandwiches.

"Drink!" he exclaimed, as he uncorked a flask of Greek wine.

"But we shall be robbing you of your lunch," exclaimed Jack and Dick Harvey.

"Not at all," returned the gentleman heartily, adding with a laugh, "some day perhaps we may return the compliment by robbing you in a similar manner."

It was impossible to refuse what was offered so willingly and in so cheerful and jocular a manner.

Unbuckling the straps that supported their revolvers from their waists, to assist digestion, they placed them on the grass at their sides and sat down to their meal, and in a very short time the sandwiches and wine were disposed of, much to the inward comfort of the Englishmen.

The brief repast being over, Zavella said, as he took up his wallet—

"There, now you will have strength for your journey if you feel inclined to take it."

"I do," said Jack.

"And I," joined in Dick Harvey heartily; "I wouldn't miss the echo on any account."

The journey being decided upon, they started again.

During the walk the Greeks took care to keep their companions engaged.

They pointed out every object of interest on the road, and narrated the circumstances connected with each.

This made the time pass rapidly, and Jack and Dick were quite surprised when they found themselves at the foot of the hills.

The bright, smiling appearance of the scene had faded into a cold sternness.

Before them lay the mountains, grand and imposing in their massive outline, but rugged and somewhat depressing in their solitary aspect.

Along the rocky path they proceeded.

"Is this echo far amongst the rocks?" asked John Harkaway, as they proceeded.

"Not far," answered the guides briefly.

Jack fancied the tone of their voices was less courteous, and their manner of speaking more abrupt than it had been.

Twice he had observed them whispering together.

"I say, Dick," he said at length to his comrade, as they went along, "I've a slight suspicion."

"Suspicion!" Dick echoed; "of whom?"

"Our two courteous friends ahead," replied Mr. Harkaway.

"Oh, impossible!"

"Nothing's impossible, my dear fellow."

"But I think you're mistaken; such gentlemanly, generous fellows——"

"They might have had a motive for their generosity. Remember, we're in Greece."

"But what makes you suspect these gentlemen? Have you any reason?"

"My reasons for suspicion are slight, certainly—hardly perhaps deserving the name, but still they are suspicions."

"Well, anyhow, we have our revolvers," remarked Dick; "and after the rubs we've had in our time, I rather fancy we're a match for a couple of Greeks."

"I should hope so, or a couple of dozen either, for that matter," laughed Jack; "and so——"

Whatever else Mr. Harkaway was about to remark, was abruptly interrupted by the voice of Carjani.

"We're very near the echo now," he called back over his shoulder.

Almost immediately after they branched off into a narrow defile, from which they abruptly emerged into an open space, a sort of amphitheatre cut out by the hand of nature in the rocks.

"Here we are at last," exclaimed the guides.

The two Englishmen gazed round them with some curiosity.

On all sides, save where the defile severed them like a deep gash, the mountains rose in a steep slope, with rough, irregular projections dotting their sides like huge warts.

Here and there were dark recesses, that seemed to suggest caverns within their yawning jaws.

After contemplating the scene for some little time, Dick Harvey remarked—

"It looks a likely place for an echo."

"Yes," replied Jack; "let's hear what it's like."

As he spoke he uttered a loud hallo.

But the echo did not reply once.

"What's the meaning of this?" he exclaimed.

"Perhaps the echo isn't in a good humour to-day," suggested Dick; "try again."

Again Jack's voice rang out through the thin air.

Still no echo.

He turned towards the spot where the Greek gentlemen had been standing.

They had disappeared.

"Where the devil are they gone?" he cried.

He was answered by a mocking laugh.

And the next moment a gigantic form of hideous aspect appeared on a projecting rock.

"You are come to listen to the echoes," exclaimed the giant in a harsh, grating tone; "ha, ha! you will hear none but the echoes of your own death shrieks."

CHAPTER XXXV.

MYSTERIOUS DISAPPEARANCE OF MRS. MOLE—A PAIR OF BLACK KIDS.

"THIS is really the happiest moment of my life," exclaimed Mr. Mole, as he entered the lodgings that had been prepared for him in the main street of a little Greek town.

"Indeed, sir!" said young Jack; "then you have a still greater happiness to come."

"Indeed, my boy! What is that?"

"The joy and happiness of meeting Mrs. Mole once more."

"Yes, I shall indeed be delighted."

But Mr. Mole's countenance did not appear very expressive of delight.

"The fact is, my dear young pupil, my public duties as adviser and chief director of our expedition had effaced all recollection of Mrs. Mole from my mind for the moment."

"Well, had you not better run down to dad's place and see her, sir?"

"Beg pardon, sir," said one of he

sailors, who had brought up Mole's luggage, and who had been stationed near enough to hear part of the talk, "but your good lady ain't to be found."

"Where is she, then?"

"Shiver my timbers if I knows!"

"Man, do you mean to insult me?"

"As how, axin' your pardon, sir?"

"By that indecent and insolent allusion to the splintering of wood. Why, man, my timbers have been shivered to atoms more than once, and I assure you the operation is too unpleasant to form the subject of a jest or a profane oath."

The seaman went away, and the professor continued—

"As my wife is not here, I think the best—in fact, the only—thing we can do is to make ourselves as comfortable as circumstances will permit till she returns."

"All serene," was Jack's response.

"I abominate slang phrases, Jack; but——"

"But, Mr. Mole, don't you think it would be as well to inquire where Mrs. Mole is gone?"

"Ah! perhaps so."

Young Jack ran to his own home, which was not far off, and soon gained the following important items of information.

First, that the noble house of Mole was expected to receive a material addition.

Second, that Mrs. Mole had gone to the house of an English nurse.

Third, the address of the person with whom she was at present located.

Mole himself regretted that he was unable to search for his wife, and then he retired to try a new bottle of rum.

Young Jack and his constant friend, Harry Girdwood, sat down to concoct what the former called "a jolly lark with old Mole."

Mr. Mole took little or no trouble to find his wife's residence, and the elder of the members of the party, guessing that the youngsters were up to some game, did not enlighten him.

However, two days afterwards Mole found a mysterious-looking letter on his table.

"Now who can have written this?" said he. "I don't know the hand, and yet I suppose there are no English here except our party."

"The best plan would be to open it, sir," said Jack; "then you can see who it is from."

Mr. Mole broke the seal, and read as follows—

"SIR,—Your conduct lately has had a very ill effect both physically and mentally on your wife, who at present is undecided whether to return or inflict upon you the heaviest vengeance human hatred is capable of.

"You had best see her, and endeavour to calm her mind. If you decide on this course, you must go at once *by yourself*, to the three palm trees behind the town. The moment you reach them, you must bandage your eyes, and wait. If you fail to do this, dread

"VENGEANCE."

"What an extraordinary epistle!" exclaimed Mole. "But I suppose I must go, or Heaven only knows what will happen."

He hesitated a minute and then set off.

He reached the spot, and waited in fear and trembling.

Ten minutes—half an hour elapsed, and no sound was heard.

Mole got more uneasy each moment.

"I begin to think the confounded brigands are at the bottom of this adventure," he muttered. "No doubt their spies told them Mrs. Mole was on shore, so they knew how to work on my feelings as a husband and—ahem!—a father."

A pause, and a slight application to his bottle.

"Under these circumstances, I have a great mind to go home. Of course I shall be very sorry to leave poor Mrs. M. perhaps in the hands of the villains, but black wives abound on these continents, while the whole world contains but one Mole."

He had just finished his soliloquy and his second sip of rum, when a hand was laid on his shoulder, and a gruff voice, which Mole fancied he had heard before, said—

"Move not on your life; make only an attempt to turn your head and you are a dead man."

The next moment Mole found a bandage bound tightly over his eyes.

Then the voice repeated—

"The Herr Professor back will not go, surely?"

"Heaven and earth! Have the—the Greek brigands enlisted German soldiers?"

"No, surely not; but get up and come."

"Was it you wrote the letter to me?"

"Without doubt, Herr Professor."

Mole then, with a little help, managed to get upon his wooden pins.

To his great surprise, another hand then grasped his other arm, while a shrill feminine voice said—

"Well, we have caught him nicely, Dr. Frankenstein."

"Frankenstein!" exclaimed Mr. Mole. "Frankenstein on my right hand, and—who knows?—perhaps the monster on my left. Oh, dear me, if ever I get back to England, you don't catch me leaving it again in a hurry."

"Silence, Herr Professor, or I your mouth will gag with my knife."

"I'm in the hands of brigands, to a certainty," thought poor old Mole; "but

"NERO IS IN GREAT DANGER FROM HIS FRIENDS."

I must rescue Mrs. Mole from the villains."

"What are you going to do with me, brigands?" he asked, after he had walked some distance.

"We shall introduce you to some people whom you have not seen yet. But be silent."

They led him onwards till he perspired.

"Up one step, Herr Professor—that is it. Now halt, and we will take the bandage off your eyes."

Mole stumbled up the step; his captors turned him about two or three times, and then pulled away the handkerchief that covered his optics.

Mr. Mole stared and blinked, and saw —within three inches of his nose—*a large brass door knocker.*

"What the deuce is this?" he demanded, turning to his conductors, who laughed loudly.

Mr. Mole rubbed his eyes, for at first he could scarcely believe them.

A second look, however, convinced him that his captors were none other than young Jack and Harry Girdwood.

"A pair of young villains!" the angry professor exclaimed, as he lifted his fist, and smote Harry on the head.

"Gently, professor," said Jack, jerking a string he had attached to Mole's left prop. "Don't you see the instructions?"

"Bother the instructions! You said you were going to introduce me to some people."

"Behold them!"

Jack as he spoke, pointed to the door, where, just below the knocker, two kid gloves were displayed.

The gloves were the blackest that could be procured, and were numbered "One—two."

Beneath was a card, inscribed with the words—

"*Knock gently.*"

"That applies to me, sir, as well as the —kids," remarked Harry Girdwood, rubbing his head.

"My dear boy," said Mole savagely, "if I only had you under my sole charge, I'd apply something else to you."

"Shall I knock gently, sir?" asked Jack.

"You may tap at the door if you like, but I don't know why you have brought me here."

"To see Mrs. M——"

"And two black kids," interposed Harry, pointing to the gloves.

"Though I hate slang, I think I may venture to make the vulgar remark that you have been 'kidding me' pretty successfully," said Mole.

Young Jack's furious attack on the knocker soon brought a response.

The door was hastily opened by a hard featured woman of middle age.

"Wha may ye be waitin' for?" she asked in the broadest Scotch accent.

"My good woman, do you live here?"

"I dinna live in ony ither place."

"Here is money for you."

"I dinna tak' siller for tellin' folk whaur I live, but if there is onything else I can do for ye, maybe I may then condescend to tak' yer siller."

"I wish to know if Mrs. Mole lives here."

"She does," replied the woman.

And having given our readers a specimen of her dialect, we shall for the remainder of the chapter put her words in a form which will be intelligible to all.

"May I be shown to her apartment?"

"Mercy on me, my good man! where are your notions of decency? Shown to a lady's room, indeed!"

"But Mrs. Mole is my wife."

"I don't believe it; the poor soul said many times that her husband was a very handsome man."

"It is true. My dear Jack, won't you tell this good lady that I am speaking nothing but truth?"

"This is certainly Mr. Mole," said young Jack. "He was my father's tutor, and is mine now, and considered by the ladies a very handsome man."

"Well, I suppose it is all right. Come into the hall." Mole entered.

"And are you thinking to go upstairs with those wooden legs?" asked the strong-minded woman.

"Well, my dear lady," said Mole, "you would not expect me to go upstairs without them."

"Hold your tongue, and sit down on that chair," said the Scottish woman, pointing to a bamboo structure just inside the door.

The woman's manner was so imperious that poor Mole felt afraid to disobey her command.

Mrs. Cameron then produced several pieces of waste canvas and a ball of twine; and went down on her knees.

"What are you going to do with me?"

"Put out your right foot," she said.

"What for?"

"What for, you great gowk? Do you think you are going to stump upstairs and downstairs like a two-legged donkey? No, you must have your feet muffled, so as to make no noise."

He was an unresisting captive, was poor old Mole, and in a very short time his strong-minded female captor had ornamented each stump with a bundle of rags like a great poultice.

"Why, Mr. Mole, you look as if you had the gout," exclaimed young Jack.

"Master Harkaway, I think my age, my position, and my numerous misfortunes should protect me from your ribaldry."

"All right. Here, let me give you a lift upstairs; now then, Harry."

Between the two boys, and with the strong-minded Scotchwoman pushing behind, Mole was hoisted up to a large room on the first floor.

"Hush!" said Mrs. Cameron, as she placed a chair for Mole, seating him with his back towards a curtain, which hung entirely across one end of the room.

"But where is my poor wife?" asked Mole in a whisper.

"Ah, poor dear creature," responded Mrs. Cameron in the same low tones; "I must go and see if she is still alive."

Mrs. Cameron then disappeared behind the curtain.

Minute after minute passed.

Mole's face expressed the greatest anxiety, while the boys seemed scarcely able to restain their laughter.

But he was not kept long in suspense, for Mrs. Cameron returned.

"Now, sir, behold with joy what I have for you. Look at the pretty little dears, the sweet little chicksy-whicksies."

Mole turned pale as he perceived that on either arm the nurse carried a black baby not many hours old.

"Good Heaven!" cried Mole, "this is too much. What is the meaning of it?"

"The meaning of this!" ejaculated Mrs. Cameron. "Why, the man is mad. Mr. Mole, do you mean to deny your own offsprings?"

"No, no, no," cried Mole, "but this is more than I expected. Are you sure there are no more?"

"No more? Why, the man is never satisfied. There, just kiss 'em, will you?" said Mrs. Cameron.

Mole placed his rum-smelling lips to the infants with about as much pleasantness as if they had been a brace of black bull-frogs.

Then he said—

"Whatever shall I do with them? Do take the little wretches—no, I mean the dear little babes—away, or they will cry, and I hate squalling children. Where is my wife?"

"Never mind about your wife; sit down and pay attention to me."

Mole obeyed.

Mrs. Cameron placed the children in a cradle behind their parent's back, and then drew up a chair to his side.

"Dear me, I never was so worrited to death in all my born days!" exclaimed the woman.

"I am very sorry——"

"You ought to be proud. But just give me my bottle of medicine, will you? I must take it reg'lar, or else my spasms comes on awful."

Mole handed the good lady a bottle duly labelled—

"The draught to be taken every half hour."

Mrs. Cameron uncorked the phial.

"Is it good for the nerves?" asked Mole.

"Yes; I am but a poor, weak woman, and require a deal of keeping up."

Then, after a pause, she added—

"I wish to talk to you; the fact is, I don't think Mrs. Mole will live long, and I can't think what made a fine, handsome chap like you go and marry a black woman."

Mole sighed.

"After all," he said, "she has been a good wife to me."

"That's her artfulness. She was afraid you'd get a divorce in America, or some of them outlandish places as you've been to; mark my words, you'll have a divorce very soon."

"Woman!" exclaimed Mr. Mole, loftily; "what do you mean?"

"Mean? Why, the poor dear ain't long for this world."

"Not long for——"

"It's true; I never see death on anybody's face so plain as hers."

"Death! Good Heaven, if my wife dies, what will become of those helpless infants? But I beg pardon; half an hour has not elapsed."

This last remark was called forth by the fact that Mrs. Cameron had again uncorked her medicine phial.

"Half an hour. Well, I know that. Sometimes I require it every quarter of an hour; but I will tell you what to do with the black kids. Bring them up by hand, with a bottle," said the nurse, as in a fit of abstraction she handed her own bottle to Mole, who in an equally abstracted manner placed it to his lips.

"Yes, that is good; bring 'em up with a bottle, and when they are old, they will not depart from it."

"Capital! excellent idea—medicine, I mean," said old Mole, smacking his lips.

We may as well explain at once that the medicine the nurse found so necessary was nothing more nor less than good old navy rum.

So no wonder old Mole praised it.

"But, good Lord, Mr. Mole," said the nurse, snatching the bottle out of Mole's hand, "there ain't much fear but what a fine handsome man like you would soon get another wife—a white one, I mean."

"No," said Mole; "if my wife should die, I will not marry again. Who would have me, I should like to know, with two wooden legs and two black babies?"

"Why, you need not look far for someone," cried the old woman sighing.

"I don't understand you."

"Why, Mr. Mole, how dull you are! You ain't half such a gallant young man as I thought."

"I believe the woman is mad!" exclaimed Mole, rising.

"Sit down," said Mrs. Cameron, giving him a good tap on the head with a hearth brush.

"Knock gently," said the two boys and Mole simultaneously.

"You are such an old teaser, Mr. Mole, but I didn't mean to hurt you, so sit down and take another dose out of my medicine bottle."

To this Mole readily agreed.

Young Jack and Harry Girdwood were all this time close by the cradle in which the black babies were slumbering.

Mrs. Cameron continued—

"You know, Mr. Mole, I am a poor, lone widow—not bad-looking, perhaps, and I shouldn't mind changing my state."

"You certainly have my permission to do so, my good woman."

"Ah, you are an old teaser, Mr. Mole. What I mean is—you know—I should like to change my name to——"

"It's changing to white!" exclaimed young Harry Girdwood.

Mole and the nurse looked round.

Both boys were still by the cradle, apparently thinking of nothing but the babies.

"Harry, what is the matter?"

"I beg pardon, Mr. Mole, but one of these babies is certainly changing its colour. It is nearly white."

"One of my babies turning white! Dear me, so it is," said Mr. Mole and the nurse, as they staggered to the cradle, the old woman putting her arms round the professor to support him, or herself.

The fact is, young Jack had discovered some violet powder, which he had gently applied to the infant's face, thus turning it from black to light brown.

But Mole and the nurse were both too fuddled to think of such a trick; so after remarking that it was a wonderful freak of nature, they returned to their seats.

There was a pause for a few minutes, then Mrs. Cameron, having taken another dose of her medicine, and given Mr. Mole his dose, said—

"Mr. Mole, you know what I mean. If your wife dies, you must marry me. I adore you."

"Impossible—oh!"

The interjection was the result of another smart application of the hearth brush from the nurse.

"Sit down, and don't be a silly old teaser."

Mole, who was thoroughly frightened obeyed, and received another tap to remind him that he must not rise without permission.

"Oh—oh! knock gently."

"Now, Mr. Mole, take another dose, there is a good man; and, tell me, when is the happy day to be?"

"I—I can't marry you before my present wife is dead," said Mole.

"Of course not, my dear, but I doubt if she will last through many days."

"And then ?"

"And then, of course, there is the funeral. What do you say, my dear Mole, to the second day after the funeral ?"

"Don't you—you don't think it's—it's just a little too soon ?" cried Mole, trying to rise from his seat.

"Not a bit," said the nurse, as her hand wandered towards the hearth broom again.

Mole noticed the movement, and exclaimed—

"Well, then, Mrs.—my dear, I mean, let it be as you wish."

"You darling old chap, why did you not say so before? But, you old rascal, you left me to do all the courting, you did, you old teaser !"

And Mrs. Cameron first gave Mole a sharp tap on the head wth the brush, and threw her arms round his neck, and kissed him in a way that fairly astonished not only him, but his two young pupils.

We are also inclined to think that some-one else was just a little bit astonished.

At all events, a voice that hitherto had not been heard began now to take part in the conversation.

"Isaac Mole, Isaac Mole, Isaac Mole !" it said, "if you marries dat white woman, my ghost shall haunt yer !"

The old nurse did not hear the voice, but stood looking lovingly at Mole.

Poor Mole turned, and to his great astonishment, beheld the countenance of his black wife looking from the curtains at the end of the room.

"Oh, horror !" cried Mole, starting up; destruction ! my mind will give way;

what a terrible situation to be placed in —a white woman who will marry me against my wish, the ghost of my black wife to haunt me, and two blessed black infants to bring up by the bottle ! Oh, it is too much !" and poor Mole threw himself against the door, tearing the few hairs from his head in despair.

"Oh, Mr. Mole, Mr. Mole ! you cruel villain, you will be hanged," cried Mrs. Mole, shaking her head between the bed curtains.

Mole stretched out his hand, saying—

"My dear, I didn't know you were there."

"I'm here, Isaac, but I'm gwine to die. You false man, to make lub to dat 'ere—oh, oh, oh !" and Mrs. Mole fell down in a fit of hysterics.

Mrs. Cameron was by this time half seas over; however, she managed to attend to Mrs. Mole, and got her to bed again, where she lay feebly moaning and occasionally muttering a threat to haunt her husband after death.

At length these sounds ceased altogether, and Mrs. Cameron, who had "pulled herself together " a little, exclaimed—

"I think she is dead !"

Mole was in a very maudlin condition, and the boys got him away to a little hotel near at hand.

The old nurse also was taken care of, and someone sent to attend to Mole's poor black wife.

"It's rather a sad ending, Harry," said young Jack.

"Yes. I wonder what poor Mole will do ?"

"Have some more rum, of course."

CHAPTER XXXVI.

A TOUGH FIGHT.

WE left Harkaway in the power of the brigands. At least so it seemed, for instantly, from one of the chasms among the rocks, sprang forth four equally hideous-looking ruffians armed with ugly knives, and stood before the travellers.

There was no mistaking the object for which they had been lured to that quiet, out-of-the-way spot.

Jack Harkaway's keen instinct had not been at fault.

He had been right in his suspicions.

The two gentlemanly Greeks, Zavella and Carjani, were nothing more than men trappers.

The treacherous guides did not re-appear.

Having trapped the game, they left

their comrades to hack it to pieces, whilst they went to hunt for more.

The two Englishmen, thus ensnared, looked sternly at the ruffianly crew before them.

But each had passed through too many hairbreadth escapes, and fought too many hard battles, to quail in the slightest.

They were more incensed at their position than intimidated.

The first thing they did was to snatch their revolvers from their belts and cock them.

"Now, you vagabonds," cried Jack, addressing himself not only to the men, but also to the giant on the rock, who was evidently their chief; "if you do not instantly crawl back into your burrows as quickly as you came out, in less than ten seconds not one of you will be alive."

At this imperative threat the ruffians laughed hoarsely.

"Upon them! bind them hand and foot," shouted their captain, whose name was Mavrocordato.

Jack Harkaway pointed his revolver deliberately at his head.

"Recall that order, or I fire," he cried.

"Ha, ha, ha!" laughed the chief, mockingly. "I fear you not; seize them!"

Jack instantly pulled the trigger of his weapon.

But no report followed.

The ruffians jeered loudly.

"I'll stop your laughing, you ugly brutes," thought Dick Harvey, as he also pulled the trigger.

But with no better effect.

Neither of the revolvers would fire.

But there was a good reason for this.

The polite Greek gentlemen had very cleverly removed all the caps from the nipples whilst their guests were eating their lunch.

The things as firearms were perfectly useless.

The position of their owners was now somewhat desperate.

"Upon them!" shouted Mavrocordato to his men.

The ruffians rushed forward.

"Go in, Dick, tooth and nail; it's our only chance," cried old Jack, as he gave the foremost of the party a smashing blow with the handle of his revolver.

"Trust me," responded Dick fervently, as he imitated his comrade's example, and

almost split one of the brigands' thick skulls.

The ruffians slashed away like furies with their long crooked dirks.

But their opponents had planted themselves with their backs against the rocks.

And both being good swordsmen, they were able to ward off their attacks.

Our English heroes were not even scratched, whilst the brigands had already received some ugly knocks.

This work was too slow for their leader.

It irritated him.

"Ascend the rocks, one of you, and crush them with stones from above," he shouted, fiercely.

One of the banditti obeyed this order.

But Jack and Dick, not wishing to be crushed in this wholesale way, removed from their post, just as a huge mass came crashing down where a moment before they had been standing.

This was exactly what the chief desired.

"Now," he shouted; "make short work with those Inglese."

But he did not know the sort of customers he had to deal with.

Driven from the rocks, the Inglese placed themselves back to back.

They had now two dirks that they had wrenched from the hands of the brigands.

And with these they resisted the combined attacks of their four adversaries.

Mavrocordato grew more and more enraged as he watched the futile efforts of his myrmidons to beat down the Englishmen.

Again the whistle was applied to his lips.

Two more of the band answered the summons and joined their comrades.

Jack and Dick Harvey had warmed to their work, and they warmed the brigands in return.

The ruffians were battered severely.

The chief began to swear (in Greek).

"Down with the dogs!" he shouted.

The men were also furious at the blows they had received.

And now that two more were added to their number, they yelled like demons, and fought like tiger cats.

And, at length, Jack and his companion, although their pluck was still unabated, began to show symptoms of exhaustion.

Dick Harvey, too, had received an ugly thrust in the arm, and the loss of blood made him feel faint.

The brigand chief, whose eyes had eagerly watched the strife, noticed this.

"Lay on, Vulpiotti; lay on, Cazzaro," he cried, exultingly; "they're giving way."

"It's a lie, you cowardly ruffian; we're not," shouted Jack, as he rammed the butt end of his revolver between Vulpiotti's gaping jaws, and half way down his throat.

At this moment, Dick Harvey said to him, in a hurried whisper—

"We must make a rush for it. I shan't be able to keep on my legs very much longer."

"All right, Dick, my boy," returned Jack, cheerfully, "here goes then; neck or nothing."

As he spoke, he rushed in amongst the ruffian throng, scattering them right and left.

Their knives flashed around him, but he heeded them no more than so many bodkins.

Just then, Dick Harvey, in an effort to follow him, staggered and fell.

Jack was at his side in an instant.

So were his foes.

And taking advantage of his momentary distraction, they threw themselves upon him, and bore him to the ground.

The next moment, he and his wounded comrade were bound hand and foot with ropes.

Utterly helpless.

Mavrocordato shouted triumphantly, and advanced towards them.

"So," he grinned, derisively, as he looked down upon his fettered captives, "you are knocked off your feet at last."

Old Jack was in a tremendous rage.

"You do well to insult us now, you hulking cowardly hound!" he cried furiously; "you who dared not strike a blow yourself."

The tone of bitter contempt in which these words were spoken irritated the brigand chief.

"What is that you say?" he demanded, sternly.

"That you're as cowardly as you're high," foamed Jack.

"Ha! you dare to call me a coward, me, Mavrocordato?"

"Yes, I dare! If you are not a coward, loose my hands and feet and fight me man to man."

"I would," replied the bandit, "if I did not expect to get more by your life than your death."

"Not you," sneered Jack, regardless of consequences; "you're afraid. I tell you so before your band."

A terrible oath burst from the bandit.

"Soul of my father," he shouted, as he clutched his sword; "he says I am afraid."

"Yes, and a coward," thundered Jack. "If not, prove it."

"I will prove it, to your cost," exclaimed the chief.

Turning to his followers, he said—

"Untie the ropes of that English dog."

In an instant the order was obeyed.

Jack Harkaway sprang to his feet, ready for the fight.

But Jack was unarmed, whilst the brigand held a drawn sabre in his hand.

"I warn you beforehand that I shall kill you," he said.

"If you're not killed yourself first, I suppose you mean," retorted Jack, sarcastically.

"Ha, ha!" laughed the chief, in a mocking tone. "If you are able to beat me, I promise you your life and freedom."

"And my friend?" asked our hero.

"And your friend's, too," answered the Greek.

"Then consider yourself beaten," replied Jack, with perfect confidence.

"Give the hound a sword," cried the brigand chief.

"Anything you like; only don't waste time. Give me a weapon."

At the signal from the bandit, a sabre was placed in Jack's hand.

It was little more than half the length of the formidable weapon wielded by the bandit chief.

But what of that?

Jack inwardly exulted as he grasped it.

He was a splendid swordsman, and felt confident of victory.

"Now, you ruffian, on guard!" he cried.

The weapons crossed.

From the enormous height and bulk of his opponent, our hero looked quite small in comparison.

Mavrocordato was not a pure Greek.

He was of Austrian extraction.

But he had lived many years on Greek soil, and had become naturalised, although he was indebted to a Bohemian father for his gigantic stature and massive limbs.

It was evident he reckoned upon making his English opponent an easy prey.

Little did he dream of his skill in whose hand he had ordered a sword to be placed.

Had he had the slightest suspicion of the truth, Jack Harkaway would have been still lying bound and helpless on the ground.

The combat commenced.

The brigand attacked fiercely, with heavy sweeping blows.

Jack, laughing to himself, turned them aside as lightly as feathers.

Mavrocordato was surprised and not a little irritated at the small effect he had produced with so much exertion.

He redoubled his efforts, but could not touch his strong-wristed, quick-eyed adversary.

Presently he received a deep wound in his brawny arm.

He uttered a yell of pain as he felt the keen steel, and slashed away more furiously than ever.

"Ha, ha," said Jack, "how liked you that thrust in your arm? Look out, for the next shall be your cheek."

Suddenly the brigand received a terrific cut across his cheek.

He had already lost half his nose and an ear in former conflicts.

But this last wound drove him mad.

He howled like a wild beast.

His weapon whizzed through the air with sharp hisses.

But he struck nothing else, whilst Jack's sword once more took effect upon his wrist.

No longer able to wield his weapon with one hand, he grasped it in both, and breathing forth bitter maledictions, he pursued his nimble opponent, who led him a dance round the rocky arena, to the great wonder of his myrmidons, who stood looking on.

But the gigantic ruffian, with all his strength, began to feel the effects of his wounds, from which the blood trickled freely.

He was rapidly becoming what is called "groggy."

He staggered and struck wildly and at random.

Jack Harkaway, on the contrary, was almost as fresh as when he commenced.

But he had to keep his eyes pretty sharply open to avoid a chance blow, one of which would have been more than sufficient to cleave his skull in twain.

Suddenly, with a final and desperate effort, Mavrocordato rushed in upon his foe.

Down came his weapon with crushing force.

It was his last blow, for Jack caught it on his sword, almost close to the hilt, and by a swift turn of his wrist, jerked the giant's weapon from his grasp.

The latter, exhausted with this last outburst, toppled over like an uprooted oak, and fell with a dull crash to the ground.

"Yield, ruffian," cried Jack, as he sprang towards him, and pointed his sword at his throat, feeling strongly inclined to put an end to his atrocities and his life together.

But prudence restrained him, and he contented himself with saying—

"You are beaten, as I told you you would be, and I claim life and freedom for myself and friend."

"Bravo, Jack," murmured Dick Harvey, who had come to himself, though he had no power to render any help.

"Yes, yes, you shall have both," gasped the bandit, as he felt the sharp steel tickling his windpipe; "you are free."

. Jack Harkaway sprang to his comrade, and knelt down to sever the cords that bound him.

But ere he could accomplish this, a noose was thrown over his shoulders and drawn tightly, whilst he himself was borne to the ground.

The treacherous Mavrocordato had given a signal he had not observed.

To his dismay he found himself once more a prisoner.

"Coward, liar, scoundrel!" burst from Jack Harkaway's lips, "you shall repent this."

"You shall repent it," growled the bandit. "A rope, quick!"

A rope was instantly brought.

Quickly it encircled the neck of Jack Harkaway.

At the sight of his friend's peril, Dick

Harvey burst into a paroxysm of indignant horror.

"Hold, you murderous wretches!" he shouted, desperately; "what would you do?"

"Hang your comrade first, and you afterwards," was the startling reply.

All appeal was thrown away.

Jack was dragged to the rock, and one end of the rope passed through a strong iron ring. It was an awful crisis.

"Now," cried the brigand chief, "you shall die like a dog."

But ere the fatal deed could be accomplished, a loud shout was heard.

The next moment, a party of friends came hurrying along the narrow defile, and dashed into the arena.

This party consisted of Jefferson the American, and his staunch friend, Brand the dwarf, closely followed by young Jack Harkaway and Nero the monkey.

In an instant Jack and the sagacious animal had unbound his father and Dick Harvey.

Jefferson, who was a host in himself, and who rivalled the brigand chief in bulk, strode forward like a young Colossus, his six-barrelled revolver in his hand.

"'Tarnal thunder!" he exclaimed; "what sort of an echo do you call this?"

There was no answer.

The treacherous guides who had lured them to the mountains, as they had previously done their companions, had again disappeared.

"There are no echoes here but the echoes of treachery," replied Harkaway at length; "this is a nest of murderers, and your arrival has saved our necks from the halter. There is their leader."

As he spoke, he pointed to Mavrocordato, who made a desperate effort to escape, but the American was down upon him in an instant.

"Not so fast, you black rascal," he shouted, as he seized and dragged him back.

The bandit once more fell crashing to the earth.

Jefferson set his foot upon his breast.

"Now, if you stir an inch, or move an eyelid, by Goliah, I'll crush you into immortal smash!" he cried.

John Harkaway's voice echoed his.

"Let us seize those murderous vagabonds," he shouted.

In the instant the ruffianly crew, who stood looking on in a bewildered manner, were seized and bound by Jack and Dick Harvey and Brand the dwarf.

Young Jack, who was very expert at tying knots, assisted, whilst Nero the monkey amused himself by making gridirons on the ugly faces of the brigands, and pulling out handfuls of their hair and beards.

In the meantime the American giant had pinioned the arms of the burly Mavrocordato with a strong leathern belt he wore.

"I hardly know what to do with you," he said, as he flourished his revolver in ominous proximity to the bandit's head; "I feel strongly inclined to save all further anxiety on your account by giving you at once the contents of this."

John Harkaway suggested—

"Better not take the law into our own hands. Let justice have her due."

"But is there any justice to be found in Greece?" asked Jefferson.

"I think so in this case."

"Very well, then; I spare him," said the American; "shooting is too good for him. A bullet for a brave man—for a cowardly cur, a rope."

"Bring 'em along," cried Harkaway.

"Get up, Hercules!" exclaimed Jefferson, ironically, as he dragged the brigand to his feet.

"Don't you think it would be a good idea to thrash these fellows over the mountains with a rope's end before you give them up to justice?" suggested young Jack playfully.

"Capital!" cried the American giant, with a stentorian laugh, in which all joined, except the prisoners.

Some ropes were quickly knotted by Jack in a decidedly sailor-like fashion.

"I think they'll do," he remarked.

"Let's try," said Jefferson, as he took one and gave his prisoner several slashing cuts with it across his shoulders.

Mavrocordato howled like a wild cat in a steel trap.

"If they're all like that, they'll do capitally," replied the American coolly; "there's real grit in 'em, and no mistake."

"And now drive the ruffians on," said Jack Harkaway.

"We're ready."

"I say, dad," called out young Jack, "I vote we turn over old Blunderbore"—this was a nickname for the bandit leader—"to Nero; he'll stick to him."

"By all means," replied his father.

"Here, Nero, look after this black thief," cried our young hero, as he pointed out the burly ruffian to the monkey, and placed a knotted rope in his paw at the same time.

Nero perfectly understood the order, and proceeded to look after his charge.

With this intent the animal scrambled up the giant's back and perched himself upon his shoulders, grinning with delight, and whacking away at his head with the knotted rope.

Being pinioned, the bandit could not dislodge him, and furious with pain, he darted off along the rocks with heavy lumbering steps like those of an elephant, swearing and howling with pain.

The rest of the gang, with a rope's end apiece falling hard upon their backs, followed, also swearing and yelling.

In this way, the band of marauders was driven like a drove of wild bullocks into the town.

They were safely lodged in prison, and shortly afterwards received the reward of their merits.

From that time forward there was no more talk about the echoes of Mount Calviero.

CHAPTER XXXVII.

THE FUNERAL.

THE boys had not gone very far on their way home when they saw two gentlemen in English dress approaching.

"Hurrah!" shouted young Jack. "Here's my dad and uncle Dick."

"Mr. Harvey is not your uncle."

"What's the odds, so long as you are happy? If he's not my uncle, he is a great deal better than a bad second cousin."

The two boys raced forward, and quickly informed their seniors of the supposed death of Mrs. Mole.

"Rather a serious matter," said Harkaway, senior. "Hadn't we better look up old Mole, Dick?"

"That's no use, governor. He's three sheets in the wind now," said young Jack.

"Perhaps," said Harvey, "we had etter go to the house, and if Mrs. Mole dead, make arrangements for giving her decent funeral."

"Quite right, Dick. Come along."

Accompanied by the two boys they proceeded to the house of Mrs. Cameron; and, as a knock at the door elicited no response, they did not scruple to enter and ascend the first floor.

There they found Mrs. Cameron asleep on the floor, with her medicine bottle empty by her side, and, to their intense surprise, Mrs. Mole, whom they supposed dead, dressed and to all appearance as well as could be expected.

"Why, the boys told me you had gone t'other side of Jordan, Mrs. Mole," said Harvey.

"No, massa; I only hab one fainting fit, an' then get up again to look after Mole."

"Well, I am glad of that. But this woman on the floor?"

"Bin habin' rum, and makin' lub to my Mole; her breff smell of rum like Mole's."

"But even that smells better than Robur, doesn't it, Mrs. Mole?" asked Harvey.

"Dere ain't much difference," said the resuscitated lady.

During this time, the Harkaways, father and son, had been talking together.

"Do you feel well enough to move to my house, Mrs. Mole?" said Harkaway.

"Yes, Massa Harkaway. If you carry one of my beautiful babies, I kin carry t'oder, and off we goes."

"Thank you, but I'm not much of a nurse; perhaps Mr. Harvey will oblige."

"Mr. Harvey will see you—home, but he declines playing at nurse girls. Harry, my boy, will you?"

Now Harry Girdwood was at all times

very anxious to show his gratitude towards those who had rescued him from the depths of misery, so he at once consented to carry one of the twin babies.

So Mrs. Mole, Harkaway, senior, Harvey, and Harry Girdwood set out, leaving young Jack to look after the house and the drunken old nurse, as well as to arrange a continuation of the joke upon old Mole.

After a time young Jack, being satisfied that Mrs. Cameron was in a sleep from which she would ·not wake for hours, went out into the town and made a few purchases.

When he returned, Mrs. Cameron was still snoring.

"Come along," said Jack, in a loud whisper, and there entered a Greek carpenter carrying a plain coffin.

"Inglese master not bury her," said the man, pointing to the nurse. "She not die yet."

"Serve her right if I did—but no. Put the coffin here, and now help me to fill it."

With the assistance of his new ally, Jack stuffed the coffin with waste paper, old iron, rags and bricks.

"Now screw on the lid."

This was soon done, and having so far completed his arrangements for the funeral, Jack proceeded to call the mourners.

Assuming as mournful an air as possible, he proceeded to Mr. Mole's lodging, and informed him that everything was ready.

The old tutor had only half recovered from the effects of the rum, and objected to the haste with which the whole thing had been done.

"Can't be helped, Mr. Mole; I am very sorry, of course, but then the authorities insist on it."

"But I have no black clothes, my boy."

"Must get some made afterwards. Come along."

Thus urged, Mole put on his hat.

"Well, but what is to be done with the lovely twins, Jack?" asked Mole.

"Well, sir, that is your business. You are strong, and would look well with one on each arm walking about your native village."

"No, no; I must consult with that strong-minded party, Mrs. Cameron. No doubt she will attend to their little wants for me."

Sunday and Monday were summoned, and the four mourners proceeded to the house where the coffin was.

"Dat a great pity, 'bout de folk up at de cemetery," said Sunday, with a sly wink at Jack.

"Yes, indeed."

"What is that?" demanded Mole.

"Why, sir, I am very sorry to have to add to your grief, but the funeral will have to take place in unconsecrated ground, the deceased not having been a member of the Greek faith. So I have arranged that it shall take place in the large garden at the back of the house, where there is a splendid willow tree."

Jack kept on talking till they reached the house, where the Greek carpenter and another native were waiting, together with a very sedate-looking gentleman in blue spectacles, who explained that he was an officer of the government, come to see that the funeral was performed in a proper manner, according to the sanitary regulations of the country.

A few whispered words between this gentleman and young Jack; then the coffin was lifted up by the two niggers and the two Greeks, and conveyed down to the weeping willow tree, where it was decently placed in the earth, and covered up.

The government gentleman made an entry in his book, and departed; as did also Jack and all the rest, except Mole, who remained behind to arrange with Mrs. Cameron about the removal of Mrs. Mole's effects, etc., etc.

*   *   *   *   *

It was late when Mole reappeared among his friends, and he presented a most decided appearance of having drowned his sorrow in the flowing bowl.

Harkaway, senior, was not present; but Dick Harvey, young Jack, and Harry Girdwood received the disconsolate widower, who, looking round rather vacantly, said—

"Goin' to be—hic—married 'gain—hic—to-mor——"

"What!" exclaimed they all.

"Dear friends, sorry Mrs. Mole would die. Leave me two black kids, can't nurse 'em self, goin' to marry old Mac

—hic—no, not—hic—Mac, I mean, Cameron—nurse."

"It's impossible," said Harry.

"So soon after poor Mrs. Mole's death too."

"Not imposs—possible; must be done—hic. Will Harvey nurse my innocent babies? If he's my friend, he will say—hic—'Yes, Mole, dear old friend, I will nurse your dear children, and—hic—bring them — hic — up like a fond — hic — mother.'"

"No, no, Mr. Mole, you have two arms left, and you must nurse your blessed babies yourself; besides," continued

Harvey, "the Greek priest won't marry you, and there's no Protestant clergyman here."

"Pack of stuff! There's consuls——"

"Quoted at 92⅜ in the last papers we received," observed Harvey.

"Surprised at such levity," said Mole, wagging his head gravely. "It's British consul I mean. He can do it or-right—legal, every—hic—thing."

And, with this lucid explanation of his meaning, Mole dropped forward on a sofa, and his friends permitted him to go to sleep, which he did instantly, snoring like a bull-frog in convulsions.

CHAPTER XXXVIII.

EXECUTION OF MOLE.

"So Mole thinks he is going to be married to-morrow," said Harvey, lighting a fresh cigar. "The old man ought to know better at his time of life, and with such an experience too."

"I believe it's that old nurse; she bullies him fearfully," said Jack, junior, "whacks him if he won't say he loves her."

"Well, we must have some fun out of this, Jack, my boy. Do you know where the British consul lives?" asked Harvey.

Young Jack did not.

"There is no British consul here, Mr. Harvey," said Harry.

"But I've seen the office up in the town, youngster."

"The consulate is removed to Syra now, sir; they left their old plate on the door though."

"Oh—Jack, a word in your ear."

Harvey whispered for some time, then Harry Girdwood was taken into the conference, and finally the two darkeys, Sunday and Monday, were sent for.

It was quite two hours before they separated, and even then there was more work to be done.

Monday had to go to the house where the name of the consul appeared, and make some arrangements.

* * * * *

Morning came with all its radiance.

It was at least nine o'clock before Mole could raise his throbbing head from the pillow.

"Now then, Mr. Mole, if you are going to be married, you had best make haste," said young Jack. "The young and blushing bride, only fifty-two years old, and twenty-two stone weight, is at the door; shall I send her away?" cried Jack.

"No, don't, please, Jack. I'll get up. That woman will kill me if I don't marry her."

"Just as you please, Mr. Mole. By-the-bye, there has been a messenger from the British consul's place to say you must not be later than eleven o'clock."

Mole gave a prolonged groan, and in a short time Harvey could hear his wooden stumps playing upon the floor as the old tutor performed his toilet.

"You don't look much like a bridegroom certainly," remarked Harkaway, senior.

"I don't feel like one. Ah! my dear Harkaway, if you respect me, pray find someone to take the bride off my hands, and I will make a present to the party of my two beautiful infants."

"No, Mr. Mole, you must go through it now; the lady of your heart insists upon wedding you."

"Well, then, I must meet my fate like a man," said Mole. "But where are the boys?"

"They have been sent away. So come

along, Mr. Mole; let us go for the bride, as it seems we must fetch her according to the country custom."

A vehicle had been provided for the occasion, and placing Mole in it, they drove off to the residence of Mrs. Cameron.

Harvey very politely led her downstairs and handed her into the carriage. In ten minutes' time they stopped at the door which bore the plate of the British consul.

"Marriage party?" asked a Greek, who opened the door to them.

"Yes," said Harvey.

The Greek led them to an inner room, fitted up as a kind of counting house.

Here was a gentleman, who wore blue spectacles, a thick bushy beard, moustache and whiskers, and a barrister's gown.

"Mr. Mole, I presume," said this individual.

The happy bridegroom bowed.

"You wish to be married?"

"I will," responded the bride, who had been studying the prayerbook.

"Certainly; join hands."

"Pardon me," said Mole, "but isn't this rather irregular, Mr. Consul?"

"Certainly not. It's a civil marriage, and we can dispense with a great portion of the ceremony."

"But I—oh! Mrs. Cameron, that hurts."

The irate bride, who had no notion of delay, had given Mr. Mole a stinging box on the ears.

"Remember your promise, Mr. Mole, and make haste and get the marriage over."

"Come," said the consul, "I can't permit this in my office. If you are going to be married, join hands; if not, leave the house."

Mrs. Cameron thrust out her eleven-and-a-half-sized glove, which Mole took as affectionately as he could.

"You both swear that you are of the full age of twenty-one years?"

"Fifty-one, both of them, if they are a day," said Harvey.

"If you was half a man, Mr. Mole, you'd stop that fellow's tongue," exclaimed the bride. "Never mind; wait till we are married; I'll teach you your duty."

"Silence!"

Mrs. Cameron held her peace.

The official went on—

"If anyone now present knows any just cause why these two persons should not be joined together in the bonds of matrimony, let him now speak, or else for ever hold his peace."

"I forbids the bamms!"

The words, pronounced in clear, ringing tones, caused everyone to look towards the doorway.

Mole staggered, and would have fainted had not the strong arm of Dick Harvey propped him up.

There, in the open doorway, stood his black wife, and behind her a Greek woman with the two babies.

Harkaway, the elder, was in the room, endeavouring to look stern, but failing in the attempt.

"Mr. Mole," said he, "I have always been ready to overlook your weaknesses, but I cannot stand by and see you commit bigamy."

"Bigamy! Ho, there! Demetrius, Brailas, Lascaridas, Xenos! Where are my guards?" shouted the consul.

Immediately there entered four men, dressed in the uniform of the Greek army, two of whom were Moors.

"Bigamy has been committed; take away those abandoned ruffians and shoot them."

"Sir! I beg your pardon," said Mole, "but as I am not married to this—this—ah, lady yet, I imagine bigamy has not been——"

"Silence, scoundrel! Is that coloured lady your lawful wife?"

"Certain——"

"Will you be silent? What made you come here to try and impose on me?"

"I thought——"

"You have no business to think. Prisoner, you have been guilty of high treason and contempt of court of the first degree. What have you to say in your defence?"

"Your excellency, I——"

"Hold your tongue."

"Sir, I don't wish to marry Mrs. Cameron; it is all her fault; she brought me here by force; but, sir, is this a court of justice?"

"Certainly not. I hereby convert it into a court-martial. Away with him! Drag away both the disgraceful villains. Shoot them in the back yard."

Mole and Mrs. Cameron were forthwith forced out to the enclosure at the back, and placed against a high wall.

"Two minutes to prepare for death," said one of the Moors, and leaving a Greek sentry in charge of the prisoners, the others withdrew.

Meanwhile, the consul, tearing off his beard, threw aside his barrister's gown, and dismounting from the stilts he had been standing on, disclosed the laughing features and form of Jack Harkaway, junior.

"How's that, dad? Ain't I a good actor?"

"Capital; but here comes Harry."

"Got the physic, Harry?"

"Yes."

And Harry produced two bottles, labelled—

"The mixture, Mrs. Cameron," and "The draught, Mr. Mole."

"It's good stuff. The chemist says if they take a drink, and cork it up, it will explode."

"Nothing dangerous, I hope."

"No, Mr. Harkaway, only rum, and I've had something put in it to make it effervesce."

"All right. Now, Mrs. Mole, come and see your good husband shot."

"Bad husband! Gib him a good fright."

"Certainly."

The whole party then proceeded to the yard, where the culprits were found.

Mrs. Cameron was on her knees, endeavouring to remember some of the prayers she had learnt in her youth; while Mole, propped up against the wall on his stumps, looked the picture of misery.

He cheered up a little, especially when Harry slipped a bottle into his hand.

He uncorked it, and took a good drink.

"Well, Mr. Mole, we have been speaking for you to the consul, but he will not pardon you, therefore you must prepare for death."

"But I would rather live. Just consider, what will my poor babies do without me?

"My dear," said he, addressing his wife, as he forced the cork into the bottle; "intercede for me. The consul will listen to you."

"No, Isaac. You bad man, you no care if I die."

"Yes, my dear. I was really very sorry, but this woman made me promise to marry her."

"I'll never do it again," whimpered the nurse, as she also took her medicine.

"It's no use," said Harvey. "We have been talking to the consul, but he won't relent. Heaven have mercy upon you, Mr. Mole."

"Oh, dear, oh, dear!" groaned Mole, as the three other soldiers re-entered the yard.

"I hear you are to be shot with explosive bullets," whispered Harry Girdwood, "so your sufferings will soon be over. Good-bye, old friend."

With this little bit of comfort he withdrew, while Mole and Mrs. Cameron, also fainting with fright, propped each other up back to back.

The soldiers went through the form of loading; they raised their guns and fired.

The four reports were as one, but immediately after there were two other explosions, the bottle in Mr. Mole's pocket and that in Mrs. Cameron's having burst, causing them to believe that they had received the explosive bullets.

"My heart is burst; good-bye, Jack," groaned Mole, falling as gracefully as his wooden legs would permit; "remember your old Mole."

"Oh, Lord! All my inside is blown out," groaned Mrs. Cameron, falling; "oh, poor me."

Thinking the joke had now been carried to sufficient length, Harkaway senior stepped forward.

"Mrs. Cameron," said he, "I think you had better give up your matrimonial projects, and retire to your own house; let this be a caution."

The lady endeavoured to rise, but was unable.

She had severely injured her leg in falling.

The others, after a hearty laugh, also retired—leaving Mole to receive a good lecture from his wife, who, however, soon forgave him.

As for Mrs. Cameron, her leg grew worse, and eventually had to be amputated.

Like Mole, she had to hobble through life on timber.

"Serve her right," said Mrs. Mole, to her dear and faithful husband, Mr. Mole.

CHAPTER XXXIX.

TORO'S RESOLVE—THE BAG OF JEWELS IN THE DEAD-HOUSE—ROBBING A
CORPSE—A SCENE OF TERROR.

TORO waited in great impatience for the hour when he could safely venture upon the daring expedition that he had in view.

The jewels and money which Hunston carried stitched in the lining of his coat must be his.

They had been their joint property, and was not he the sole person who could have any claim to them?

Beyond doubt.

Persons might have been found, with the assistance of Toro and Hunston—had he been alive—who had certainly a prior claim to the valuables.

Yet Toro felt that they were his, and come what might, he would not be robbed of his own.

Accordingly he waited until the whole of his particular ward slept.

And, when all the long spacious dormitory was hushed in slumber, he sat up and groped beneath his pillow for his knife.

He had contrived to secrete that about his person, in spite of the close and vigilant search which was made of his garments upon his entrance into the lazaretto.

Besides the knife, he had secured a small lamp, which he had ready now for work.

Slowly, gently, he arose and glided off his bed.

The guardian of the ward lay dozing in his chair, not ten feet from where Toro stood, and as the latter's bed creaked, he half opened his eyes.

"Eh, what? Who's there?" he mumbled.

And while Toro clutched his knife firmly, the old man grumbled and muttered incoherently.

Then he slept again.

Aye, slept and snored.

Toro stepped out towards the door, the boards creaking with a noise which, to the Italian's anxious ears, seemed loud enough to awake the dead.

Slowly, cautiously, he gained the door.

He passed through, and then he began to breathe again.

Toro's destination was the dead-house of the lazaretto.

The dead-house was a separate building altogether.

To reach it, he was bound to pass out by the hall door.

Toro stepped on, but barely made any progress in the hall, where his boots seemed agreed with the stone paving to create a discord, and creak out words of warning to those on guard.

Down went Toro on his knees, and he crept along, holding his knife between his teeth.

The Italian brigand was very desperate now.

Had that hall-porter woke up, it is probable that there would have been another customer for the dead-house of the lazaretto that night.

Luckily for him, he slept, all unconscious of the brigand's presence.

The bolts stuck.

He used a deal of bad language, but as it was under his breath, and moreover in Italian, there is no need to shock the reader with it.

"Ha, ha!" he muttered, in real satisfaction.

The door was open.

He was outside, at liberty.

Yes, at liberty, for he was so far ungrateful for the benefit of that excellent charity as to regard his life there in the light of bondage.

He crossed the spacious courtyard, and there, upon his left, stood the dark, ugly mausoleum, the dead-house of the Greek lazaretto.

There was a dull, dim light, twinkling feebly through a small window in the building, and this served him as a guide.

"SUNDAY STARTED, BUT HELD HIS KNIFE STILL READY."

He groped his way along until he came to the door, and felt for the catch.

But there was none.

The door gave way slowly before him, and as he passed through, closed behind him with a spring.

The click startled him, for now he was alone with the dead — Hunston, his comrade, and Jack Harkaway's old schoolfellow and bitter foe.

The position was unpleasant.

Still, he had come for the special purpose of doing the business in hand alone and unseen; why should he then fear?

Yet fear he did, bold, burly ruffian that he was.

His nation are proverbially superstitious, and, for a superstitious man, it was not a pleasant locality.

But, in his greed for gold, he had gone through worse scenes than this.

All was gloom and darkness.

But, by degrees, his keen vision pierced the obscurity, and he began to distinguish the ghostly objects by which he found himself surrounded.

It was a long, vaulted chamber, with rows of shelves all round, upon which was a grim array of coffins.

In the centre of the room was a long table fixed upon trestles, upon which rested two coffins.

These were the last silent visitors to the dead house.

Toro shivered a little as his eye rested upon them.

But he did not mean to shirk his self-set task.

With a slow but firm hand, he removed the lid of the nearest coffin, and placed it noiselessly down.

He could not endure the faintest sound then.

Why?

Did he fear to disturb the rest of those silent occupants of the long ugly boxes?

No.

He knew well enough that all he could do would not accomplish this.

The dead would never notice his intrusion did he fire cannon beside them.

Never, never!

And as his thoughts wandered, he started and looked around.

Was it fancy, or did the coverings of the dead really move?

"It must be the weakness of my nerves that causes this feeling," thought Toro. "Away with such childish folly."

But he felt a sinking at his breast, and he wondered at the unaccountable dread which had fallen upon him.

Had he grown womanish? he asked himself.

It was not the first time that he found himself in the presence of death.

Not the first by a great many times.

Beneath the sheet was the shroud of the ghostly occupant.

Now to ascertain if the first was Hunston, it was but necessary to draw back the top cover of the winding-sheet.

Yet his courage almost failed him at this moment.

He had to pause a long while ere he could screw it up to the requisite pitch; but he did it, and then he saw—not Hunston, but a withered old man, with an open mouth and sunken cheeks and a horrible grin.

A pair of glassy eyes were open, and fixed as it seemed in menace upon the bold man who thus broke in upon the silent repose of the dead.

The ruffian gasped.

He drew back and let fall the cover of the shroud.

In his first sensation of fright, he would have made for the door; but he could not find it at once, and he managed to conquer that impulse and stick to his self-set task.

He reflected upon his wretched, penniless condition, and he bethought him of the object of his visit there.

Hunston's hidden treasure must be his at any cost.

Averting his gaze from the other coffin, he passed on to the next, and here, screwing his courage up to the requisite pitch, he stretched forward his hand.

A moment's irresolution here occurred.

No more.

Fighting desperately with his superstitious dreads, he dragged back the shroud from the face of the corpse and then drew cowering back.

"How horrible!" he thought.

How weird and ghastly do the dead appear.

He gained courage presently and returned to face it.

Yes, it was Hunston, surely enough.

Hunston in the flesh, if not in the spirit, yet far less changed corporeally than Toro had expected to find him.

Traces of his last sufferings were to be seen in his face plainly enough; yet he could not think that this looked like the face of a dead man.

The face was pale, it is true, yet it was not the pallor of the grave.

"Poor Hunston!" mused Toro, as he gazed upon the face of the dead man, "he was right enough in his sad predictions, but I did not think that it would come about so very soon; but now for his money bag. Now for it."

It was to be done, and therefore the quicker the better; but although he did his best to assume an air of boldness, he felt unnerved.

His hand shook like that of a palsied wretch as he fearfully withdrew the winding-sheet.

His hand jerked against the body once, and then he started back horror-stricken; his heart leaped to his mouth and his hair dressed up on his scalp.

Had the dead walked, he could not have been more scared.

"What a fool I am!" he muttered in a subdued tone.

The murmur was whispered in the four corners of the dead-house, and echoed back to his frightened ears a ghastly moan.

He plucked up by degrees, and tremblingly returned to the body, when just as his hand rested upon it, the clock of the chapel tolled the three-quarters.

He started again.

How every sound affrighted him!

"Only fifteen minutes more," thought Toro, "before they come. I must be quick."

He groped along the coffin for the bag, but there was no sign of it there.

"They have robbed me!" he gasped; "I am cheated, swindled by these pious thieves! But I'll be revenged; I'll fire this accursed den. I'll burn them all in their beds—I'll—I'll——"

He paused for breath, and for dire threats of vengeance, for although pretty fertile in this sort of matter, his invention seemed to fail him now.

He could think of nothing worse than burning his benefactors in their beds.

"What's that?"

His hand touched something hard against the left side of the body.

He pressed eagerly down and felt the outline of the bag itself.

"Hurrah!"

Here it was surely enough.

He dragged back the sheet, and caught at the bag, but the white drapery yet enveloping the body baffled him.

Do what he would, he could not find the end of it.

Well, it was useless repining, so he set to work with his knife and cut out a square piece of the sheet.

In the midst of this task, the lamp he had brought flickered and gave up the ghost, and then the only light proceeded from the feeble oil lantern hung upon the wall at the further end of the chamber.

This startled him and caused his hand to slip, so that the knife struck the corpse and penetrated a good inch.

There was no particular harm in this, nor would the fact have been worth mentioning but for a remarkable look of the linen as he withdrew the knife with a jerk.

A long, dark stain showed where his knife had pierced.

He looked on with a vague sensation of fear, for he at once knew the nature of the stain.

Blood!

"Why, how's this?" he gasped aloud. "Dead men don't bleed!"

But now his hand grasped Hunston's jewel bag, and greed got the better of fear.

He dragged at it, and having to apply greater force to it he bent over the body, when suddenly, to his intense horror, it moved!

"Great mercies!" he faltered, closing his eyes.

At that instant an icy hand fastened upon his throat, and as the Italian felt the hideous touch of the cold hand, he gasped for mercy.

His tongue clung to the roof of his mouth—he endeavoured to cry out—but in vain.

A slight gurgling noise was heard in his throat.

"It is the death clutch!" was all he could articulate.

And then he fell over the body half insensible.

CHAPTER XL.

ALARMING NEWS—THE ENGLISH VISITORS—TORO REBELS—THE MAD WARD—
THE PADDED ROOM.

AT the moment that the brigand Toro fell fainting over Hunston's body, the great bell of the lazaretto rang out a loud peal of alarm.

Clang! clang! clang! went the iron tongue, and in the space of a few minutes all the place was in an uproar.

Toro, horribly frightened, felt his brain on fire with the confusion prevailing.

He fought with the hand that pressed upon his throat, as soon as he had recovered his senses sufficiently to realise what was going forward.

The alarm bell brought him to his wits again, and he began to understand now the danger he was running.

He remembered the tales of the previous days about sacrilegious people who had robbed the dead, and the thought of the penalty for sacrilege roused him to action at once.

With a mighty effort he struggled up and set himself free from the clutch that had held him, and dragging himself up, he found himself—face to face with Hunston. Yes, there was Hunston, sitting up in his coffin—bolt upright!

Toro started back aghast with fright.

The pale face of Hunston was close to his, and his glassy eyes fixed steadfastly on him.

But the explanation rushed into Toro's brain.

In his frantic endeavours to free himself from the singular entanglement with the corpse, he had dragged it up into a sitting posture.

He thrust it back, but to his intense dismay the right arm was thrust out again, and at the same time a low moaning voice breathed his name.

"Toro."

The Italian reeled back.

He stared at the body with eyes half starting from their sockets.

"Hunston!" he gasped, barely above a whisper.

The body of his former comrade gravely bowed his head.

Toro stared, frozen with terror.

Cold drops of perspiration stood out in big beads upon his forehead.

"Speak, Hunston, speak," breathed the wretched man in accents of unspeakable horror. "Do you live indeed? Do my eyes cheat me, or is this some devilish juggling of the fiend himself?"

"Toro."

"Yes, yes, speak," cried the Italian, eagerly. "Speak, if you are really alive."

"How cold it is!—I'm so thirsty—don't leave me here alone," came in a low tone from Hunston.

Toro burst forth into a fit of hysterical laughter, and sprang forward to raise Hunston up in his arms.

"You're alive—alive!" he cried wildly. "My poor *camarado*, the sound of your voice warms my heart, and sends the blood through my veins at fever pace. Hurrah, hurrah, hurrah!"

Hunston looked on as one stupefied.

He could not at all comprehend what had taken place.

What he had had was neither more nor less than a species of cataleptic fit, and it had lasted so long that it had fairly baffled the doctors.

The probability indeed is that he would have passed away in this trance, but for an accident.

That accident was the slipping of Toro's knife in the body of Hunston, in the clumsy efforts to cut away the bag of jewels.

But there was no time for explanation now.

Before Toro could utter another word, the door was burst open, and five or six armed men entered the place.

"See there," cried the first to cross the threshold, "behold him!"

"Down with him!"

" Let him pay the penalty for his sacrilege," cried another.

" Death to the villain who does not respect the sanctity of the grave," quoth a fourth, who was the head of the lazaretto, and they made a show of rushing upon the Italian.

" Stand back, if you value your lives !" thundered Toro, plucking up now that he had had time for reflection.

" You have proof that I don't respect the dead. Here is ample proof that you don't respect the living."

" Hah !"

" What does he say ?"

" I say that you do not respect the living," retorted Toro, boldly.

" Audacious scoundrel !" vociferated the head of the lazaretto.

" Do you want proof ?" cried Toro. " If so, look there."

Saying which, he pointed to Hunston, and then for the first time they caught sight of that startling spectacle.

Startling indeed.

The dead alive.

The new comers stared at Hunston sitting up in his winding sheet, and then at Toro, and next at each other.

" Is it possible !" ejaculated the head of the hospital. " Does he then live ?"

" See for yourself," was Toro's reply.

But Hunston set all his doubts upon this point at rest, by asking in dry, husky tones for drink.

" My throat is parched and burnt," he said feebly. " In pity give me a drink of water."

Some drink was got, and Hunston revived rapidly.

" What is this horrible place ?" he asked, with a shudder.

Someone was about to furnish the required information, but the head of the lazaretto interfered.

" Hush !" he exclaimed. " Do you, signor," he added to Toro, " explain to your friend that this is the surgery where he has been brought, as he has been so long in a trance that an operation might have been necessary; the shock of learning the truth might be too much for him in his present condition."

Toro approved the idea, and translated It faithfully; but Hunston was by this time fast recovering his presence of mind.

" For a surgery, Toro, it bears a very close resemblance to a mortuary; this," he added, pointing to the linen shroud, " is more like a shroud than a table cloth, and the box I sit in might also be taken for a coffin. Was I not right when I predicted that I should be laid out here ?"

" Yes, right and wrong."

" How ?"

" It is only a sham death, you see. You have vitality enough in you yet, Hunston, to live the best man here out "

Hunston shook his head.

" I doubt that."

" I feel sure of it; and after all I was right, since you are living now, and have cheated all the doctors."

*   *   *   *   *

The restoration to life of the English patient made an extraordinary excitement.

Toro made the best tale he could of his share in the business.

The first question asked was naturally what induced him to break into the mortuary.

He had anticipated this question, and he was prepared with a suitable reply.

" I dreamed that my friend and foster brother was in danger of being buried alive," he said; " the thought of it haunted me, and I no sooner heard of his supposed death than I was determined to see for myself. So I waited till all was quiet, and then I crept out—determined at all hazards to learn the truth for myself. You know the rest."

They vowed that this was the most remarkable instance of correct presentiment that had ever come to their knowledge.

The treasurer of the lazaretto, who had a keen eye to his duties—the increasing the funds of the hospital—saw a chance of making capital out of this.

He got a highly-coloured version of the story circulated, although, in all conscience, the tale was sufficiently startling as it stood—for the purpose of drawing visitors to the place.

Now visitors were always expected to help the charity by a small donation.

Visitors came in shoals after the first day, and they bled pretty freely, so it was an excellent accident for the lazaretto.

The result of this was that when Toro and Hunston wished to take their depar-

JACK HARKAWAY AND HIS SON'S ADVENTURES.

ture, the head doctor, prompted by the treasurer, would not hear of their leaving.

"But we are well now," urged Hunston.

The doctor smiled with a pitying air.

"So you think. But if you think you are well, I have my professional reputation at stake, and I know better."

Toro lost all patience.

His fiery blood was up, and he blurted out—

"Well, signor doctor, well or ill, we will stay no longer."

"Do not be foolish, my good man," said the doctor; "it is not alone for your health that you must stay, but for your interest."

"Interest," said Hunston, "what interest?"

"While you were ill—in that trance, we had some rich English visitors here—very rich."

"What of that?"

"Everything. Why, they were all greatly interested when they heard your case mentioned, and they were very liberal to the charity—very liberal. They will no doubt come again when they hear of the extraordinary case, and if they come, no doubt they will be lavish with their money as before."

"So!" exclaimed Toro, violently, "you want to keep us here to make a show of us."

The doctor smiled.

"That's rather a rough way of putting it, but if we did——"

"If—if——"

"Yes," pursued the doctor, coolly; "what then? You cannot aid the funds of the charity upon which you have lived."

"Bah!" cried Toro, furiously; "you want to make us a show for fools to gape at."

Hunston, less impetuous than his comrade, had been thinking the matter over, and hoped to turn it to account.

If these rich English were so very lavish with their wealth, might not a few judicious words bring help from them?

Help for the two interesting invalids themselves, as well as assistance for the hospital funds.

He hastily explained this to Toro.

"When do you expect these English to come here?"

"Perhaps they will come to-day. I will ask."

He called one of the attendants.

"Did the English gentlemen, the Signor Harkaway and his friends, say when they would come?"

"Yes, sir; to-morrow morning."

Toro and Hunston started.

"Did you hear?"

"Yes. Let us make sure. Ask him."

"What name did you say?" demanded Toro, trying to look indifferent.

"Harkaway," was the reply. "Your friend here," he added, indicating Hunston, "is smiling at my pronunciation of the name, perhaps."

"No, no."

"Why did you ask, then? Is the name known to you?"

"Not at all—not at all!" exclaimed Toro, eagerly.

His manner attracted the doctor's attention.

"The name is known to me," said Hunston, who perceived Toro was making a mess of it.

"Hah, I thought so," said the doctor; "he is, as I supposed, a man of note in England?"

"Well, perhaps scarcely a man of note," said Hunston; "but I happened to have heard his name."

"*Corpo di Bacco!*" ejaculated the Italian, "it matters little whether he be rich or poor, I for one don't want to be shown as a prize pig or stuffed monkey; and what is more, I mean to go, and go now."

The doctor changed colour.

"So you mean to go," he said, giving him a curious look.

"Yes."

"Very good."

He touched the bell as he said this.

A minute after three men appeared upon the threshold.

"This patient has become troubled in the head," he said, significantly, "and he must be kept apart in a padded room."

Toro started.

"A padded room!" he exclaimed.

The doctor smiled.

"You'll soon learn all about it, my poor fellow," he said.

"About what?" demanded Toro, anxiously.

"About your sanity, and also about

your doctor. Amongst other things, they'll teach you to be obedient to your doctor."

Toro remarked the meaning smile of the doctor, and he was about to expostulate, when suddenly he was seized by two of the attendants, and his arms wrenched back.

The third attendant fastened them by the wrists very dexterously, and then he was powerless to act in his own defence.

Toro blustered and swore and made a great noise.

The doctor ordered him to be taken to the padded room.

"You'll like to receive your visitors yet."

"Never!" said Toro. "You may do as you like in this infamous den, but I'll see no one."

"How can you help it?"

"I'd make it very unpleasant for you by my explanations."

"Bah! they will know it is but the raving of a madman."

"Not when I relate how generous they were on the first visit, and that I am kept here to work upon their sympathies, and——"

The doctor broke in here impatiently.

"Take him away," he cried; "to the padded room with him."

The order was obeyed, and as he left the doctor said to himself—

"He's right there; that is checkmate. Of course I cannot have them see him—the big-headed fool! The other is more tractable, I suppose."

He thought it best to keep them apart, but Hunston soon persuaded him to the contrary.

"He is very obstinate," said Hunston, "but I could soon bring him to his senses."

"Do you think so?"

"I am sure."

"My own opinion is," said the doctor, with a searching glance at Hunston as he spoke, "that the name of the visitor sounded unpleasant to him."

"No, no," interrupted Hunston.

"Well, go to your friend—perhaps you may be able to calm him."

"I'll try."

The doctor called his attendants, and gave orders for Hunston to be sent to the other patient.

When Hunston entered the padded room, he found Toro fastened hand and foot with cords.

He was scowling fearfully.

"Be careful," whispered the latter, hurriedly; "they are listening at the door."

And then he said in a loud voice—

"Come, come, old comrade, the doctor only spoke for our own good. Let me persuade you; they are quite frightened with your wild behaviour."

Toro grunted.

"Pretend to give way by degrees," whispered Hunston.

"Well, I won't be driven."

"That's it," exclaimed Hunston; "but the good doctor wants you as a great favour——"

Signs were exchanged, and Toro appeared to assent in a grumbling manner.

To have changed too suddenly might have aroused suspicions.

And then they heard footsteps retreating along the stone-paved passages.

As the last echo died away in the distance, Hunston turned and exclaimed—

"We must escape to-night."

"We will," said Toro.

"To-morrow Harkaway will again cross our path, and then it would be too late."

"Too late indeed. Escape is the word, and if I can get that cursed doctor's throat in my grip, I will have his life."

CHAPTER XLI.

WHEREIN MR. MOLE TAKES SPIRITS WITHIN AND SEES A SPIRIT WITHOUT.

Of course Mole came in for a vast quantity of badinage from his friends about the marriage and execution.

Mrs. Harkaway, in particular, rebuked him very severely, as also did "little Emily," who, however, soon relented, and asked the old tutor a variety of questions concerning his adventures with the brigands.

"Are you not sorry you went on shore there?" she asked. "Only think how much better it would have been if you had stayed on the ship to take care of Mrs. Mole. If you had done so, the brigands would never have had a chance of capturing you."

"My dear Miss Emily," said Mr. Mole, "it will ever be a source of satisfaction to me to remember that I was a prisoner in the hands of those miscreants at the time of that memorable attack upon the house in the wood upon Magic Island."

"But you were out of the way of the fighting," said little Emily, slily.

"Out of the way?" iterated Mr. Mole indignantly; "no, I was on the way to give the scoundrels what they so richly deserved."

"Dear me, I did not know that," said Emily.

"Not know it? Goodness me! why, I thought everybody knew what my share in the work was."

"I know," said young Jack, who was present, "that Mr. Mole rendered very great service."

Mr. Mole knew well the chaffing spirit of the family, and had his misgivings about young Jack.

He shot a sharp glance of inquiry, but young Jack returned it with the demurest possible stare, and Mr. Mole was led on to indulge in his constitutional weakness for lying and exaggeration.

"I was left alone for some little time," said Mr. Mole, "and I soon contrived to get free; so I watched the fight in great anxiety, as you may suppose."

"Yes, I should," responded young Jack, drily.

"I saw one of the brigands coming in my direction, so I waited until he was close by where I was hiding——"

"Hiding?"

"Yes."

"Oh, then, you did hide?"

"For strategic reasons," responded Mr. Mole.

"I see."

"Well, just as the poor man was close by, I pounced out upon him and disarmed him."

"Poor fellow!"

"You will say poor fellow directly," said Mr. Mole; "he was in such a state that I was forced to kill him."

"What?" cried little Emily.

"Or he would have killed me."

"You had no choice then."

"None, but I was merciful; I took off his head at a single stroke of his own sword."

At this there was a general chorus of "Goodness gracious!" in which little Emily and young Jack were joined by other voices.

The latter belonged to Dick Harvey and Magog Brand.

"Goodness gracious!"

But the addition to his audience did not in any way dismay Mr. Mole.

He had been indulging to some slight extent, and in his case the old proverb, *in vino veritas*, was exactly reversed.

He never pulled the long bow so hard as when his brain was heated by the fumes of alcohol.

"At a single stroke!" he said, planting his right wooden leg firmly down; "and can you wonder at that?"

"Singular to relate, we can," responded Dick.

"You all know my reputation as a swordsman in my youth," said Mr. Mole.

"I ought to have heard it," said Dick.

"You know, when I was your age, I have faced some of the greatest experts with small arms. You have heard of Angelo, the great fencing master?"

"Yes."

"He, Angelo, the great fencing master, would not face me."

"Very rude of him to turn his back."

"Of course he didn't do that. I mean he dared not face me with the sword. He knew I was too much for him."

"I don't wonder at that," said Dick; "you are almost too much for us, too—eh, Mr. Brand?"

"That he is," laughed the little gentleman; "but I say, Mr. Mole, how are those beautiful fair—no, I mean, your splendid dark twins getting on?"

"My children, I confess, are dark," said Mole, "but then, you see, I have one advantage—they do not require washing so much as your pale-faced children, and you know that saves some amount of crying. However, I wish I had a chance of showing you what I could do if my courage was put to the test."

He drew himself up to his full height, and stood not only on his wooden legs, but on his dignity likewise.

Now, strange to relate, as Mr. Mole spoke, he strutted off to the window with an air of lofty patronage just as a deep shadow fell across it.

Next minute, two men passed along, one limping, and leaning upon the other.

The limping man looked up and peered into the room through the glass, and he faced Mr. Mole, their eyes divided by the window, but really not twenty inches apart.

Mr. Mole staggered back.

His face was ghastly pale and his lips bloodless.

Stranger than all, he was thoroughly sober in an instant.

"Good Heaven, Mole," ejaculated Dick, "what has happened?"

Mr. Mole made some faint sound, but they could not make out exactly what he said.

Fright had rendered him inarticulate.

"Have you seen a ghost?"

Mole nodded.

"I have," said he, in a hollow voice, "the ghost of the Italian brigand, Toro."

"Toro!"

"Yes; and not only Toro, but Hunston also."

There was a general rush to the door and window, but no signs were to be seen of the two men.

Both had disappeared.

"My opinion is," said Magog Brand, "that the ghosts have been conjured up by the spirits Mr. Mole has taken as refreshers."

And this view was generally adopted, in spite of poor Mr. Mole's protestations, in spite of his deadly-white face and staring eyes.

CHAPTER XLII.

TORO AND HUNSTON—THE ESCAPE FROM THE LAZARETTO—OUT OF THE WINDOW— A TUSSLE AT THE GATE—A VERY WARM CHASE.

THEY were inclined to laugh at Mr. Mole, and treat the whole matter as a fit of imagination.

This we have seen.

What we have yet to see, however, is how much truth there was in his wild exclamation.

This you may learn by reading what follows.

*   *   *   *   *

Toro and Hunston looked about them in that padded room, and mentally reckoned up the chances of escape.

They were meagre.

The door was fast enough.

So fast, indeed, that it would have defied the exertions of an experienced burglar, armed with proper instruments, to demolish it.

There only remained one chance for them—the window.

To this, therefore, they devoted all their attention.

The window was solidly barred.

This was not a very hopeful beginning, but they were not easily discouraged.

The dreaded visit of Jack Harkaway and his party filled them with dismay; and, come what would, they must get clear of the lazaretto before the morrow.

Toro clambered up to the window by mounting upon Hunston's shoulders, and, once there, he held on.

"Where does the window look out to?" asked Hunston.

"Can't see yet," replied Toro, tugging at the bars. "I must get my head out first."

"Pull the bars away."

Toro grunted.

"That is more easily said than done. I can't move them."

"Here, take my knife; loosen the mortar in which they are set."

"Good."

He set to work again; and, after persevering for some few minutes, out came one of the bars.

"Bravo! Now look," said Hunston, eagerly. "What do you see?"

"The roof of a low building."

"Which?"

"I scarcely know it; yet stay——"

"Is it slated and slanting, on one floor only?"

"Yes; I know it now. It is the dead-house, I remember."

"I thought as much," said Hunston. "Tell me, what is the drop?"

"Perhaps twelve feet, or perhaps fifteen; not more."

"Good."

"Now, a little more patience, a little more work, and then——"

"Hist!" ejaculated Hunston eagerly.

"What is it?" demanded Toro, in an excited whisper.

"Someone coming."

"In the corridor?"

"Yes."

Toro, without a word, slid down to the floor, and, with one of the bars, he made a strong wedge in the crack of the door, which would certainly impede its opening.

Another bar, which was not so thick, he thrust into the keyhole, and thus spiked the lock.

"There, that will spoil their curiosity," said he, with a chuckle; "and now look to the window."

Hardly were the words uttered, when the door was tried upon the other side.

The key was thrust into the lock, but of course, it could not turn, thanks to the spiking with the iron bar.

After a few moments' fumbling, Toro could hear a voice, in vexation, mutter—

"Why, they have given me the wrong key."

"I don't think so," replied another voice outside.

"This one will not turn. We must get back and see."

And then, to the intense satisfaction of the two occupants of the padded chamber, footsteps were heard retreating along the stone corridor.

Back they got to the window.

A third and fourth bar were speedily out, now that the settings were loose.

And now there was room to squeeze through.

While Toro was thus engaged, Hunston was not idle.

He had torn down the leather with which the room was hung, and slit it with his knife into strips.

These he tested in a variety of ways, and once secure enough to trust the weight of his body to, they were fastened to the only bar left in its place.

To complete all this, they had perhaps spent five minutes.

But yet it was time enough for the people to be at the door again.

The door was shaken violently now.

Loud voices were heard in altercation.

"Now we must be quick," said Hunston, excitedly.

"Hush!"

A voice without was heard challenging them.

"*Oh, Signor Italiano.*"

It was the doctor.

"*Che cosa, Signor Dottorino?* (What is is it, little Mr. Doctor?)"

"*Ho besognio* (I want)——" began the doctor.

"*Basta! basta!*" interrupted Toro, with a laugh of derision, "*ho uscité adesse adesso* (I have just gone out)."

And he wound up with a noisy fit of laughter.

The next moment Toro was out of the window.

"Be careful," exclaimed Hunston in a whisper.

"All right."

The knocking at the door of the padded room grew louder.

Hunston turned to the window in great anxiety.

Toro was half way down, and the frail rope of strips of leather upon which he trusted was cracking ominously under his weight.

The hammering upon the door became every instant more and more alarming.

If they were not quick, there was really some danger of the door being broken in.

Hunston waited only a short time, just enough to see Toro safely landed upon the roof of the dead house, before he trusted himself to the very primitive ladder.

He clambered through the window just as the doctor shouted—

"Why don't you answer? Do you hear?"

Hunston thrust his head into the chamber, and replied—

"What answer do you wish for? He will not talk."

"He! Who?"

"My friend the Italian."

The doctor grunted impatiently.

"Tell me if you have done anything to the door."

"What do you mean?"

"Why, you know well enough. You have made it fast somehow."

"If that's your opinion," retorted Hunston, in an indignant and loud voice, "you are welcome to enjoy it; but I, like my companion here, shall decline to continue the conversation, since it has taken such an offensive turn."

This was the most judicious speech he had yet made.

It was well timed too, for Toro was just then beginning to slide down the sloping roof of the dead house, and as he spoke, Hunston grasped the twisted leather and slid down.

It creaked and strained as he went down, and every moment he expected it to snap asunder.

Great was his relief, therefore, as his feet touched the slated roof below.

At the self-same moment, Toro had reached the ground.

A crash was heard above.

The impatient doctor had ordered the door of the padded chamber to be forced, and loud cries above announced that the flight of the two patients or prisoners was already discovered.

As Hunston began his descent from the roof of the dead house, the doctor appeared at the window above, calling and gesticulating in the greatest excitement.

"Stop them!" he shouted, "shut the yard gates! They are two mad patients!"

The gate-keeper ran out, and hearing the alarm, dashed to the gates just as Toro came up at a run.

"Open the gate!" he thundered at the man, "or else——"

The gate-keeper made no reply, but grappled with the fierce Italian.

Toro's blood was up, and he put forth his great strength to grapple with the man, who proved but a mere boy in his clutch.

Seizing the luckless fellow around the waist, he lifted him fairly off his feet, and hurled him violently to the earth.

He lay there quietly enough, never offering to move or stir.

Hunston was by this time at the gate, and dragged at it with all his strength, but in vain; it closed with a spring that held it fast.

"A thousand devils!" cried Toro; "open the gate!"

"I cannot," replied Hunston.

The startling sound of the alarm bell was now heard, and several men were seen issuing from the main entrance of the lazaretto.

Toro rushed at the porter, who lay motionless upon the ground, and with a mighty effort dragged him up on to his feet.

"Now, fool!" he hissed in the man's face, "open the gate, or you haven't a minute to live."

He flourished his long knife in the man's face as he said this, and half frightened him out of his seven senses.

There was a murderous expression in the brigand's face as he looked into the frightened man's eyes, and he felt that his life was in jeopardy.

He obeyed Toro with great alacrity.

"Close it after me," said the savage Italian, "and stop pursuit, for if we are caught, your life shall answer for it."

And so the fugitives passed through the gateway just as eight or ten men flew rather than ran up in hot chase.

Now both Toro and Hunston were fleet of foot, and having a tolerable start, they contrived to render pursuit hopeless within ten minutes after they had got through the gates of the lazaretto.

"Phew!" groaned Toro, when they drew up to get breath, "that was a narrow escape!"

"Indeed it was," answered his panting comrade; "I thought it was all over with us."

"And I too, nearly; but we have done them. We bid good-bye to the lazaretto, and we laugh at our friend the doctor."

They then made for the town, where they converted some of their valuables into cash and procured themselves new garments for the purpose of disguise.

CHAPTER XLIII.

THE DANGER INCREASES—HOW HUNSTON WAS DOGGED, AND WHAT CAME OF IT— THE KNIFE—IN THE WOODS—A STARTLER—DOG BITE DOG.

TORO and Hunston were right when they made such frantic efforts to escape from the sight of the Harkaway party.

The hue and cry was already hot enough; they did not wish to add Harkaway's influence to that of the authorities of the lazaretto in hunting them down, and as the two adventurous ruffians were in the lazaretto under assumed names, they would in all probability have escaped the attention of our friends but for the accident of their recognition by Mr. Mole at the window.

Harkaway made his way to the lazaretto, and there having got a full description of the two men who had succeeded in escaping, he could not have a doubt left in his mind that they must be indeed his old enemies, Hunston and the Italian bravo.

As soon as he was satisfied in his own mind about this, Jack Harkaway went to the police and gave information.

"They are the most vindictive wretches in the world," he said to his old chum, Dick Harvey, "and the sooner they are caged the better, for while they are at large, I don't feel that our children are safe."

"Quite right, Jack," said Dick. "As family men, we ought to grow prudent some time or other; although, if I tell the honest truth, I don't like putting the police on them."

Jack stared.

"Not like it, Dick!" he exclaimed.

"Well," said Dick, "if I confess my real sentiments, I should like to tackle them again myself. I think it is our duty and our mission to make them 'smell agony,' as the American wags say."

Old Jack fired up at this.

Like an old war-horse, he snorted at the smell of powder, however far off.

But prudence had come upon him with years, and he thought of the peril in which his boy and little Emily had been placed by the machinations of their old enemies.

"If we were alone in the world, Dick," said Jack, "it would be all fair for us, but we must not forget our obligations."

"Of course not."

So the police had the job of hunting down Hunston and Toro handed to them.

From that hour the chase after Hunston and the Italian ruffian grew unpleasantly hot.

Wherever they presented themselves they were beset by huge printed placards, offering rewards for their apprehension.

Moreover, the description was exactly given. But this was not the worst.

Two days afterwards there appeared a second notice, in which, in the middle of a long placard, in the native type, were two names, printed in big capitals of the Roman alphabet—

HUNSTON AND TORO.

"How on earth can they have got at our names?" asked Toro, in amazement.

"There is but one way," replied his companion.

"And that is?"

"Through our old enemy, our bitterest foe in the world."

"Harkaway?"

"Of course."

"Malediction on him; accursed be the day that he first saw the light—may——"

"Stop, stop," cried Hunston; "more work and less noise. Just oblige me by thinking your curses; let them be deep rather than loud. The present business is how to get out of this part of the country."

Toro was silenced.

"You are right, Hunston," he said, "although you have a devilish aggravating way of expressing your opinions."

"Pshaw!" ejaculated Hunston, impatiently, "learn to pay less attention to mere words and more to the services rendered. Let us go out of the town as fast as our legs will take us."

"Agreed."

They fixed upon a meeting place about a mile from the city walls, and then they separated, the better to throw the Greek police off the scent.

The appointed meeting place was by a well, or mineral fountain of water.

It was nightfall when Hunston ventured forth from his lurking place, for he was possessed with a strange fancy that he was being watched by a tall, dark man, who had turned up unexpectedly in three different places where he, Hunston, had been that day.

This watching made Hunston particularly uneasy in his mind, and so he determined to put an end to it.

He walked along to the outskirts of the town, where houses were only at rare intervals, and sauntered by gardens and orange groves, until he thought he had tired out the spy, for so he had, until then, designated the tall dark man.

"I was wrong, after all," he said, half aloud, "for he has left me to my own devices, after all."

And then, as the very words were upon his lips, his tall friend suddenly popped up before him.

Hunston started back, greatly alarmed.

"Don't be afraid, Mr. Hunston," said the dark man in very good English; "I hope I see you well."

Hunston gasped again.

Firstly, at hearing English spoken by the new comer.

Secondly, at hearing himself addressed by name by a stranger.

"You don't remember me?" pursued the stranger.

Hunston, taken completely off his guard, replied—

"No, I can't say that I do."

"I thought not; but I want you to walk back into the town with me."

Hunston felt just a little uncomfortable now.

There was a dash of command in the speaker's tone which told its own tale.

"What do you wish me to go that way for?" he asked, when he could muster up courage.

"Only a freak."

"I don't understand you," began Hunston.

"Don't you?" said the dark man, with a very unpleasant laugh; "oh, you very soon will. Come."

"Gently, gently," said Hunston, who had got back some of his scared senses by this time. "If you will explain your business with me, and tell me who you are, I am willing to make an appointment with you."

The dark man laughed out loud at this.

"My name," he said, "is Piffari. A curious name, is it not? My business," he added, deliberately, "is simply to take you back to the town with me."

"Take me back?"

"Yes."

"What do you mean?"

"Hunston, you are my prisoner," he answered, in the same calm tone.

Saying which, he clapped Hunston on the shoulder.

"On what charge?"

"Various. Come along, or I shall use force."

Hunston got back his *sang froid* by this time, and he walked back a little way.

He looked forward and backward, to ascertain if there were any witnesses about, while his hand slowly stole into his tail pocket.

He carried a long dagger knife there.

"You are mistaken in addressing me," said Hunston, with an assumed air of offended virtue, "and I warn you that I shall seek redress from our consul."

"Yes, do so, by all means," replied the singular dark man, in the pleasantest way in the world.

" I'm curious to know, sir," answered Hunston, "how you have been led to adopt this very strange course of conduct with me."

" Sir," replied the stranger, with great politeness, "your curiosity upon that point will doubtless very soon be satisfied now."

" Very good."

By this time Hunston was gripping the dagger knife nervously in his sound hand, and suddenly he made a dash at his unwelcome companion with the other.

"Ha! Mr. Hunston," said the dark man, catching the mechanical hand by the wrist with the greatest ease, "that is very unkind."

He might have spared his sarcasm, for this was a trap.

Down came the dagger-knife when he least expected it, and with such violence that it pinned him fairly through the body.

The dark man gasped, then quivered from head to foot, and then he gave way at the knees, and sank upon the ground—lifeless.

" That's done," said Hunston, greatly relieved in his mind.

He wiped his knife upon the victim's garments, and then, with a final glance about him, he hurried away as fast as his legs would carry him, never looking once back at the murdered man.

*   *   *   *   *

" Toro."

" Hunston."

" Here."

" Good."

And the two villains met.

When they came to compare notes, they had a good deal to go through upon both sides.

Toro more than Hunston.

The latter's story, in fact, was soon told.

It was only the story of another tragedy in which he had played the chief part again.

Toro listened silently until Hunston concluded.

A smile of devilish triumph shone in his eyes when Hunston came to the episode of the assassination.

" So perish all our enemies, Hunston," he said, violently, "and now let us get out of this part of the country as fast as we can."

" So say I."

They made for the woods until they came to a thickly-grown part, where progress became a matter of difficulty.

" This is a capital spot for an ambuscade."

" You are right there, Toro; half a dozen stout fellows could hold this place against a precious big force."

" You are right: but there is little fear of any such danger here."

" Why, have you never read any accounts of the awful atrocities that these Greeks commit?"

" They must be almost as bad as the Italian brigands," said Hunston, slily.

" Worse, worse!"

" I regret one thing," said Hunston; "we ought to have bought a rifle each and some ammunition."

" They would only have proved a burden to us," replied Toro.

" They would have enabled us to go shooting here; I don't see how we shall get on for food without firearms."

" Something is sure to turn up."

Something had.

A loud commanding voice was heard, and armed men sprang up on all sides.

In less time than it takes to record the fact, they were covered by a dozen rifles.

They staggered back, then held up their hands to show they were unarmed.

The robbers crept on, still pointing their guns at the two victims.

" Move or speak, and you are dead men!" cried a deep voice.

CHAPTER XLIV.

HOW TORO AND HUNSTON FELL INTO A TRAP—CONDEMNED TO DEATH—
LAST CHANCE.

SEVERAL of the brigands pounced upon Hunston and Toro, and bound them hand and foot.

"Well," said Hunston, when he had recovered from his first surprise, " this is dog bite dog, with a vengeance."

"Take us to your leaders," said Toro, presently, to the brigands surrounding him.

"You will not find them more easy to deal with than we are ourselves," said one of the brigands.

"We will take our chance of that," said the Italian.

They were bandaged with handkerchiefs across the eyes, and led along for about three hundred yards.

Then the handkerchiefs were removed.

The two adventurers now found themselves in a clearing in the midst of a thickly-wooded country.

The spot was well chosen.

It was so admirably concealed by its natural position that no one would, by any chance, come across it.

There was a little natural grotto of great beauty facing them, and a miniature waterfall which furnished the brigands with a pure drink.

But neither waterfall nor grotto caught their attention any more than the other beauties of the surrounding scenery.

They only had eyes for the mob of armed men which filled the place.

There seemed to be no end to them.

They lined the open space, and from their steady, silent manner gave the lookers-on the impression that they were a disciplined force, far more so than any of the lawless hosts of a similar character with whom they had been connected in bygone years.

In the centre of this striking picture stood the captain, leaning, as it were, his arm upon his carbine.

He was not a very formidable-looking fellow, although he was certainly a handsome man, and one of rather striking appearance.

"Capitano, your servant," said Hunston, bowing.

"Excellency, my homage to you," said Toro, in his turn.

"Gentlemen," returned the captain, " my best welcome here."

It began well.

So they hoped that they would have no trouble with the captain.

In this, however, they were doomed to disappointment.

They had a great deal of trouble, as we shall see.

"We have been in search of you," said Toro.

"Indeed," returned the captain, smiling incredulously; " then you are no doubt grateful to my people for bringing you to me so soon."

"No and yes," answered the Italian. "Yes, because we were anxious to meet with you. No, because of the rough usage we experienced on the way."

"Indeed, I fear you must blame your own resistance."

"We made none."

"Then consider the extra precautions taken as a compliment to your very bold appearance."

"We hope to prove ourselves bold in more than mere appearance," said Toro.

"No doubt, no doubt."

The tone of the brigand captain showed that he was bent upon humouring them, and yet it made Hunston vaguely uneasy in his mind.

"Now, gentlemen," resumed the captain, proudly, " allow me to proceed to business, for we have weighty matters before us to go into as soon as your affairs are disposed of."

"By all means," cried Toro.

"Tell me then," said the brigand captain, " what are your respective positions?"

"TOBO FRANTICALLY WAVED HIS HANDKERCHIEF—A SIGNAL GUN WAS FIRED."

Toro and Hunston, instead of replying, could only look at each other in rather a puzzled manner.

They could not frame a reply to this question.

Hunston, being the man of superior education and tact, found a way out of the difficulty.

"We have no position," he answered. "We have been what you are, and our wish is to join you."

The brigand eyed him sharply.

"Join us?"

"Yes."

"Humph! That is, to live on our earnings instead of starving."

"No," thundered Toro, vehemently, "no."

"No; our intention is to work, to show you that we can bring as much to the general coffers as the best man among you. We are no idlers."

The captain mused in silence for awhile, and then he said—

"Enough of this. Tell me what ransom you can offer if I should spare your lives?"

"Ransom!" echoed Toro; "why, we haven't a friend in the world."

"Ransom!" exclaimed Hunston, "not a rap."

"Then you know the consequences," said the chief, with a lowering glance.

Hunston was silent.

Toro shrugged his shoulders.

"We can't keep useless men here," said the chief, sternly.

"You will not send us back."

"No."

"Good; we shall soon show you how we can merit the good thoughts of the best of you."

"No," continued the brigand captain, ignoring the latter speech, "for we cannot trust men back who have been as far as this."

"What mean you?"

"Simply this," returned the captain, in an ugly voice, "that you will be shot at daybreak."

An unpleasant silence succeeded this speech.

"We had better have remained in the town," remarked Hunston; "the police could not have treated us worse."

"Then you had got into a mess there?" demanded the captain.

"Yes."

"How?"

"One of the gendarmes would have detained us, so I killed him."

The brigand captain's face brightened at this, and Toro cheered up.

Hunston had secured the sympathy of the lawless chieftain.

"Why, that is as good as a ransom," said the latter; "we can sell you to the police."

This was a staggerer.

A death blow to their hopes.

And with this the chief haughtily dismissed the subject.

But Hunston was not to be disposed of so easily.

While Toro contented himself with storming and swearing, Hunston's busy brain was at work.

He had got into a terrible mess, but he did not intend giving up without a struggle.

"One word before your excellency goes," he said.

"Can you find the ransom?" demanded the captain.

"No, but——"

"Enough; to-morrow morning at daybreak I shall see you again, for the last time."

"Stay, you shall hear me."

"Shall!"

"Aye, shall," said Hunston, with determination; "if I cannot give you a ransom, I can leave you a legacy."

The brigand chief stopped short at this.

"A legacy?"

"Yes; a legacy of hate."

"Thank you, I have a fair store of it already, and need not your legacy."

"Perhaps," retorted Hunston, quickly; "but my legacy offers you not hate alone, but a rich booty as well."

These words caught the captain's ears.

"What mean you?" he asked.

"This; in a word, our purpose in joining you was to get your aid to secure a rich countryman of mine."

"An Englishman?"

"Yes."

"Where is he?"

"Hard by. Not a league from hence. This man, who is our bitterest enemy, is rolling in wealth. He could buy up your kingdom, and his ransom would fill your pockets for life."

He paused. The captain was evidently interested in the tale.

"Go on."

"This man is a dare-devil, a rash fool that you can lay hands on if you will, for he runs into danger for the simple pleasure of encountering it."

"Indeed ; he must be an extraordinary man."

"He is."

"His name ?"

"Harkaway."

The captain stared, and started back as though he had received an electric shock.

"What !" ejaculated the brigand in a voice of thunder ; "Harkaway again !"

"You know the name ?" said Hunston in surprise.

"Know it !" reiterated the captain ; "it is eternally dinned into my ears. I have heard this Harkaway spoken of as one beside whom Achilles was but a braggart, a second Hercules and an Apollo all rolled into one."

Hunston winced.

To hear his old enemy thus praised was bitter as gall to him.

"You at least need not sound his trumpet," he said, "for he is your sworn foe."

"Now you say too much," retorted the captain fiercely ; "he knows me not."

"Not personally, perhaps, but yet he is your enemy unseen. He is the sworn exterminator of your trade. He has made his mark in Italy, where a whole band fell before his unceasing efforts at their destruction. In America he made his presence known to others, and here his purpose will be, unless I am greatly mistaken, to hunt you down."

The captain looked in silence as Hunston proceeded.

The words sank deeply into his mind, and with good reason.

He remembered the visit of that same Harkaway, the redoubtable Englishman, to a neighbouring mountain, whither he had been decoyed under pretext of hearing a famous echo, and how Harkaway had fought the captain, defeated him, and given him up to justice.

The brigand captain had not forgotten how several of the brigand band had been treated, nor that Harkaway had brought them to their doom in a way that the slow-going authorities could never have done alone and unaided.

The brigand chief brooded long and silently over this.

Meanwhile both Hunston and Toro passed a precious unpleasant time of it.

They were placed under a strong guard, and treated as men under sentence of death.

At daybreak they were to die.

*   *   *   *   *

Towards three o'clock in the morning both Toro and Hunston dozed off.

They had been sleeping perhaps fifteen or twenty minutes, when Hunston was aroused by a hand being placed upon his shoulder.

"Awake."

The prisoner started up with a cry of alarm.

"So soon ? The day has not dawned yet."

"Do you wish to see a priest ?"

The prisoner shuddered at these ominous words.

"No."

"Will your comrade ?"

"Ask him."

The other prisoner was aroused, but he also declined the aid of priest or pastor.

"I have lived a brave man," said the Italian, "and I shall show you Greeks how a brave man can die. I have faced death too often to be afraid of it, whenever and wherever it comes. Only I would sooner have died with a sword and rifle in my hand."

"If you want no priestly aid," said the man, "you can sleep again for twenty minutes. By that time the firing party will be called."

With this he left them.

As soon as he was out of hearing, the two prisoners carried on a brief conversation in English.

The only tongue to which they could safely trust here.

"What shall we do, Toro ?"

"Do ! what is there to do ? Stand up and receive as many bullets as possible, so as not to writhe long in the agonies of death."

"Do you give up then ?"

"What else is there to do ?"

"One thing."

"What is it ?"

"Make a rush for it."

"To what end?"

"To escape."

"Bah! impossible; we should be shot down or cut piecemeal before we got a dozen yards."

"Well," quoth Hunston, "what of that? It would be more satisfactory to die in harness than be shot down like dogs. Besides, poor as the chance is, surely there is a chance."

Toro reflected.

"You are right. We can only die," he added, with an air of determination. "Let us try it."

"We must be cautious; then there is no need to spoil our chance by imprudence, after all."

"True."

"And now that we are agreed upon that, Toro," added Hunston, "let us settle what next to do when we are clean away—if——"

"Ah, 'if'—a very big 'if.' I think it is a waste of breath to sketch out anything further. We shall not escape."

"You're a Job's comforter," retorted Hunston, "but I prefer taking the hopeful side of every question. If we escape, make for the lazaretto."

"Why, in the name of the fiend, there?" cried Toro.

"Not to stop there. Get past there to the sea, and try to get on board some ship as a stowaway. For between the gendarmes and the brigands here, we shall never be safe in this cursed place; either party will discover us."

"You are right," said Toro; "when shall we make the attempt?"

"Now."

They arose quietly to their feet, and Hunston led the way upon tip-toe for eight or ten yards, when suddenly they found themselves confronted by a dark, shadowy form.

"Where are you going?" asked a cold, calm voice in the Italian language.

They had not a word to reply.

So suddenly had the speaker appeared, that they taken completely aback.

"I want a word or two with you. You Englishman, I mean."

They recognised now the voice of the brigand captain.

"Speak, captain," said Hunston, recovering himself.

"Is it true that Harkaway, the Englishman, is near this spot?"

"Yes."

"You swear!"

"I swear."

"And would you still pledge yourself to this if death by torture were to be the penalty for the discovery of your falsehood?"

"Under any circumstances I would swear it by any oath you could prescribe," returned Hunston, boldly, "for it is true. Harkaway, the enemy to brigands, is near us."

"Admitting that, now tell me could you help me to the capture of this hero, Harkaway?"

"I could."

"How?"

"Many ways."

"One will suffice," returned the brigand captain, coldly; "I don't like those who protest too much."

"One, then, shall I name? There is a means of decoying Harkaway alone into your power."

"Hah!"

"What think you of it?"

"Very good, if the plan be fair. How would you set to work?"

"Simply by writing a letter."

"This Harkaway is a man of more than ordinary discernment," returned the brigand captain; "your letter would have to be something cunning indeed to entrap him, after that adventure which cost the lives of so many of our best followers, and of a gallant chief among the number."

"Let me have paper and pen and ink or pencil, and I will draw up a letter at once, so that you shall see the whole scheme."

"Have you thought it out?" asked the brigand.

"I am now thinking it out," was the reply.

This answer caught the brigand's attention.

The ready wit it promised gave him hope and secured his interest in the scheme.

He called out to some of his followers the necessary instructions.

While they were gone, Hunston turned to Toro, and said—

"Old comrade and companion of many

a danger, you saved my life recently; I shall return the obligation just now, I think."

"I hope so, Hunston," returned the Italian.

Hunston then proceeded to sketch out the following letter—

"*To* MR. JOHN HARKAWAY.

"If you care to see once more in life a wretched man, who in bygone years was known to you as Hunston, come at once with the bearer of this note, whom you may implicitly trust. The writer's dying wish is to expiate as far as may be the crimes of his past days, the more especially those with which you have been directly associated. It is needless to point out that the roads are infested with brigands, that it would be in the highest degree imprudent to come unarmed or unaccompanied by a good, strong escort. The unhappy man who pens these lines with such infinite pains has but recently escaped from the hospital of the lazaretto, and in his flight has sustained the severe injuries which preclude all possibility of his recovery. The end is merely a question of days—perhaps only of hours."

When finished, he scanned it through, and then, apparently satisfied with it himself, he handed it to the captain of the brigands.

He made a hurried translation of it into Italian, and then in silence awaited his comments on it.

The captain said nothing, but Toro was full of critical remarks.

"It will excite suspicion at once," remarked Toro, "to try on the decoy dodge."

"The invitation to bring assistance with him will put him a little off the scent——"

"And put us off the chance too," said Toro, "if he should do so."

"If your letter brings him far enough out of the town, I know how to act," said the captain.

"Nothing is easier," said Hunston, "provided that we can find a messenger trusty and courageous."

"We have plenty of men ready to accept the risk," returned the captain; "brave men are not scarce amongst my followers."

"Doubtless."

"What do you say to the scheme?" demanded Toro of the captain.

"I think it practicable," was the reply.

"And are you willing to try it?"

"Yes."

Toro's countenance brightened visibly at this.

"Let us have it carried out without loss of time, capitano," said he eagerly, "for I long to see our old enemy laid by the heels. Once let me see him at my feet, and I can die contented."

The brigand captain was silent for awhile.

He reckoned up his plans and the chances of success.

And then he gave out his decision.

"At dusk to-morrow the attempt shall be made," he said, "and if successful, not only shall you have your lives, but a rich share of the booty we may make by it, and, if you desire it, a post of trust for each of you in my band."

The brigand captain then, without another word, left Toro and Hunston in charge of three of his band, each armed with sword and musket.

CHAPTER XLV.

ON THE HIGHWAY—THE LOVERS AND THE BRIGANDS—AN ADVENTURE WITH A
RICH BISHOP.

A LITTLE later in the morning, the captain of the brigands came to Toro and Hunston with a fresh proposal.

"I am about to give you a proof of my confidence in you," he said.

"Captain," returned Hunston, "you shall find that your confidence is not unmerited."

"I hope so."

Then he summoned the whole band by bugle call, and when they were assembled, to the number perhaps of sixty odd men, he made the following short address—

"These two men here," he said, "are comrades; they come to join us. Let the oath of allegiance be administered to them, and then we must forget that they were ever with us other than as friends."

The oaths were then taken by Hunston and Toro.

The wording of the oaths was of too horrible a nature to be repeated here, nor, indeed, is repetition at all necessary.

Suffice it to say that the ceremony was not altogether wanting in solemnity, and that all alike appeared to be impressed with it.

When it was done, the captain sent the men upon their respective errands again, while he resumed his conversation with the new members of his band.

At this point there came up a brigand in hot haste with news.

This was a scout.

He had discovered that a wealthy prelate was going to travel in his carriage, very poorly attended, through the very heart of the brigand's scene of action.

"The bishop counts upon the sanctity of his office for protection," said one of the brigands.

"He shall have more blows than protection from me," said the captain; "I owe him a turn."

"Pardon me, captain," said one of the brigands, "you know that it will make the superstitious folks about here very bad indeed against us if anything happened to a bishop."

"I can't help that," said the brigand captain, shortly; "if his lordship will insist upon travelling over our property, he must pay toll just as well as any ordinary priest or layman, and he shall pay smartly for it, too, if I have any luck to-day."

The expedition was got up by three men.

The captain in the first place.

Next were Hunston and Toro.

The purpose of this the reader has already discovered.

It was simply to test them before they ventured upon a matter of greater moment.

He procured them disguises, and then they set out for a favourite spot upon the high road, along which my lord bishop was pretty sure to pass.

Here they waited for about an hour, when a scout, at a considerable distance from the spot, blew them a signal.

"His lordship is on the way," said the captain to his two new recruits; "stand close and take the word from me."

"Good."

"I will see to the reverend gentleman alone; he is not very formidable."

Barely were the words uttered, when they heard the jingle of bells, and a carriage appeared in sight.

"Hide you away," said the captain, hurriedly.

They obeyed, and the carriage rolled up to where the brigand chief sat, hat in hand, upon the bank.

As the pair of ponies came trotting up to the spot, the brigand arose and seized the bridles with a sudden firmness that stopped them in their trot, and sent them rearing back almost upon their haunches.

"Charity, monsignor, charity," said the brigand, in a regular mendicant's drawl.

"Audacious scoundrel!" ejaculated the reverend gentleman.

"Charity, my lord," repeated the brigand, as before.

"Let loose the heads of the horses."

"Alms, my lord bishop, for a poor miserable sinner."

"There, then," said the bishop, testily; "take my blessing, and stand aside."

"Thanks, holy father," said the brigand. "A poor man's best wishes for your goodness, but I would fain have solid charity with it."

"I have nothing."

"Indeed you have."

"Insolent!"

The brigand chief, in the coolest manner possible, left the ponies' heads, and came to the carriage window, where he thrust his head in.

"Could your lordship not manage me a few hundred francs?"

"A few hundred!" quoth the bishop, aghast.

"A thousand," said the brigand, coolly, "if possible."

"Poor wretch!" said his lordship, "he's mad."

"Not very, father," returned the brigand; "only my head has been fired with the tales of your almost fabulous wealth, which appears hard, whilst I and the likes of me are hungry."

"It is false," answered the bishop, promptly; "I have no wealth. Never a penny of my own have I."

"Excuse me, my lord," said the robber, "but that must be my purse, then, that I see beside you."

So saying, he stretched forth his hand and took up a weighty velvet sack of money, that was held tight together by a thick silken cord.

It jingled with a rich metallic sound, that spoke of gold.

But before he could get it through the window the bishop had produced a long-barrelled pistol from under his robe, and dealt him such a smart rap upon the knuckles that the bag fell to the bottom of the carriage.

Then he lunged sharply out, and thrust the pistol muzzle into the robber's face.

"You are mistaken," he said, with great calmness. "That is a bag of medals and holy relics."

"So I perceive now," said the brigand, coolly. "I have lost my spectacles, and you would never believe how near-sighted I am."

"Ugh!" grunted the prelate, "accept my blessing alone this time, and make way."

The brigand withdrew and made a profound obeisance.

"My lord, I shall remember you in my prayers."

"Pray don't," retorted the prelate, hurriedly.

And with this the ponies were whipped up, and the little carriage rolled off, the bishop's admirable coolness having saved his money bag.

Toro and Hunston crept out of their hiding-place.

"Well," said the brigand captain, laughing heartily at his own failure, "what do you think of that reverend gentleman?"

"Wonderful!"

"Great courage."

"And presence of mind."

"Both," said the brigand. "His coolness almost lost me mine."

"Hark!"

"What's that?"

"A bugle."

"A signal from Livoni the scout."

The signal was heard again, and then the brigand captain made his reply.

The counter-signal was heard in the course of three minutes, and the captain said—

"Two persons are coming, it would appear by the signal."

He proved to be correct, too, for in the space of a few more moments up came a couple in sight.

"A brace of lovers spooning," suggested Hunston.

He was not far out, for there soon appeared in sight a youth and a girl, leaning lovingly upon each other, and evidently so engrossed by each other, that they had never a thought for anything else in the world.

But there was a startler in reserve for them.

Just as they got by the brigands, they popped out of their hiding-places and seized them.

The girl shrieked, and hid her face in her hands.

The young fellow turned upon his

assailants, and snatching a gun from the hands of one of the brigands, felled the man to the earth with the butt end.

The next moment the gun was pointed in a direct line to the brigand captain's head.

But before the trigger could be pulled, Toro threw his huge carcase upon him, and held the young Greek as though he had been in the hug of a bear.

" It is useless to resist," said the captain, as the young man was disarmed and held fast; " please oblige us with all the valuables you have handy."

" We have nothing, sir," replied the trembling girl, " nothing indeed, sir."

" Oho !" quoth Toro, who was busily engaged in turning out the lover's pockets, " what is this ?"

" Yes," said the young Greek, with a bitter smile, " it is my money, my fortune —two lire.* Take it, my gallant friends, and I can go without my dinner."

" 'Twill do you good."

" That's kind."

Meanwhile, the brigand chief had turned over the maiden's pockets, and lighted upon nothing more valuable than a letter.

" Who's this from ?" said the brigand captain laughing; " our young swain here ?"

" No, indeed, sir," answered the trembling girl. " It's an answer to Mr. Mole's note from the contessa."

Hunston pricked up his ears at this.

" A letter from whom ?"

" The Contessa Maraviglia," said the girl.

" To whom ?"

" To his excellency Mr. Isaac Mole, sir."

Toro and Hunston exchanged significant glances.

" Do you hear that ?"

" I do."

They spoke in English, and signed to the captain to be upon his guard while they pursued their questions further.

" Mr. Mole is your master, then," said Hunston.

" No, sir," returned the girl; " but he is my master's friend."

" Who is your master ?"

The girl stared.

" Everybody knows my master," she said; " everybody in this part of the country."

" Perhaps I am an exception," said Hunston, " if you will only say what his name is."

" He is a great English milord, the millionaire and English prince, Monseigneur Harkaway."

In spite of themselves the three robbers stared again.

It was certainly an extraordinary coincidence.

" Harkaway !"

" Yes, sir."

" And are you taking a letter from the Contessa Maraviglia to Mr. Mole ?"

" Yes, sir."

" To—to where ?"

" To our villa."

" Why, I always understood that the English milord Harkaway lived in the great hotel."

" Did so, sir; but within the past few days only he has taken the Villa Del Popolo for his and his friends' occupation."

" The Villa Del Popolo ?"

" Yes."

Just then, Hunston perceived something fall from the girl's side, and he hastened to secure it.

It was a key.

In her fright she did not perceive her loss.

" Well, well," said the captain, after coming to a quiet understanding with the two new recruits by signs that were unperceived by the lover prisoners, " we shall not impose any very serious penalty upon you, nor shall we detain you long."

The girl began to offer thanks at such an easy escape.

" The fine you have to pay," resumed the chief of the brigands, with a merry and mischievous look in his eye, " is a kiss to each of us."

The girl got very red in the face, and declared she would never consent to this.

" Oh, yes, you will," answered the chief, with a grin.

" Never," protested the girl, " never, never !"

" You would sooner die first ?" said the brigand, with a sham serious look.

" Yes."

---

* About one shilling and eightpence English.

"Of course. Well, we can accommodate you even there, if you wish it."

"Oh, sir!"

"Oh, yes, we can kill you if you prefer it."

The girl, finding them very yielding and easy so far, had thought that they would never dare to offer her violence.

But their words now filled her with alarm.

The blushes which the brigand's audacious proposal had called up into her cheek faded away and left her as white as a sheet.

As for her swain, he had not a word to say for himself.

"Well, we must waste no more time," said the brigand captain, drawing a long stiletto from his girdle and testing its edge with his thumb; "it's in very good condition, and you'll be out of the world almost without pain."

The girl closed her eyes and looked ready for fainting.

"I can predict, captain," said Toro, "that she will alter her mind now."

"How?" ejaculated the captain, in affected surprise; "impossible."

"I'll go further," said Toro; "I'll even wager that not only will the young lady relent, but that she will volunteer to give us each a chaste salute herself, of her own free will."

"What say you, young lady?" said Hunston.

"Come, decide."

"Oh, sir!"

And as she faltered she shrank back affrightedly.

"You see," said the captain, tucking up his sleeve, "she would rather die."

This business-like preparation put the poor girl in a regular fever.

"Oh, Alecco!" she faltered, while her eyes drooped to the ground. "What must I do?"

"You have no choice," was the lover's reply.

"Pardon me," said Toro, "there is a choice—death, or a kiss."

The girl wrung her hands, and looked the picture of embarrassment.

"Ah, well," said the captain, tucking up his sleeves to the elbow, and flourishing the stiletto, "that's all, I suppose. Now for it."

He made a step forward and seized the girl by the wrist.

She shut her eyes and gave a faint scream.

"Oh, sir; oh, sir!" she faltered, "pray let me kiss you!"

"You shall not ask twice, fair one," said the brigand.

He held his face forward ready for the ceremony, and she, timidly advancing her lips, just touched his cheek with them.

"I hardly felt it," said he, roughly; "this is the way."

So saying, he seized her in his arms, and gave her a kiss that echoed again, and made her lover turn livid with rage.

It was not safe, he thought, to threaten, but mentally he vowed vengeance.

"Now, my turn," said Toro.

He didn't wait for her timid salute, but hugging the girl in his big arms, he stole a dozen kisses.

"Beast!" cried the girl, and she boxed his ears with great energy.

Hunston would not press for his share of the booty, and so the lovers were released, and they made off as fast as their legs would carry them, with a final word of warning from the brigand captain ringing in their ears.

"Savages!" cried the girl.

"Ha, ha, ha!" laughed the robbers.

* * * * * *

"This key," said the brigand captain, taking it from Hunston, "is, no doubt, the key of the house, or, at least, of some room there; and it may make our future operations easier than they would otherwise be."

END OF VOLUME I.

Our Next Volume will complete " Jack Harkaway and His Son's Adventures in Greece."
Order of your Bookseller No. 11 of " Jack Harkaway and His Son's Adventures in Greece," with which a Coloured Picture will be given.

www.ingramcontent.com/pod-product-compliance
Lightning Source LLC
Chambersburg PA
CBHW080832250626

47160CB00008B/2903